I DIDN'T DO IT

I DIDN'T DO IT

Thriller Writer Conventions
Can Be Murder

Jaime Lynn Hendricks

SCARLET
NEW YORK

I DIDN'T DO IT

Scarlet
An Imprint of Penzler Publishers
58 Warren Street
New York, N.Y. 10007

Copyright © 2023 by Jaime Lynn Hendricks

First Scarlet Press edition

Interior design by Maria Fernandez

Library of Congress Control Number: 2023902478

ISBN: 978-1-61316-411-2
eBook ISBN: 978-1-61316-412-9

10 9 8 7 6 5 4 3 2 1

Printed in the United States of America
Distributed by W. W. Norton & Company

For Ann Marie DePaulis,

the one who puts the "B," the "F," and the "F" in BFF.

Here's to 44 more years.

PROLOGUE

Thursday Night

Kristin Bailey should've been a nervous wreck the night before the awards ceremony. Instead, she calmly sipped a glass of Merlot and chatted up the other nominees for the Thriller of the Year award. She clinked glasses with Kevin Candela, Marco Crimmins, and Larry Kuo, not a care in the world. The only one missing was Vicky Overton, whose flight was delayed from Florida.

"Are you nervous about tomorrow?" Kevin asked.

Kristin adjusted her signature headband and gave a slow shake of her head. "For the ceremony? Nope. But I'm Panel Master at seven-thirty tomorrow morning for *Trauma, Drama, or Revenge*." She groans at the time. "So early."

Kevin smiled. "I know. I'm attending that one. I'm speaking at three tomorrow for *Big Screen or Small Screen*."

"I'm planning on going to all the panels I can muster. It's great that so many authors are attending this year. I can't wait to meet everyone in person."

Kristin had made the move to New York City from Iowa years before, and now her new hometown would be hosting every

New York Times and *USA Today* bestseller for the next few days at Murderpalooza, the premiere thriller conference.

Larry, eyes glued to his phone, spoke next. "People on Twitter are saying they think Kevin is a shoo-in to win the M-TOTY." This is what everyone in the industry called the award.

"I think so too. I loved your book, Kevin," Kristin said. "Yours too," she added, looking at both Larry and Marco. "And Vicky's. It's just an honor to be nominated."

It was the requisite phrase that authors used whenever they were up for an award. Kristin won the Agatha two years prior. It *was* an honor to be nominated. She never felt more at home than when she was among her peers.

"Let's get a picture of us for Twitter. All the nominees," Larry said.

"We should wait for Vicky," Kristin said.

"Right. Well, whatever, she's late. We can get another one tomorrow."

Kristin didn't feel right about that, for so many reasons. They shared the same agent, and she liked Vicky, despite recent actions that said otherwise. But that was a secret, for now.

The four of them huddled together for a selfie. Larry uploaded the picture, tagged all of them, and put it out onto Book Twitter, where everyone attending the conference would stalk the Murderpalooza hashtag for the next two days.

Kristin scanned the bar and caught eyes with Mike Brooks. He was one of her best friends in the business, but few people knew that. Tonight, they had to avoid each other. They didn't want people talking. He gave her a quick nod and snapped his head back to his company: Davis Walton. Kristin knew Davis from a writing group in the Midwest. They also shared an agent. Now, she only spoke to him when she had to. Davis was a completely different person since he got a publishing contract, one that she despised. She knew the real him.

A half hour later, Kristin got the text she was waiting for and knew she had to go back to her room and wait. Just as she was about to call it a night, Vicky Overton walked in with her boyfriend, a developmental editor named Jim Russell. They both looked beat—glassy eyed with slumped shoulders. Kristin assumed it was from the long day of delays and travel, but it could've been something else. She knew Jim well enough to know his expressions.

Vicky already had a tote full of books, and she seemed to be seeking out authors to have them signed because yes, authors fangirled over each other. Jim's eyes met Kristin's, then he immediately put his head down, trained to the floor. She was sure Jim didn't want Vicky to see them chummy. They said hello to a few people, and Vicky waved at Kristin and smiled, which made her stomach turn.

The guilt.

As Vicky and Jim left the bar, she stopped to talk to someone familiar. Vicky even pointed the girl toward Kristin, and when they locked eyes, Kristin lost her breath.

Oh no. Forget panels, awards, and presentations. Her stalker was there. *That* made her nervous.

1

VICKY OVERTON

Friday, 11:30 A.M.

It's a Friday afternoon when I decide I hate my agent. Having flown to New York City from Florida to attend this conference, I assumed she'd be waiting with open arms. But no. Penelope Jacques is late, as usual. This is the second time I've met her in person and the second she's been late. Should've been a red flag, but I was a newbie writer and saw her as my savior. After years of rejection, I took the first offer I got. Not that she's a bad agent in general, she just is for me.

Meanwhile, I've already downed a nice cold glass of wine, waiting at the restaurant on Park Avenue for our working lunch. Working, meaning I'm determined to ask her why she isn't. My debut novel was a moderate success. It's up for the highly coveted Murderpalooza Thriller of the Year award, though I'm sure it won't win *("but it's such an honor to be nominated!")*. It's why Penelope said I should attend the conference in person. The flight is a write-off, and the conference comps two hotel nights for nominees. Mini vacation for me and the boyfriend—he insisted on coming. He's in the industry too, but he doesn't have to be at this conference.

So far, Penelope hasn't done squat with my second manuscript, and she takes forever to respond to my emails. It's frustrating because I've been such a great client—I stick to deadlines she gives me, and I don't complain. I finished my third manuscript, and she hasn't had time to read it yet. She didn't even answer my pitch for my fourth book. I started writing it anyway because that's what writers do. We can't sit on our hands; we prefer them tapping at a keyboard. I hope she likes it and has time to read it once it's complete.

I check my watch. Fifteen minutes late. Almost twenty. My boyfriend Jim wants to do touristy things this afternoon, and now we're going to have a time crunch. All I know is that I have to be back at the hotel bar by five o'clock. That's where all the authors gather for some liquid relief after days filled with meetings and panels, before editor and agent dinners. Jim said he would spend the time beta reading my third manuscript, even though I already told him about every plot twist that happens in it. I can never be trusted to keep my mouth shut when it comes to plots and secrets. I get too excited.

Finally, Penelope blows in. She's around forty by my estimation, taller than average, and wearing black pants and a light pink silky tank top, which already has sweat marks poking through. She's holding her long dark hair off her neck. It's almost eighty-five degrees out, but once you've spent thirty Junes in Florida, it's hard to notice the heat. As she approaches the table, I see a pound of makeup sliding down her freckled face, forming different colored lines down her cheeks.

"My Vicky!" she exclaims with flourish, arms spread out after she drops her hair. When I stand, she air-kisses me on each cheek (she's French, after all) and then hangs her obscenely huge designer leather bag on the back of her chair. "So sorry I'm late. My call with Davis Walton's film agent ran over."

She grabs a paper cocktail napkin and blots her face as I seethe about being last year's news. My debut novel got lots of attention on Instagram, but I didn't get a TV or film deal. This year, it's all about Davis Walton, from his spread in the *New York Times* to his starred reviews in the trades and his inking of a blockbuster movie deal. All three months before his book even comes out. Penelope has been laser-focused on everything Davis, and it's likely why I've been getting zero attention. She has her favorites.

"Your hair is different," she says.

It's no longer mousy brown—one of those color-depositing conditioners has made it a bit darker with a purple hue, almost violet. I love it. The creative part of me likes to stretch boundaries. Brunette, blonde, and redhead seem so boring now.

"How's Davis doing?" I ask because I have nothing against him. We follow each other on social media platforms and banter on occasion. Authors are great like that, always cross-promoting each other. I look forward to meeting him in person tonight; we got in too late last night to socialize. Our flight was delayed for hours because of lightning storms in Tampa, and later, Jim acted weird and claimed to be tired from the travel. We passed through the bar where everyone gathered, said hello to a few people, and I got some books signed, but that was the extent of it. A half hour, tops. Davis was there with Mike Brooks and a few other authors, but they were surrounded by adoring fans so I didn't interrupt.

Anyway, it's not Davis's fault Penelope isn't doing her job. I'm happy for him.

"Oh, Davis is busy, always promoting something," Penelope says. "Bee has put the entire marketing team behind him."

Bee Henry. Everyone calls her Bee, because no joke, the woman's name is Banana Henry. She's the editor in chief of the Biggest of the Big publishers. She was so enamored with Davis's novel in acquisitions that she overspent on his advance at auction. Really, what debut gets a two-book, seven-figure deal? I'm aiming for five figures on my next contract. Now Bee has to make that money back, so it's all systems go for Davis.

"Speaking of Bee—have you thought about sending her my second novel?" I ask, hopeful.

Penelope placed my debut at a boutique publishing house, and they only wanted one book—I was considered risky as a debut. They call it "boutique" instead of saying they have no marketing and publicity department, and I'm pretty much on my own. Jim lent me some money, even though we were only dating a few months at that point, and I took some of my savings and hired a publicist to get the word out there. She was good at her job, and now I'm up for the holy grail award, even though my sales haven't gone through the roof. I'm hoping the continuing award buzz around my book will make me an attractive option to someone like Bee Henry and her plus-sized marketing department.

Having only met her once before, I can't read Penelope's face, but she's tapping her fingers on the table and then waves over a busboy and asks for water. Her bronzer has oxidized on one side of her face from the heat, and the blotting makes her look like she has a rash.

"I already sent your second manuscript to Bee's team, and they passed on it," she says.

That's news to me. How could Penelope not tell me that the biggest publisher out there isn't interested? What is her actual plan for me? I hate that I think that: *actual* plan. I'm a writer—it's a crutch word and should be deleted, but really, what is her *actual* plan? Also, what did I expect from someone named Banana? My empty wine glass mocks me, and suddenly, I'm parched.

"Actually," she continues. *Actually.* "I've sent it out to a bunch of places, and no one wants it. Why don't we shelve it? Just write a new manuscript."

My heart sinks, and I want to tell her that this relationship might not be working, but I freeze. She obviously forgot that I recently completed one, and she forgot about my pitch for Book Four. That's how little I mean to her. What do I do with the twenty thousand words I've already written? I will *not* cry in front of her, even though I want to.

Instead, I say, "I really wish you would've communicated this to me earlier." I *really* wish. Another crutch word. Delete. "I could've done a rewrite before we wore out the available options. Has there been any editorial feedback I can work with?"

Her eyes narrow. "I think we should go in a different direction."

We, because we're partners again, after she's been ignoring me for months. Thank God her cell phone rings and stops the absolute rage I'm about to expel out of my wine hole.

She winks and says, "I have to take this, you understand?"

It's probably Davis. Golden boy.

As she answers her phone, I tap my brain for my backlist of ideas in case Penelope the Dream Crusher decides to squash my Book Four idea. Do I write about the best friend with a secret? The wedding that never happened? The husband who murdered his coworker? By the look on Penelope's face, you'd think she was informed that her husband just murdered a coworker.

"I'll be right there," she says quietly and hangs up. Her tear-filled eyes turn in my direction. Her mouth opens to talk, but nothing comes out. She blinks several times in disbelief and finally says, "Kristin Bailey was found dead in her hotel room by housekeeping. Stabbed."

"What?" It's the only reaction I can muster.

Kristin Bailey is the female counterpart to Davis Walton, and I say that even though Davis got more money, more accolades, and more attention than someone who was far more talented than he was. Kristin's novel is also up for the M-TOTY, and I got an advance reader's copy of Davis's book due out in the fall. There's no comparison in the writing—Kristin is better—but Davis is a man. *Here's your cookie with a bag of money, MISTER awesome.*

Still. Murdered? It's hard to wrap my head around it. Who would want to kill her? I mean, besides me. Bad joke. Friendly competition and all that. Crap. Us thriller writers call that motive, don't we?

Penelope holds the cloth napkin to her face and sobs; Kristin was her client too. I don't know what to say. I inch my full glass of water toward Penelope, and she grabs it and takes a gulp, then dips the corner of the napkin in and dabs it under her eyes. The heavy cloth against the tears and the makeup makes it look worse, but I don't tell her that.

"The hotel is trying to keep it quiet right now. They don't want chaos at the conference. I have to go. We can pick this up another time, right?" Penelope says. "Let me call Davis really quick."

Another time? She's actually dialing Davis's number right in front of me. *Actually* again—delete. I flew here for this meeting and for the show tonight. The rest of the afternoon is going to be nothing but madness now. Kristin was murdered in her room. Am I going to be able to enter the hotel? It's a crime scene.

My text message beeps as Penelope gathers her bag. My cell is face down on the table, and I turn it over, expecting Jim, but it's from an unknown number.

Did you know Kristin was sleeping with your boyfriend Jim? Check his texts. Maybe you're next.

2

DAVIS WALTON

Friday, 11:30 A.M.

What the hell is that noise? A vacuum?

I turn over, and the clock reads eleven-thirty. A.M. or P.M.? The blackout shades are drawn. Wait. It's the morning. I see a shimmer of light.

Fuck, I slept until almost noon. Again. Missed the morning panels. Housekeeping must be vacuuming the hallway. I better have put up that *Do Not Disturb* on the door because I'm stark naked. Of course I did. Not my first rodeo.

Beside me, the bed is empty but was slept in. I brought that girl up here last night, right? What a mistake that was, but she—Janie?—threw herself at me. It was at the bar, after the introductory panels. After dinner with my literary agent Penelope, my film agent Susan, my publisher Gary, my publicist Billy. Everyone came out to celebrate me over hundred-dollar steaks. Why not? I'm worth it. I'm Davis Walton.

Once I got back to the hotel, *to get a good night's sleep,* I stopped for a nightcap. What's going to make me pass out better than more alcohol? I wanted to catch up with some other writers too, ones I hadn't yet met in person. Mike Brooks was holding court at the bar, I remember that. We got along great, like I knew we would. I tried not to brag, while he lamented about his failures. The guy was supposed to be the next Lee Child. He was—a decade ago, anyway. Four massive *New York Times* bestsellers, back after the turn of the century. His fifth was panned. Books six through eight chased his early fandom, never living up to the hype of his name. Supposedly, he's got something new with a co-author, all a big secret right now. Something that's supposed to take the industry by storm.

He should brace himself for more failure. Maybe he hasn't read the industry press releases, but I am the storm.

Our beers turned into tequila shots, then scotch. You know, gotta look the part. By the time my sport coat came off and my sleeves were rolled up, everyone at the conference wanted a piece of me. Other agents slipped me their cards, *just in case.* At only thirty-three, I'm the toast of the whole Murderpalooza.

By the time the girl whose name might be Janie showed up with her friend, I only had one eye open. I remember she was short, barely came up to my shoulder even as I sat on the bar stool. Her hair was long and dark, and she was plain—no distinguishable features that I can recall, though she looked a little familiar. Small industry. My hangover haze is preventing me from remembering mundane details. Mike Brooks had long since scurried home to the ball and chain on the Upper East Side where he lives, and Janie made a move (the fingers, all five, through my mop of dark curls), so I responded. The pit bull friend with the wedding ring, Connie, kept pushing her on me and me on her.

I'm savvy enough to know what Janie wanted. A story to tell her friends. How she fucked the big shot from LA. I get enough tail, but I guess she convinced me. I guess shit happened, even though I don't remember, because I see a condom wrapper and a stray lipstick on the floor.

Truth is, I don't remember leaving the bar. I could've had both of them last night.

My phone is in my pants pocket on the floor next to the wrapper, so I rise from the bed and retrieve it. After typing in my passcode, it's a barrage of green banners. I'll never get used to a hundred texts and missed calls every morning. The move from Illinois to LA last year was a good one, and perfectly timed since Penelope Jacques came knocking on my email less than a month later, wanting to represent my book and promising great things. Her agency is the top book-to-film agency in the country, and they hold the rights. So far, she's been keeping her end of the bargain. I'm in Book of the Month for September, she got it in Reese's hands, even though she doesn't feature men, and there are full-page ads in every trade and entertainment magazine in the country. That's in addition to being the number one most anticipated release on every website. The book sold to three foreign territories for translation so far. I'm making Penelope rich.

While I listen to voicemails (industry shit, people wanting to see me, have some *face time*), I open the blackout shades, and my pupils shrink like my dick in the pool. Ouch. I blink a bunch of times and look for my sunglasses, which I find on the desk. I put them on and look out the window, down forty-eight floors to the street. My publisher got me the penthouse suite. God, I'm sunglasses-inside cool.

Still, I have an outside, so I might as well use it. I grab the hotel's pen and notepad and open the sliding door to my private balcony. It's really more of a terrace, red and gray brick with planters holding multicolored flowers. Two chaise lounges are at the far end near a mini fridge. There's a wrought iron table with an umbrella and four chairs, and I scrape one back as I delete, delete, delete the voicemail messages one by one. It's amazing how this high up, I can still hear the incessant horns from the traffic below. Does no one know how to drive in this city? I'll take the LA gridlock and smog over this noise any day.

The phone rings again as I'm listening to my messages, and it's Penelope. I smile before I answer so she can hear it in my voice. We writers have a commonly used phrase that only translates on paper: *he smiled, but it didn't reach his eyes.* No one thinks that or says it out loud. Ever. I make sure my smile reaches my eyes. I'm Mr. Nice Guy, *humble* according to *GQ* and everyone I interact with.

"Hey, Penny, what's up?"

It's a nickname I gave Penelope the first time we talked, and she was so enamored with me that she lets me—*only me*—call her that.

There's a sniffle. "Davis?"

She says it like a question. "Yes, it's me. Is everything okay?"

"No. It's Kristin Bailey. She—she was found in her room. Stabbed."

"What?" I move to the chaise lounge and open the mini fridge. Empty. Fuck. I need a drink to get through this. "Holy shit! Is she okay?"

"She's dead, Davis."

A million things go through my mind.

I'm off the hook.

"Oh my God. Where are you?"

"I sat down for an early lunch with Vicky Overton, but I'm leaving. I'm going to the hotel. Can you meet me near the bar in a half hour? Don't say anything to anyone yet."

"Absolutely. Do you need me to do anything?"

"No. Just don't talk to any press if they're there. Wait for me."

She hangs up. Don't talk to press? That's like telling a politician not to tweet. I'm a natural in front of the camera.

In the bathroom, I attempt to turn the lights on again. When I checked in yesterday, I had no idea what I was doing. Why were lights on an iPad attached to the wall? It's not like I'm unfamiliar with an iPhone, but I don't understand the icons in the dark, and when did switches go out of style? When everything is turned on, I jump in the shower to wash off the alcohol and Janie, and all I can think about are the promises Kristin Bailey and I made to each other. Does this mean I don't have to deliver anymore? Admittedly, her out of the way isn't the worst thing for me, unless she told someone what she knew.

With a towel wrapped around my wet lower half, I wipe the steam from the mirror, grab my phone again, and start to clear my text messages. The ones that come from strange numbers always start with "Hi, this is so-and-so, we met at so-and-so." When I see a text from an unknown number that doesn't start that way, I'm curious.

All it says is, *I know about your deal with Kristin. Maybe you're next.*

3

MIKE BROOKS

Friday, 12:00 P.M.

"What time are you coming back?" my wife Nicole asks me.

I pull on my sports jacket despite the heat I know is outside because Nicole shut the windows. She's lived in New York City her whole life—born and raised—and she enjoys fresh air and car horns. When Nicole closes all the windows, she's trying to trap the cool air inside, which means the heat outside is unbearable. We have AC units in every room in our Upper East Side prewar classic six. Nicole has been begging to move to a splashy new building with central air, but I like old things. I think this with a cringe as I see the sides of my dark hair turning rapidly grayer than they used to be. My pants are a little tighter every day. Pushing fifty is no joke.

"It's just lunch with Vita," I say.

"Mmm," she says. Then adds, "I'm surprised she hasn't dropped you yet." She says it under her breath but loud enough for me to hear. I don't blame her for nitpicking on me for the better part of five years.

Sure, she married me at the height of my fame a decade ago. I was thirty-seven and on my fourth *New York Times* bestseller, one of which became a movie.

Four more books and ten years later, and I haven't had a hit since then. That being said, my latest project will be my way back in. I'm trying a very avant-garde approach, with a co-author that I'm being hush-hush about. I have over fifty thousand fans making all sorts of guesses from my newsletter, but so far, no one knows who it is. Not even my wife. My agent, Vita Gallo, emailed pitches to editors trying to garner interest right after I turned it in to her.

"Vita still believes in me. She's got meetings scheduled with a number of editors over the next few days to try to sell my new book in person. This conference is a good thing."

Nicole fluffs up her bleached hair while facing the mirror, then puffs up her surgically enhanced fortieth birthday present under her dress—she had the twins at thirty-five and wanted a "lift" at forty, but somehow that turned into D-cups. Satisfied, she sits at the edge of the bed and buckles a heel, getting ready to meet a friend for lunch.

"Are you going to let Vita know who your secret co-author is?" she asks as she stands, turns her back to me, and lifts her hair off her neck.

"No." I zip up her red structured blouse. "I told you, that's done by design. The intrigue and the guessing are getting buzz. The other author doesn't want anyone to know."

"Doesn't want anyone to know or doesn't want to hitch themselves to the titanic?" She raises a perfectly groomed eyebrow.

Yes, I know, I'm sinking to the bottom of the ocean faster than that billion-carat blue diamond necklace.

"I'm sorry," she says quickly, putting her hand to her head. "Everything has been such a roller coaster lately, and I've been feeling a little neglected. You've been working on this for almost a year. Plus, I haven't been feeling well. I don't mean to take it out on you."

When I first met Nicole, I was thirty-three. She was a plus-one at my third book release party and writing for *The Atlantic* after giving up on her novel. She worked her way to me, and I noticed her immediately. It was her perfect nose. It's got to be what plastic surgeons have on display as the ultimate "after." And it's natural. I thought about how good we'd look in photos.

Of course, that's something narcissistic authors think. Everything is about us, and the reality, I've learned, is that no one cares about us more than we do. Reader reviews online? Everyone else glosses over them while we obsess. Trade reviews? We look for our own—I can't remember the last time I read a trade magazine to see what they were saying about *other* writers.

The last five years, I've been struggling with my slow-burn detective-crime-drama audience when most bestsellers seem to be splashy commercial beach read thrillers with a million twists. My longtime publisher, after eight books, finally dropped me last year. Vita had told me I should just say who my secret co-author is so she can tell potential editors and the rest of the literary world.

No way. I signed a confidentiality agreement. Even Nicole doesn't know who I've been spending my nights with for the better part of a year.

"I know, honey, and I'm sorry this book has taken up so much of my time. But good things are coming. Vita believes in me," I say again.

Nicole stands in front of the mirror and applies gloss to her lips, presses them together, and smiles, rubbing her teeth with her index finger like a junkie testing the quality of cocaine. She's not listening to me. I can't really blame her. I've been so damn boring lately, and I turned into an old man this past year, almost forty-eight, while Nicole just turned forty-one. For me, it's dinner at six and bed at eight. When I'm home, that is.

"Oh, before I leave, how'd last night go?" she asks, finally interested. I had texted her that I was with Davis Walton, the go-to boy. The one everyone wants to be.

The old me.

"Good," I say. "Davis was still there when I left. He was fine, surrounded by women."

Davis is a damn lothario if the gossip websites and whisper networks are to be believed.

No one has hit on me for half a decade. That comes with being a has-been.

There was that one time . . .

"I bet they were all over him. Must be nice to be that young." She smirks.

Burn.

"I've got to go and meet Donna," Nicole says. "The kids get dropped off from camp at five-thirty, and Janina will be here to greet them if I run late. I assume you'll be late again tonight?"

What would we do without our part-time nanny, Janina? I nod. "Lunch with Vita, then I'm going to check out the panels and meet up with some of the others at the bar and grab a quick bite before the ceremony. I've been chatting with Suzanne Shih and Dustin Feeney. They're both clients of Vita's, so we made plans."

Her eyes squint. "I've heard of Dustin. Who's Suzanne Shih?"

I don't meet her gaze. "New. Young. Vita signed her about five months ago, and I only met her once. I think they're done with edits, and Vita is about to shop her book. I read the unedited manuscript. It's good."

It is good. It's going to sell this week at the conference. Everyone likes the splishy-splashy *friend-with-a-past-secret-wrecking-everyone's-life* novel. Hopefully, there's an editor out there who likes old white male smokers in trench coats and fedoras trying to solve mafia crimes.

Nah. That's my old stuff. My new project is the shiny new thing everyone is looking for.

My phone rings. Vita.

I hold up an index finger to Nicole like I'm an important person who needs a moment of quiet for a super important call. "Hey, Vita, I'm walking out the door," I say.

Her Italian accent booms through my cell. "No, no. Don't come!"

Holy shit. She's dropping me. My career is over. My face must show my panic because Nicole silently mouths *What?* I'm sure she saw the color drop from my forehead to my neck. I certainly felt it fall.

"There's been a murder," Vita continues. "Kristin Bailey. *E morta.* She's dead. They found her in the room. Stabbed."

A high-pitched piercing sound runs through my head, like microphone feedback, and I feel my brain split in two. Kristin Bailey is dead. She was my friend. "I've got to go. I'll meet you at the hotel anyway. Holy shit."

"Don't tell anyone. The hotel is trying to keep it quiet, but it already made Twitter."

Twitter. The bane of every author's existence. "I'll see you soon."

I disconnect and slide the phone into my jacket. Disbelief washes over me, and I picture her face. Smiling. Concentrating. Working. Two computers open, a stack of notebooks with hand-written notes, printed pages so she could sort her plot. She had a frantic calm about her, which radiated to those she knew. She was Black on her mother's side, Brazilian on her father's, and a real beauty. She always wore her relaxed curls pushed back in a headband and little white collared shirts tucked into trousers. Loafers. A preppy. I don't know one person who didn't like her.

But someone killed her. Kristin Bailey is dead.

I keep repeating it in my head. *Kristin Bailey is dead.* It can't be true.

I loved her, but not in a romantic way. She was a great person and a terrific writer. She was my friend, and now she's gone. I swear I think all of that first. Then the selfish part creeps in: am I going to be able to sell this book, as mine only, now that my secret co-author was just murdered?

My text beeps as I head to the door, and I retrieve my phone from my left breast pocket. It's from an unknown number, and I know I go pale again.

I know you wrote the book together. How convenient for you. Maybe you're next.

4

SUZANNE SHIH

Friday, 12:00 P.M.

Wipe the smile off my face. Just try.

Shuffling to the door with the other writers, I can't believe I'm here. I can't believe I had breakfast with *my agent* Vita this morning. Thank God we went off site because I heard the eggs at the buffet are cold and rubbery and usually gone by eight A.M. anyway. I can't believe I'm at Murderpalooza and *my agent* is going to talk to real live New York City editors about my book! I'm going to be famous. I am. It's all I've ever wanted.

My friends in suburban New Jersey couldn't believe it last night when I sent them pictures of who I was hanging out with at the bar. Okay, I wasn't really hanging out with them, but they were there. Oh-Em-Gee, Davis Walton! Mike Brooks! My favorite, Kristin Bailey, was also there, but I couldn't introduce myself to her. Vicky Overton passed through with some guy I assumed was her boyfriend. I almost fainted when she spoke to me and even said she'd meet me for drinks today when everyone is back here later tonight. Better believe that's going to be plastered on my social media. Most of my friends are still in grad school or working entry-level jobs, but I'm going to be an actual published author soon, hobnobbing with the entire mystery/suspense/thriller section of Barnes & Noble. All before I turn twenty-four next month!

I'm just leaving the *Showing vs. Telling* panel that the conference is hosting. That was another one where I bounced around on my seat, trying to contain my excitement about the authors that were speaking and the people who were sitting around me. In the flesh. When I say I've idolized these writers, it's an understatement.

My shoulder hurts from the tote bag of books I've been lugging around since this morning. Did I put twelve hardback new releases on my parents' credit card? Yes, I did. One day, someone will be just as excited to be carrying mine around. When I'm famous.

"Great streaks," a young woman says to me as we amble out of the conference room, then smiles and sticks out her hand. "Hi, I'm Tara Kretz. First time here?"

"Hi, thank you! Yes, first time. Suzanne Shih."

"Nice to meet you."

I shake her hand, then absentmindedly touch the pink streaks I recently got in my long, sleek, black hair. My mother wanted to kill me when I got home from the salon. My parents are too "traditional." But I'm an artist. Writing is art. I get a lot of inspiration from my sorta-boyfriend Constantine too. We've only been together a few months. He dropped out of school and he's in a band—my parents will drop dead on the spot when they meet him, with his bleached hair and piercings and tattoo sleeves.

Plus, half the people here have rainbows in their hair. My people. I did decide to dress more conservatively than my usual punk rock style. Though I'd normally be in torn jeans, leather, and lace, I had on a short sleeved black dress—with pockets. The female holy grail.

"How did you like the panel? Exciting stuff, right? Do you have rep?" Tara asks.

Rep. So cool. So, so cool. "Yes, I recently signed with Vita Gallo. She's putting my manuscript on sub soon. She's got a lot of meetings set up today. It's nerve-wracking."

Tara nods. Her strawberry blonde, non-rainbow-altered waves are the perfect accent to her peaches and cream complexion. She's probably only a few years older than me. Definitely under thirty. She's wearing a black skirt, a tank, and a blazer, which I wish I had with me because it's freezing in this place. I peg her as quiet and sweet. "Nice. I'm with Jeff O'Malley. We just sold to Bee Henry's team last week. Angela Rivera is going to be editing."

I've seen Angela's name in the acknowledgements of at least half a dozen books I've read. "You'll be in great hands." God, I think I would just about die if Bee Henry bought my book.

Tara glances at her watch. "Hungry? I hear they have good tapas plates at the bar upstairs."

Despite being a moody rocker, Constantine always describes me as "bubble gum happy" and said I'd be truer to my personality if I wore frilly pink stuff, whatever that means. Wouldn't that be the way, me looking like a stick of Bazooka Joe. I'll admit, my cheeks hurt from the smile that's been on my face all morning already, and now, a friend to lunch with.

Wipe the smile off my face. Try.

"That sounds great!" I have to stop speaking like everything I say has an exclamation point at the end. But again, I can't help it. Bubble gum happy. "Do you think I have time to run upstairs and drop this bag off in my room? I've been dragging it for over three hours."

Tara reaches into her purse and yanks out two books. "From last week's *New York Times* list. These aren't getting any lighter either." She laughs.

Only two books? She doesn't have what it takes to be famous.

The mood changes as soon as we get to the makeshift lobby area. People stand around, their own tote bags packed to the brim with books. Some even have small wheelie bags full of them. Now, where obscure chitter-chatter used to be in the background, people are hushing. And *shushing*. And there's an authoritative voice commanding everyone not to loiter but to go to the left, up the stairs, and to the main lobby. Which is fine, that's where we were going anyway. As the people part, I see lots of men in police uniforms.

Uh oh. I push the feeling down that they're looking for me and clutch my huge studded leather tote closer to my body.

"What's going on?" Tara whispers, a line forming between her brows. Maybe she is over thirty?

I shrug. *Please don't let this be about me and what happened this morning.*

The chatter slowly gets loud again, a mix of surprise and panic. Some people are holding their hands over their open mouths while staring at their phones; others have their palms over their hearts. Voices get louder. Someone screams *Oh my God!*

"What happened?" I ask a man beside me. Wait, that's not just a man, that's Kevin Candela. I've read two of his books, and he's up for the M-TOTY award tonight. However, it seems like an inappropriate time to fangirl because something serious is definitely going on.

He turns to face me, sweat on his forehead. "I can't believe this is true, but on Twitter, they're saying Kristin Bailey is dead." It doesn't register at first because *omigod* Kevin Candela is speaking to me, and then . . . what?

"Dead?!" Tara shouts. "Holy fucking shitballs!"

So much for quiet and sweet.

At least I know what the commotion is about now. It's not about me. But it will be. Crap.

Then the worst, the most *oh-no-it-didn't* thing happens. The elevator doors open and surrounded by four uniformed men and someone wearing a jacket that says *Coroner* is a stretcher. The gasps are audible as someone points and shouts. There's not a person attached to oxygen being wheeled out to an ambulance. It's a fully zipped body bag being wheeled out to a waiting van.

Afraid I'm going to be sick, I cover my mouth. Not Kristin. Please, no.

I'm sure I look awkward the way I slither my arm into my tote. I brought three of Kristin Bailey's softcovers from my own collection at home, and I wanted her to sign them. My idol is . . . dead . . . in a bag. This can't be happening. She died thinking I'm crazy. I'm not. I never got to fix it, and now she'll never sign my books.

The chatter turns into gasps, and some people are visibly crying. I didn't know Kristin personally, no matter how much I wanted to or how many email interactions we've had. I assumed I'd meet her in a friendly tete-a-tete with some other authors tonight when she'd see how *normal* I really am, but that's not going to happen now, is it?

Worse, I just know I'm going to get questioned for this. That's not how I pictured myself becoming famous. My phone dings from my purse, sobering me. I try to open it inconspicuously as to not reveal my Kristin fan club inside. I look at my phone in my hand. It's a text from an unknown number, and when I swipe it, my heart stops.

I know you were stalking Kristin. Does anyone else know? Maybe you're next.

5

VICKY OVERTON

Friday, 12:00 P.M.

While Penelope was still here, in front of me, downing water and crying, I texted back *???* from under the table to the unknown number telling me that not only is Jim cheating on me with a dead person, but also that I might be next. I didn't want Penelope to see my shaking hands. I hope my reaction was appropriate, doing the stuff I make my characters do when they find out shocking news. The hand over the mouth, the wide eyes, the *omigod*. She's a literary agent, not a psychologist. She'd never be able to tell I faked it, but mixed feelings is an understatement if the text I just got is true. Kristin and Jim? I can't accuse him until I find out what's going on.

My phone lights up, and the text I sent to that number has come back as undeliverable. Who the hell sent it?

Penelope was late, then took off before we got into the meat of what I need to discuss with her. But instead of lunch with me, she called *Davis* right in front of me and asked *him* to meet her at the bar. She even stuck me with the bill—*even*—delete—for my lone glass of wine. Well, okay, I'll be honest, I just ordered another one and closed out the tab. As she would say, *C'est la vie!*

Once I pay the bill, I text Jim. I have to wrap my head around this, and I need to get a look at his phone. My texts let him know there was an emergency, that Penelope took off, and I'm free for the rest of the day. I won't give him details until he's in front of me, because his reaction will give me fodder for my books for years to come: *I knew he was faking it because the guilt registered over his face; the short gulp of breath, the slow blinking* . . . He writes back immediately and tells me to stay where I am and he'll meet me for lunch instead since he has nothing else to do.

I bet. His mistress is dead.

He asks me where the place is, and I tell him the corner and cross street. The clientele around me looks like the power lunch crowd with button downs and slacks and "let's put a pin in this" and "circle back" talk. I find myself eavesdropping on some conversations, wondering if anyone from the conference is here. Kristin's name is never mentioned, so I assume they're all bankers and lawyers and advertising execs. When I finally flag down the waiter, I apologize for closing the tab so quickly and ask him to restart another just as Jim walks in. He's easily recognizable, especially in the city. It's probably because of how he dresses. He screams *I'm from Florida!* with his Adidas flip-flops and stupid hat. I shrink in my chair a smidge.

Jim is always super tan—*super*—delete. His black hair below his cap ripples in waves, likely from the humidity, because this is what it's like most of the time at home in Florida. Against his bronzed skin and shocking blue eyes, he's a vision. Always has been.

Jim spots me and waves like he's nine years old and just spotted Mickey next to Donald Duck and heads toward me. As he gets closer, I see the hat logo and notice it's Tampa Bay Lightning. Is he trying to get us killed in New York Rangers country? My knuckles are white with rage, gripping to the wine glass, and I have to restrain myself from throwing it at him even though I want to cry at the thought of him cheating on me. Get the facts first. It could just be a bad prank.

"Hey, babe." He pecks me on the cheek and sits down across from me, in the seat my agent occupied twenty minutes earlier. Before she left to go deal with the *omigod not Kristin Bailey!* situation. "What happened? Why did Penelope leave?"

Jim is simple, and that's one of the things I love—*loved*—about him. I don't even know how to feel, and I push the tears down. He's *swears* he didn't come to the conference to network, only to support me. He's secretive about who he works with, anyway. All he's ever told me is that five *New York Times* bestsellers are clients. Who? No idea. *I have to keep my clients' privacy. No one wants to admit they need help in this industry.*

Now I know why he's here. Secret lover time.

We met at a small writing conference in St. Petersburg about four years ago, and I hired him to edit my book before I searched for an agent. He worked absolute magic on it, but we didn't get together until about a year and a half ago. I ran into him at a restaurant where his friend was bartending. We remembered each other, made a date to "hang out," and the rest is history. He always says how happy he is.

Now I question everything. Was he really visiting his parents in West Palm last month or was he up here, with her? I made him a gourmet meal when he came home because he complained about his mother's cooking. Meanwhile, he was probably squiring Kristin around to Michelin-rated restaurants. Because I read so many thrillers, my mind flies to lacing his coffee with antifreeze or stabbing him in the neck with the butter knife in front of me. Why don't I, though? Because I'm not a stupid character in a stupid book who turns into a murderer for no reason. I need to be strategic about this if it's all true. I still owe him money, and honestly—he's brilliant.

"What took you so long?" I snap. Shit. Didn't mean to sound so cross. I'm still reeling from the *Kristin-Bailey-is-Jim's-girlfriend* news.

He shrugs. "I got lost."

"I told you it was thirty-ninth and Park. It's walkable from the hotel."

He grabs Penelope's untouched water—I haven't yet found a way to turn it into wine, so help me Jesus—and gulps it down. "I don't know my way around the city, so I took a cab. But the cabbie asked me which corner once we got here, like I know what direction I'm facing. Then he started screaming 'North? South? East? West?' like I knew what the hell any of that meant. Anyway, he turned down thirty-ninth and let me out, and I kept walking and ended up on a different avenue altogether. Turns out, I was right across the street originally, but what do I know?"

Did he not see the huge sign with the restaurant name in big block letters *on the corner of 39th and Park?*

"So," I start, taking a long sip. "I have news."

The waiter comes over, and Jim orders a Michelob Ultra, bottle, no glass, and I cringe again. We're not at a dive bar watching football.

"What news? Did Penelope sell your book?" he asks, his large blue eyes unblinking.

I make a noise, one I don't mean to because *GAH* he's probably expecting a paycheck so I can return that borrowed money, and I have to smooth this over. "No. Apparently, it's been turned down a lot. But that's not what I have to tell you."

His eyes narrow. He never liked Penelope. Called her a predator as soon as she signed Davis Walton and turned ninety percent of her attention to him.

"Turned down? What are you talking about?"

I wave my hand in front of my face. *No big deal.* Sure. "No, that's not it. She left because she got a disturbing call." I pause for dramatic effect. *Feast on this.* "Apparently, Kristin Bailey was found murdered in her hotel room this morning."

There's a moment. A ping. A nanosecond. His eyes glaze and recover. Good liar. Thanks for the reactions, which I'll be penning in my next novel. Here's your cookie.

"Oh. Wow." He swallows, and his Adam's apple bounces in front of me like it's a bobblehead on my dashboard. Hula dance, bitch. *Hu. La. Dance.* "Isn't that the girl who was up for the award tonight? Against you?"

I nod.

The girl. Him and his lies.

"How did Penelope find out?" he asks.

"Don't know. She got a call from someone."

My eyes narrow, waiting for him to give something away. Now I know why he stiffened all the times his texts rang out yesterday and he ignored them. I'm sure Kristin was pissed that her lover was in New York and not answering. Then again, I was in half a coma last night. Maybe he snuck out to see her while I slept.

I may be judgey wudgey like the bear, but the earlier text message is bothering me. *Did you know Kristin was sleeping with your boyfriend Jim? Check his texts. Maybe you're next.*

So, someone here knows that she's been screwing Jim. Recently.

Who?

Does this mean I'm going to be a suspect? It's a fantastic thriller plot. The jilted girlfriend who finds out about the affair and goes stab-happy. God, those plots irk me. How often do regular, stable people turn to murder? If you're a thriller reader, you'd sleep with one eye open and trust no one—not your parents, your best friend, your coworkers, and especially not a spouse or lover. They're all fucking crazy murderers. Which means Jim is a suspect too.

But that's fiction. My more pressing issue is, how the hell am I supposed to go on record about where I was before I met Penelope for lunch?

6

DAVIS WALTON

Friday, 12:00 P.M.

The elevator stops a billion times on the way down to the lobby, the perils of being in the penthouse suite. Everyone wearing a conference badge recognizes me. I can tell because their breath catches or they try to look away. They smile at me. They know me, but I don't know them.

Even though the bar is packed, it's quiet. Morose. Everyone is getting the news that Kristin is dead, so this is her first unofficial wake. Penelope is across the room, talking to one of the agents who tried to poach me last night. Meghan something. The gossipy bitch—Jesus, her Twitter doxes everyone. She doesn't care if you're a famous author, agent, editor, or a newbie. She says what she says without apologies.

Wearing my million-dollar smile, I head over. They stop speaking as soon as I approach.

"Oh, Davis, thank God!" Penelope says, then hugs me dramatically. "Oh shit, I'm so sorry." She pulls back and motions to the bronzer and mascara stain on my shirt.

Fuck, really? This is Versace. I grab a cocktail napkin and dip it in the water glass on the table in front of them and wipe.

"It's okay, Penny. I know you've had a rough morning." She'll send me a new one. I swivel to that Meghan woman and stick out a hand. "Davis Walton. Nice to meet you." I don't need to give her up and let Penelope know she tried to poach me. She's grateful, because right before that, she looked like she was about to shit her pants.

"Hi. Meghan Morgan. I'm an agent with Nelson-Tully."

You don't say? Her card is still in my wallet.

"This is crazy. I can't believe Kristin is dead. This has to be an inside job, something to do with the conference. Who would stab her?" Penelope asks.

"Vicky Overton," Meghan says with an unapologetic scoff.

"Vicky?" Penelope doesn't bite. "Why would you say that?"

"No, no, no. I don't think she killed her. I just mean she's up for the same award tonight."

Meghan Morgan knows exactly what she's doing.

"So are Kevin Candela, Marco Crimmins, and Larry Kuo," Penelope says.

I decide to add my little something of absolutely nothing to this conversation because I don't want anyone to think the murder had anything to do with my connection to Kristin, so I shrug and decide to add my own flair. "I see what Meghan means. Only one female left now."

The small percent of Midwestern corn boy left in me instantly regrets it. Why did I say that? I don't think Vicky had anything to do with this. I'm perpetuating a lie to keep the heat off me. Kristin was right; maybe I am a coward.

Meghan whips out her phone and starts tapping away. Great. Penelope picks up a glass of something dark and fizzy, takes a gulp, and makes a face that turns her ugly.

"Can I get you another drink?" I ask her, even though she should be buying my drinks. I'm a client.

"I'm good, but I have a tab open. Why don't you order something and put it on there?"

"Thanks, I will. Have you spoken to the police yet?"

She shakes her head. "Not yet. I mean, I talked to one for a second, but I think he's an investigator with the hotel. Pearson, I think." She lowers her voice and curls her finger for me to lean in closer. "They're trying to keep it quiet in case someone from the hotel is involved. Supposedly, there was no forced entry." She straightens up and speaks normally. "I told him I was Kristin's agent and gave him my card, so I'm sure I'll have to go on record eventually. Especially if . . ." She stops. Her wheels are turning, and she whispers again. "I mean, it's targeted. Right?"

Is it someone from the hotel, or is it a conference thing? That text I got proves that someone knows my connection to her. Am I really in danger? Could I really be next?

"Right. So they don't know how the killer got into her room?" I ask.

"They don't know if it was a break-in from someone who works here and had access, or if someone was already in there with her. Or if she knew them."

"So it could be anyone at the conference then?" My eyes shift. Is the person who texted me watching? Are they here? It could be anyone—Penelope, Meghan, hell, it could be Bee Henry. And I suppose it could be Vicky too. That makes me feel better about what I said out loud.

Penelope looks up at me with her huge dark eyes. "Davis, you take care of yourself. Don't trust anyone. What if this is only the first one?"

Ha. Too late. The texter already threatened me. Should I mention it to Penelope? Nah. Not yet.

Also, Janie already got to me, and only now do I realize how reckless that was. She could be crazy, and that could've been me this morning, stabbed and left to bleed out until I was discovered by housekeeping. Man, how low rent.

"I'll be right back." I turn around to go to the bar and don't have to elbow my way through because people part like the Red Sea once they see me. At least people aren't talking about the dead girl anymore. Though they should be. How awful—I had my issues with her, but I never wanted her dead. That's bad karma. Too many writers around me have died.

I order a draft beer and take a sip, licking the foam off my lip when I turn around and—

"Davis!"

Shit. It's her. Janie.

She takes me by surprise, and I don't know what to say. She looks way younger than I remember, and it freaks me out. She better be legal. "Hey!" I say, in lieu of botching her name because I'm not a hundred percent sure I have it right. We do the awkward *do we hug or shake hands* thing, and we settle on a small hug. "Did you hear what happened?"

"Absolutely tragic," she says.

Her voice is huskier than I recall, but her image is coming back to my scotch-clouded brain. I definitely recognize that face.

"I know," I say with wide eyes and try to get out of the situation. "Hey, I hate to do this, but I don't have time to socialize right now. I have to get back to my agent. She's waiting." I point.

Her eyes widen. "Ooooh, Penelope Jacques is your agent? Can you introduce me?"

I don't know this girl, and she's asking for favors? She's probably a wannabe writer, getting rejected day in and day out. I don't say another word, just nod and wave for her to follow me, which she does, gripping my elbow from behind. When we get back to the table, Penelope and Meghan are both texting or social-ing on their phones, and I really don't want to have to botch her name but—

"Hey, Penny, this is a friend I met last night." Sure. Let's go with that.

Penelope looks at her and scoffs, then presses her lips together. "Julie Keane. What brings you to Murderpalooza?"

Julie! Not Janie. Oops. How does Penelope know her?

Julie looks defeated as her shoulders slump and her eyes water, but she blinks it away. "Just trying to make some connections, maybe find a few critique partners. I need to do tons of research. I'm sure you know this is new to me."

"Right. Good luck with your 'transition.'" Penelope says it with air quotes, then looks directly at me. "Davis, can we go somewhere private?"

"Sure." I turn to Julie. "I'll catch up with you later."

She nods and quietly makes her way over to the bar, probably to drink away the ice that Penelope just threw on her.

"What was that about?" I ask.

"Don't pal around with Julie Keane. It's not a good look for you," Penelope says with a smirk.

"Who is she?"

She laughs loudly. "A self-published romance writer trying to be a traditionally published thriller writer. She's like twenty-one, and she's been contacting everyone in the industry about this conference for the last couple months. The whisper network knows about her. She reeks of desperation."

Ah. Romance. Self-publishing. The death knell in Thriller World, according to me—it's like assuming you're going to win an Oscar when you're a soap opera star. Jesus, I slept with a romance writer. I'll deny it if confronted. Just hanging around her would take a star off my rating.

Penelope takes another long drink, finishing what was left in one gulp, and makes the ugly face again. How much alcohol is in that thing? Her phone vibrates in her hand, and she holds an index finger up to me to let me know she has to deal with whoever is texting her. I decide to catch up on social media and see what the conference is saying about Kristin Bailey.

I got to the hashtag for Murderpalooza. Twitter is brutal.

I mean, I like it—it hasn't come for me yet, and in general, people on here kiss my ass. But people really have their own take on everything that they portray as fact, and this time, it's the conference's fault that Kristin was killed. The hashtags are everywhere.

#MurderAtMurderpalooza #WhosNext #CancelTheCon #You-CouldntProtectKristin #JusticeForKristin

My notification button is lit up like a Christmas tree, with people tagging me and mentioning me and following me. I always look through my list to see if anyone worthy is there to follow back. The names of the handles normally don't make me sweat, but this one rubs me the wrong way when I see it.

@MPaloozaNxt2Die followed you.

The profile picture is the Murderpalooza logo, a bloody knife, and the page says it was created in June 2022. Today. This morning? I click on it, and it's only following four people.

Me.

Vicky Overton.

Mike Brooks.

Suzanne Shih.

I have to find out who Suzanne Shih is, but first, I need to call Mike.

7

MIKE BROOKS

Friday, 12:15 P.M.

The cab stops in front of the hotel. I drag myself out, wondering what the hell is in store for me in there. The news about Kristin Bailey is daunting. Once people find out that she is—was—my co-author, shit will hit the fan. This makes me nervous, and I loosen the tie around my neck, wondering if the moisture pouring out of me is from the heat outside or the heat I'm about to take inside. I'm either going to be a suspect or this thing will sell for seven figures and secure another movie deal. Publishing someone after they're dead is a whole business in and of itself. God knows what damning evidence is in her hotel room.

Well, besides the manuscript itself. I'm totally screwed once someone else reads it. The storyline is a little close to home.

Despite the heat, I stand on the sidewalk, trying to force myself to open the door when my phone vibrates inside my jacket pocket. I'm perplexed when I look at the screen. It's Davis Walton.

I cringe as I hit the green button to take the call. "Hey, Davis."

"Mike. Where are you?"

His voice is rushed, panicked. He should've been an actor. He's going method, and I wonder how he's going to make Kristin's death about himself.

"I'm outside, about to come in." I pause, and he says nothing. "I assume you heard?"

"Everyone heard. Stay there. I'm coming out."

"I have to meet Vita. She's waiting for me."

"She can wait five minutes. There's something going on. We need to talk."

If he knows that Kristin was my co-author, he's doing a bad job of hiding it.

"Okay. I'm right outside the main doors."

"Go down the block. I'll meet you on the corner of forty-second and Lexington. People shouldn't see us together."

The line disconnects, and as usual, Davis is calling the shots. Everyone saw us together last night, so what's the big deal? Like the sad beaten-down sack I am, I just walk. *Whatever you say, sport.*

I find a spot in the shade under an awning and remove my jacket. I'll put it back on when I eventually go inside, but it's too hot to stand here like an idiot, sweating through my shirt. I fold it over my left forearm and wait. People pass by, all strangers, though lots of them have the conference badge on. Everyone is going on with their lives, not knowing or caring how mine was disrupted. Groups of women exit lunch places with their takeout salads and afternoon coffees, and men pat each other on the back while holding the door open to enter the steakhouses for Masters of the Universe lunches. I stand, shoulders hunched, alone.

"Hey."

I turn and Davis is behind me. He's wearing jeans, and of course he looks cool. Inner jealousy eats at me. I used to be Davis. *Take a good hard look and welcome to your future, buddy. Don't get too cocky.*

Too late.

I extend my hand for a shake. "How was the rest of last night?"

He winces, then waves his hand around. *Not important. Got it.* He probably had a threesome. Because now he gets to live my old life while the industry mentally abuses me.

"Have you looked at Twitter yet?" he asks.

Twitter, the curse of publishing. Everything happens on Twitter before it happens anywhere else. Anyone can find out if they're a *New York Times* bestseller or, alternately, if they're canceled, as soon as they open the app. I try to avoid it as much as possible—it's not good for someone like me. I was famous before social media became a thing. Now what I see are the reviews of my latest work, and it's been sobering.

"No. I'm sure everyone is talking about Kristin." I gulp. "What do you think happened?"

"So you don't know who the 'Murderpalooza Next To Die' Twitter account is?"

Next to die. Sounds like the text I got. How does he know?

Davis, you shit. Davis sent me the text.

I point my finger in his chest. "What game are you playing, Davis?"

He rolls his eyes, and he should, because what am I going to do, hit him? I'm middle aged, and he's Davis Walton. "Stop it," he says, because he knows I'm being ridiculous. "I assume you got a text telling you that you might be next? Because I did too."

Okay, that's shocking. I know I got mine for a specific reason, but does Davis know about me and Kristin co-writing? I need to be careful. We have a legal-binding document that I'm to tell no one. Does that matter if she's dead? I don't know the rules. I'm not an attorney.

"What did yours say?" I ask.

He grabs my elbow and directs me around the block. I was going to resist, but what's the point? When we're against a building in the middle of a side street—less foot traffic—he takes a deep breath.

"Someone on Twitter followed me this morning. The account is named after Murderpalooza and Next To Die. It only follows four people. Me, you, Vicky Overton, and someone named Suzanne Shih."

My eyebrows dent. So what? It's following authors. Welcome to Publishing Twitter.

Still. The name. Murderpalooza. Next To Die.

I begrudgingly open my app and click on my notifications, and yes, there's a bunch of new followers, like there is every time I look at this ridiculous thing. As I said, I used to be someone. Scrolling through, I see the follower with that name, @MPaloozaNxt2Die. I click on it. Davis was right. It's only following the four of us.

It's not just following *authors*. It's following *us*. Why? It hasn't tweeted anything yet.

"Did you get a text from an unknown number this morning?" Davis asks.

I nod.

"Who's Suzanne Shih?"

My hand wipes the sweat off my forehead, no longer from the heat. "She's with Vita also. Newbie. Been with her about four or five months. We're supposed to have dinner tonight. Me, her, and Dustin Feeney."

His head shakes back and forth. "Dinner is canceled. Something is going on. Someone knows stuff." His eyes narrow. "What did you know about Kristin Bailey?"

I go stiff. No way I'm giving that up. He'll just use it against me to make me a suspect, because as soon as certain things come to light, I'm going to be suspect number one. I know this already.

However, he said he got a text message too, so I fake bravado. "What did *you* know about Kristin Bailey?"

He acquiesces. "Well, whatever it is, you can bet your last dollar that Vicky and this Suzanne girl knew something too. We need to meet up. Now. I'll send Vicky a message. Can you get in touch with Suzanne?"

I nod, but no matter who he thinks he is—*Davis Walton!*—I still promised Vita I'd meet her. "You have to give me some time. I have to meet Vita. And the panels—"

"Dude, fuck the panels. Are you listening to me?"

Dude. So hipster, so surfer, yet he's neither but it still works because he can say whatever he wants and it sounds like Grammy-nominated music coming out of his mouth. I stand my ground. I need to see Vita.

"Let me speak to Vita. Find out what she knows. You get in touch with Vicky, and I'll get in touch with Suzanne. Regroup around two?"

He chuckles. Not because it's funny, but because he can't believe I'm defying his orders. "Fine. But not around the hotel. These are your stomping grounds. Where can we go that's quiet and unassuming? And far away. I don't want to be anywhere near this neighborhood in case someone is watching us."

Despite living in the city for over twenty years, I draw a blank. The pressure. "I'll text you an address. But I have to go."

I leave him standing, bewildered. Something's got him nervous. Before going to the bar upstairs, I open Twitter again to get a grip on what's going on. Davis has me flustered, and I didn't appreciate the demands he made, or maybe I don't really understand the gravity of the situation.

The Twitter account is new—June 2022 inception—and this time, there's a tweet from @MPaloozaNxt2Die.

Tick tock, motherfuckers

8

SUZANNE SHIH

Friday, 12:30 P.M.

After throwing up in my room, I rinse out my mouth and go back downstairs to a waiting Tara. I had to drop off the heavy books, and I still need to eat now that my stomach is empty. We can't get a space at the bar for lunch, so we go across the street and find a little café that has a bunch of different salads, sandwiches, and fruit cups. We're able to get a table by the window, a nice spot to people watch. And people are visible now that the coroner's van has pulled away, the one containing my idol's dead body in a bag.

Tara sits across from me on the orange plastic chair and tears open the lid to her Turkey club sandwich, then uncaps her bottle of water and takes a swig. She's pretty, I think. The lines in her forehead have disappeared, and I begin to think she's under thirty again. She has freckles on her nose, but she wears too much eyeliner. Like I should talk—my eyes are small, so I overcompensate with heavy eyeliner and fake lashes. My parents hate it and say I should embrace what God gave me. Well, God gave me a Sephora too.

My stomach rumbles, and I look at my food on the rickety table. I went with a premade California roll and a diet coke. I grab my chopsticks when Tara gets a call from her agent. She indicates she'll be a couple of minutes and turns toward the window to have her conversation. Probably info on Kristin. I'd rather hear it secondhand from her and not look needy by inquiring about it. No sense raising any red flags. I decide to use the time to catch up with social.

First, I check my email and see there's one from the Murderpalooza conference.

Statement Regarding Kristin Bailey Death

Due to this morning's unforeseen tragedy, please take extra precautions when attending panels and off-site meetings. For now, the hotel has asked to keep this as contained as possible until they have a chance to vet all employees' whereabouts between eight and ten A.M. and review the camera footage. They have their own investigator on the case, who will be working with NYPD on the investigation. For now, the awards ceremony will go as planned at eight P.M., but stay tuned for confirmation.

Twenty percent refunds will be given to participants with the full three-day package.

Sincerely,

Jonathan DeLuca, President, Murderpalooza

A stiff statement with no heart. Refunds! They're thinking about money. How typical. A girl is dead. A fantastic, beautiful, wonderful writer is dead. But money.

Second—crap. They're going to review the camera footage. Crap!

I turn on Twitter and look up the Murderpalooza hashtag. The comments are scorching. Of course they are, because it's Twitter, and no one there knows how to play nice in the sandbox.

Really, money? #murderpalooza

Don't you have any sympathy for the family #Murderpalooza?
Sure, prioritize refunds. How dare you

OMG #Murderpalooza can't even keep anyone safe! Everyone should leave!

Cancel the ceremony you pigs! #Murderpalooza only cares about money!

Well, thank heavens we get the awards! Everyone gets to have their cake and eat it too. EXCEPT FOR KRISTIN #Justice-ForKristin #murderpalooza

Then, of course, the theories.

#Murderpalooza this is like one of the books you're promoting. Hella free publicity, no?
#Murderpalooza do you keep track of your authors? All of them?
#Murderpalooza CANCEL THE CON! This can't be random! #accountability
#Murderpalooza I wonder where @VickyOvertonWriter was this morning? Last woman standing for the award. Strange

The last one makes me do a double take. Of course it came from Meghan Morgan—the gossipy agent with the big mouth. Not that I'm going to call her out—I'm still a newbie, and she's got some pretty high-profile clients that I don't want to make waves with if I intend to become famous. Eventually, I'll need authors to blurb my book, and I feel like keeping my mouth shut is the best way there.

But . . . did she seriously just try to throw Vicky under the bus? This is a murder. A real murder, at a real conference. It's not a storyline for a book.

And she's effective! Because now I can't stop thinking about it. Jeez, I saw Vicky last night! It was only for a hot second to say hello when she was passing through with a guy, and she seemed nice and all, but what if that's a cover for who she really is? What if she's a jealous, controlling, crazy person? She pointed out—

Wait a second.

She pointed out Kristin Bailey to me last night at the bar. Was it with snark? I can't remember—I'd had a few beers. I was excited. I was surrounded by these superstars, and I didn't pay attention. I remember Kristin looked tense and that Vicky didn't go over and say hello to her. I know Kristin better than anyone here, despite her not wanting to have anything to do with me.

I click my notifications. Four new followers! And I feel like crap right now because one of them is @VickyOvertonWriter. *The* Vicky Overton followed me, and I notice my total is up to four hundred thirty-three followers. Another follower is @Author_Tara_Kretz. I smile at my new friend and follow her back. The third is @AuthorKRR3. I squint at the picture, then expand it, and yes, that's another newbie writer, Keri, who I met last night at the bar. The fourth is called @MPaloozaNxt2Die. Zero followers, only following four people. I'm about to block it when—

What did that earlier text to me say?

Maybe you're next.

I rub my eyes and look again. It's following me and Vicky and Mike, and also Davis Walton. Wow. Talk about casting a wide net.

Its one tweet says *Tick tock, Motherfuckers.*

Is this meant for me?

I wipe my forehead with a napkin when a text comes in while the phone is in my hands. I squirm into the seat. I don't want to look. I'm feeling a bit nauseated again and place my palm on my stomach to calm it down before I look.

Oh thank God. Mike Brooks.

I need to talk to you. It's important. Where are you?

My shaking fingers type back, *At lunch with a friend.*

Where? It can't wait.

Well, well, how the tides have turned.

I'm across the street. I'll be done in 20 mins. I'll text you as soon as I leave!

Crappola.

Tara hangs up and slams her phone on the table, breaking my anxiety. "Holy fucking shitballs, that was Jeff." Well, that seems to be her catchphrase. "He said the word on Twitter is that it's not random. Like, it wasn't a rando psychopath meth head who got into the hotel. So far, the security tapes are inconclusive, but they're thinking it's conference related. They think the person is still here."

Thank God the tapes are inconclusive. They'll know I was at her door this morning. But I didn't kill her! I hate that my mind flies to Vicky. I never would've thought that if I didn't see that tweet from Meghan Morgan.

But it's a good observation. Where was Vicky this morning?

9

VICKY OVERTON

Friday, 1:00 P.M.

We decide to bag lunch since Jim said he wanted a real New York City "dirty water dog" from a cart, so that's what we do. That poor waiter. Open a tab, close a tab—*sorry!*—reopen the tab, close the tab, and we won't be eating after all . . . I left him a hundred percent tip for jerking him around. I needed to walk off those glasses of wine anyway because if I get any tipsier, I'm liable to accuse Jim before I get facts. We hold hands as I act my way, Oscar-worthy, through Times Square, which smells like that hot dog Jim crammed down. I pretend everything is okay while my head is in a fog.

Jim smiles as he poses with a green M&M, and I snap a picture like I'm on autopilot and step over someone asleep on the sidewalk covered in vomit. Jim stops and places a five-dollar bill next to the man's hand. He's playing the part of tourist so well. He mentioned wanting to visit Madame Tussaud's Wax Museum and the Museum of Natural History. *Look at me! I didn't even know that author you're up against! What was her name again?* He's doing a good job of pretending that the Kristin Bailey news doesn't bother him. I know it does, but I have to check his texts before I accuse him of anything. Looks like I'm as trustworthy as he is.

The dating scene where we live in Florida isn't exactly what you see on TV. It's waitresses and fisherman, barflies and locals. And me, being a writer—well, it's not like I have a commute or fancy lunches or happy hours with coworkers where'd I'd be able to meet people. No bumping into a handsome stranger at the dry cleaners, no group of guys next to me and my friends at a power lunch. I work alone from nine to five, sometimes longer, in my one-bedroom condo that I rent, scraping by on freelance editing until my next book is sold. The first didn't sell for much—high four figures, wahoo! I've done okay with royalties. I'd be doing better if Penelope would do her job and sell my second book.

Now, my boyfriend's girlfriend—also my competition—is dead, and it doesn't look good for me. If she had any evidence of their affair on her computer or texts on her phone, I'm going to be the center of attention at this damn conference in a way I never wanted to be. And there's the whole issue of that text message I got this morning. Someone else knows. Someone else is trying to ruin me.

Jim grabs my hand and directs me away from the Disney characters and the rest of the tourists as we head east, back toward the hotel. At a red light, I check Instagram and see that Davis Walton sent me a direct message.

Hey, can you give me a call ASAP? It's important

Well, la dee da. Golden Boy gave me his cell phone number.

"I have to make a quick call," I say to Jim. "Davis Walton. He said he needs to talk and it's important."

We get off the avenue and go halfway down the side street where it's a little quieter—but only a little. Damn. The horn-honking is incessant, and it smells like hot garbage. Could I live here if I dump Jim and start over? I plug my left ear with my index finger, cradle my phone in my right ear, and wait for Davis to answer. He connects the call by saying his first and last name.

"Hi, it's Vicky Overton."

"Vicky. Where are you?"

Well, hello to you too. Davis and I know each other through social media only; his insistence is a bit off-putting. What if I'd just gotten out of the shower? Was I supposed to tell him I was dripping wet and naked in my hotel room? If the gossip is to be believed, he'd love that.

"Heading back to the hotel. Did some sightseeing with my boyfriend." My heart stabs at the mention of the word *boyfriend*.

"Don't go back to the hotel. Not yet. Have you checked Twitter?"

Oh, jeez. Twitter. Someone probably found out about Kristin and Jim, and there's probably press sneaking all over the hotel waiting to snap unflattering pictures of us. I already see it splashed on social media and the Facebook thriller reader groups that love drama. Me, with my sunglasses on, head down, and my hand in front of my face. *No comment!*

I gulp before I answer. "No. Why?" Play dumb.

"Something is going on. I'm going to ask you something and I need an honest answer."

Shit. "Okay."

"Did you get a strange text message today? One that said you might be next?"

Shit. Everyone knows.

Wait, how does Davis know something so personal? The car horns blur in my ears, and now it sounds like my canals are stuffed with cotton. I lean against a nearby building. I don't know what to say, and I have to say something soon or—

"Okay, I'll take the silence as a yes," Davis says. "Look, I got one too. So did Mike Brooks and probably some kid named Suzanne Shih. There's a Twitter account that's following the four of us. And it has a message for us only. It's connected to Kristin Bailey. We all need to talk. Mike sent me a meeting place off the beaten path. We don't want to be near anyone from the conference. I'll forward it to you. Can you be available at two?"

What he's saying isn't landing on me—is someone following me right now? I look left to right. There are people everywhere, and I don't know who I'm looking for. Is the guy with the takeout bags using food delivery as a cover? Is the well-dressed woman on the phone trying to listen to my conversation? Does the bike messenger with a knapsack have a knife?

I agree to meet him to find out. "Uh huh. Two o'clock."

"Okay, good. Hey, don't tell anyone about this until we figure out what's going on. Deal?"

I nod, then realize he can't see me. "Yes. I'll wait for your text."

"Okay, good. I'll see you soon."

He disconnects, and I hold my phone in my hand and stare at it.

"Everything okay?" Jim asks.

"Huh? Oh. Yeah." Davis said to be covert, and to be honest, I'm done with Jim for now anyway. "I have to meet up with some other writers. Something about . . ." I draw a blank. *Think!* "Davis needs to bounce some ideas off a group of us."

"Davis, huh? Didn't think he'd ever need help from anyone."

Jim keeps up with writer gossip. He knows Davis can be a little . . . extra.

"I've got to go. I'll text you later and let you know when I'll be back at the hotel," I say.

"Who else are you meeting with?"

"Just me, Davis, Mike Brooks, and Suzanne Shih. She's a newbie."

He pecks my lips, stiffly. Under normal circumstances, this would excite him. He'd get to go meet up with Kristin. But now she's dead, and that text message still reverberates.

I open my Twitter app, and yes, there's a follower called @MPaloozaNxt2Die that recently followed me. I click on it. There are only two messages.

Tick tock, Motherfuckers

One of you is next. I'm just not sure who it's going to be yet

10

DAVIS WALTON

Friday, 1:15 P.M.

When Penelope calls, again, to be a drama queen, I tell her I'm out exploring New York since I don't expect the panels to be highly attended this afternoon. It's half true.

The hair on the back of my neck has been at full attention ever since I saw that second tweet. Frantic to blend in, I walk to midtown near Times Square, then jump in a cab to take me downtown near the Freedom Tower. From there, a subway to the Upper West Side and a walk to the address Mike texted me. I took one picture with a Disney character in Times Square to save for later, but I never visited the new tower or the 9/11 Memorial, and I'm not exploring artisan cheese shops and antique stores now.

Since I'm not entirely sure I'm not being followed, I went with a covert operation. The last tweet from @MPaloozaNxt2Die was a direct threat on my life. *One of you is next.* I want to make it as hard as possible for someone to track me around town. I'll post the picture of me in Times Square later, tagging the location. Let someone think I'm there.

Right as I'm about to walk into the bar, I get another text from an unknown number.

The awards ceremony goes on, no matter what, or else. Do you understand?

I damn near shit my pants. My mind spins. My career is on the upswing and screen shots are forever, and I really hope there's nothing in her emails about what I did.

Our system was flawless. A shared email account. We spoke over edited drafts that were saved and never sent. No sent email means no received emails, which means no forwarded emails. Then again, it would be my word over a dead girl's word. I'm terrified to log into it though, in case she had any last words for me.

But I do, just in case.

There's nothing in the drafts folder. Nada. Our entire conversation was erased. Or . . . sent? I click on the sent folder, and there it is. Sent to Kristin's email this morning, right around ten A.M. My heart races and my brain goes foggy. Shit.

She sent it to herself, or maybe the murderer did it, and anyone going through her stuff will be able to see it.

My texts ding, and I jump again—that sound will forever remind me of being threatened.

When I look at the text, it's worse. It's Jonathan DeLuca, the head of everything Murderpalooza.

I'm getting pressure from the rest of the board to cancel the ceremony tonight. I'm starting to think what's the point of the ceremony anyway, considering what I did. This could be bad for both of us.

Good grief, it's like he knows about the text I just got. He's right about what he did. They were bribes I asked him for, that Kristin blackmailed me for, but the show must go on, *or else*, and yes, I understand. Now that Kristin is dead, I'm afraid of the nature of our relationship being exposed. If this thing gets canceled, whoever is screwing with me will end me. I write back.

> *Don't cancel—tell them whatever you need to. Tell them it's non-refundable and people are already complaining on Twitter*

He answers immediately.

> *I want it to go on as well, and I'll do everything I can. Just understand that Kristin being dead changes nothing between us*

Of course it doesn't. Shit, his name is all over that draft, which is now a sent email. All of this could be over. *It's all good*, I write back. I can't tell him someone else might know what we did.

I look over my shoulder one more time for good measure. I have no idea who I'm looking for—a man or a woman, old or young, Black or white, industry professional or regular person. It's driving me crazy. I don't get paranoid. I'm indestructible.

Except I *am* paranoid. Is someone really going to try to kill me? This city should be big enough to hide in. Why do I feel trapped?

The first time I came to New York, I was a kid. Where I grew up in Illinois, the Chicago Cubs ruled everything, though they never won a thing while I was a kid. One time in the summer, my parents packed up small rollaway bags for me and Alyssa, and they got a limo to the airport for the four of us. We jumped on a plane—my first time—and took a four-day, three-night-long weekend to New York. I got to see The Museum of Natural History and the Guggenheim, Central Park, Wall Street, the World Trade Center—a few months before it disappeared forever. And of course, the Cubs playing at Shea Stadium.

My parents are good people. They raised us right, with good Midwestern values. I wonder where I went so, so wrong.

I miss them. With my phone in my hand, I dial them back in Illinois. My mother answers on the first ring.

"Hello, my sweet darling baby boy."

People ponder why I'm as self-absorbed as I am. I'm a classic case for a therapist. This type of behavior is probably what started my deceit. I was always told I was too good.

"Hey, Ma. Is Dad with you?"

"He's out golfing. Should be back in an hour. Why, is everything okay?"

Now is *not* the time to say *I just wanted to say hi and I love you in case this is the last time I ever talk to you* because you just don't say that to an overbearing parent. That and I'm in shock that my father left her alone with her dementia progression.

"No, nothing, everything is fine. I'm in New York, and I remembered that time we came here for the Yankees versus the Cubs, and—"

"Oh," she interrupts. "We'll get there one day and see the baseball. I promise."

I close my eyes and hold the phone to my chest for a second. She's having a bad day. I'm going to kill my father. Why didn't he call Alyssa to watch her? Ma will probably burn the house down without supervision.

"Who's there with you?" I ask, my jaw clenched.

"Your father is here. Paul!" The sound is muffled, like she's covering the speaker. "Paul!"

Jesus. She has no idea what's going on.

"What?" It's his voice answering in the background. I exhale. Of course he didn't leave her. She just forgot he was there. "Hello?" his voice booms through the phone.

"Dad, it's me."

"How are you, son?"

I press my lips together. I can't lose it. Not now. "I'm in New York at a conference. I was just thinking about when we came here that summer. The Cubs game."

"Ah, yes. We had a great time, and they finally won a game! How are the bookish things going?"

I nod, like he can see me. "Good. All good. How's Ma?"

"Eh, well," he says. "She's been having an extended episode. Couple of days now."

Dementia is a cruel way to go.

I look at my watch. "Hey, I'm supposed to be flying back home late tomorrow night, but how about I stop in Illinois? I can catch the first flight out Monday morning and be back in LA by breakfast."

"Son, you don't have to do that. We knew when you didn't make Mother's Day or Father's Day brunches how busy life had gotten for you."

My face grows hot with shame that I passed over seeing my parents and my sister, who lives fifteen minutes away from them, to party. Narcissism is a disease, I swear. I'm the poster boy. Although is it really narcissism if I know I have it? Or is that just an overinflated ego? Thirty-three years of wearing a crown and being carried around on proverbial shoulders while everyone cheered below me will do that to a guy.

"Consider it done. I'll let Alyssa know what time I'll get in and see if she can pick me up from the airport. We can catch up. Have a big family day on Sunday. I miss you guys."

"Us too, son."

"Hey, give Ma a big hug, and tell her I'll see her soon."

We disconnect, and I hope I'm telling the truth that I'll see anyone *soon*. Now my mission is to stay alive for the next twenty-four hours.

Still cautious, I walk on a slant as I enter the dark bar. It's packed, which leaves me on edge. My head swivels left to right. I don't see Mike or Vicky yet, and I have no idea who Suzanne Shih is, but I'm sure she'll know me, so if I get accosted immediately, I'll try not to swing in defense.

There's an unoccupied high-top table in the corner, but it's got the last person's shit on it. I look at the bartender and point to it with raised eyebrows, and he nods. It's free. A busboy comes over with a bucket and dumps the plates and glasses. I jump every time they crash onto each other. Once he wipes the table down, I settle in and open my phone to post my picture on Instagram and Twitter, the one of me and the yellow dog with the floppy ears. I tag the location as Times Square and caption it *Enjoying some down time!* I order a beer from the bartender—God only knows how long it's going to take a server to get here in this chaos—and walk back to the table to see how many likes I got in the last two minutes.

Twitter has a comment on my photo already. From @MPaloozaNxt2Die.

Come on, Davis. We both know you're not there.

11

MIKE BROOKS

Friday, 1:30 P.M.

After I text with Suzanne—where is she, by the way?—I text Vita that I am running late. Following my tense talk with Davis, I need some time. To do what, I have no idea. I walk up and down the block but run into too many conference people. *Hey, Mike, what are you working on?* Pass. I end up ducking into a bookstore—ironic, I know. At least it's quiet. I grab the latest thriller with a cool cover from the table and sit on the floor in the back corner. I open the book to make it look like I'm reading, but all I do is read conference news on my phone from Twitter. And watch to see if that account posts anything new.

Of course there's another tweet, saying one of us is going to be murdered, but the Stalker Murder Account doesn't know which one of us yet. Awesome.

It's no wonder I'm hiding. I'm a coward. I'm not dying to go inside and see Vita.

Dying. Ha.

Seriously, though, what if someone is in there, ready to kill me? To stab me the way they stabbed poor Kristin? Maybe it's better to go there to see Vita and be among people. I'm easier to kill when I'm alone. Tucking my tail between my legs, I stride into the hotel, past the hordes of cops, where I find Vita with a bunch of other agents, holding court in a corner of the bar. "Hit Me Baby One More Time" is playing lightly in the background, and I get nostalgic for my "struggling artist" days. That song was always on the radio when I sat hunched over my desk, hen-pecking out my first manuscript. The good ole days, when I'd have to scrape together quarters for coffee and a lunatic from Twitter wasn't trying to kill me.

"We have a problem, Mike."

That. That's the first thing Vita says to me when I get inside.

"Vita," I say. "What? What's the problem?"

Her eyes widen, and she looks like she's aged five years since I saw her last month. Her dark curls are cut chin length and puff out like a pyramid near each ear. She's a few years older than me, by an earlier estimation when we started our careers together two decades ago, but right now she could pass for my oldest cousin Jami, who spells it that way because she's fancy. Makeup pools in the wrinkles under her eyes, accentuating their imperfections, and I thank God that I don't have to cake myself in foundation every day. I certainly don't need to highlight my age. The emerging writers with their TikToks and Instagram Lives do that for me.

"Mike, let's go over there." She nods to a corner, her charming Italian accent thick.

Slightly fewer people are over there, but that's because it's near the door to the kitchen, and I just know I'm going to get whacked by it a hundred times.

Whacked? My brain won't shut off.

We settle and immediately, *thwack*, the door opens and hits me. Startled, I bump into Vita and she bumps into the wall. This better be some devastating news she has, to have us squeezed in this corner. The scent of the grease from the kitchen hangs in the air after the door closes.

"What is it, Vita?"

Her lip twitches. "I was supposed to see Bee Henry at four o'clock, for you." She pauses. Makes a little scrunchy face. "I'm not sure I should let her read this manuscript. I'm not sure anyone should."

Ideal? No, not even a little. This was supposed to be my comeback.

But the book's subject matter, with just my name on it, is not a good situation. Worse, Vita doesn't know that Kristin was my co-author. A fleeting moment goes by where I think I need to come clean, talk to the police about it. At least tell Vita and see if she can get ahead of it.

This isn't just career suicide. This can be evidence, and evidence that does not paint me in a flattering light. I fold.

"Vita, I have to tell you something about—"

Ding. My phone. A text. Suzanne.

Where are you? You seemed frantic earlier. I'm in the lobby if you're here

My radar goes up. Right. I remember what Davis said. I need to talk to Suzanne, and we need to get to Clover & Crimson on the Upper West Side to meet the others. Find out who knows what. Why it's just the four of us that are being stalked and threatened.

"I'm sorry, Vita, can we pick this up later? Don't stress about the manuscript. There's enough to worry about with this Kristin thing."

"That's what I'm worried about. I don't want anyone else to see it. Before you go, one question, yeah?"

Of course, before she opens her mouth again, I know what she's going to ask. I nod.

"Was Kristin Bailey your co-author?"

Bingo. She thinks I killed Kristin, because of that stupid manuscript. I'm sure my face gives it away. Her eyes go wide and she steps back. She's terrified.

I should've prepared myself to answer this question, but right now it'll get me into more trouble. And I have enough trouble coming my way if the next twenty-four hours play out the way my brain is imagining they will. I grab her shoulders and give her a firm *don't-worry-it's-okay* shake.

I shouldn't have touched her. She's afraid of me.

"I'll call you tonight after dinner, before the awards show starts," I say. "Don't worry. We'll figure something out."

She nods and lets me leave. As I walk to meet Suzanne, I check Twitter to see if whoever is behind that stalker account is still trying to murder me. No other tweets. Yet. But there is a text from Davis.

Hurry up. I think I'm being followed.

Terrific.

12

SUZANNE SHIH

Friday, 1:35 P.M.

There are still people crying all over the lobby. It's only been a couple hours, and the news has spread like wildfire throughout all attendees.

This is not how I pictured my first conference. How am I supposed to build a social platform? I already got Vicky to follow me, and I fully plan on asking her to blurb me once Vita sells my manuscript, but can it sell now? The editors are freaked out. No one wants to take meetings, and people are talking about going home. How am I supposed to make more writer friends? Tara is great, but she has no pull.

I'm here for connections, to be noticed. This is my shining moment. My friends at home are supposed to be jealous of how famous I'm getting. I want to be a full-blown celebrity. So many people nowadays get famous on TikTok, but I'm smart too. I wrote a sure-to-be bestseller! Camera flashes are supposed to be blinding me. People are supposed to be shouting my name. My social impressions should be going through the roof. That's how I picture it, with me wearing sequins or feathers and posing on a red carpet with my hand on my hip for my book-to-film adaptation and everyone telling me how brilliant I am. That's all I want—am I asking for too much?

I'm supposed to make a lifelong connection with Kristin Bailey. To get her to see that I'm great. Not a stalker. Crap, I'm going to be in so much trouble before the day ends.

Mike skips down the stairs, and my stomach clenches. He sees me and raises his eyebrows. I don't know him well enough to know if that's a tell or if he's genuinely happy to see me.

A smile is plastered on my face when he reaches me. "Hi, Mike!" I say it with enthusiasm. *Please, please don't be here to bust me.* "How's your dad doing?"

Last time we spoke, his father had had a heart attack. I want him to know I remember.

"Hey, Suzanne. He's fully recovered, thanks for asking. I need you to come with me. I'll explain on the way."

One thing I've learned is not to go anywhere with a strange man. Sure, I know him, but he's like, fifty. I'm twenty-three. I've heard the stories about how older established writers try to groom younger writers. Then they try to sleep with them. Then they blame the young writer.

"I'd rather stay here. What's so important?"

He lets out a frustrated sigh. "We have to go. We're meeting Vicky Overton and Davis Walton at a bar away from here."

Okay, so the guy knows exactly how to wrangle me. Did he say we're having intimate bar time with Davis Walton? I'm *in.* Vicky too? How cool! Running in this circle will set me up for life. I nod and turn toward the door so he won't see my goofy smile. We're silent as we exit the hotel, and he's walking quickly, bopping and weaving through the sidewalk crowd as I try to keep up. We get to the corner, and he hails a cab.

"Get in," he says as he opens the door.

My stomach gets a knotty feeling again, but I do as he says. He gets in after me and shuts the door. "Eighty-first and Amsterdam, please."

I don't know much about New York City, but I do know that's not close. I'm pretty sure it's the Upper West Side. We're off the grid, and I'm afraid of being left somewhere with no knowledge of where I am. The cab makes a right, and we're heading up Park Avenue—I know it's Park because the traffic goes in both directions and there are planters between north and south.

"What's going on, Mike?" I ask.

He's sweating. Granted, it's hot, but he's also panting like a dog that just ran a marathon. Nerves? He looks like he just swallowed an orange.

"To be honest, I don't know yet. None of us do. Have you checked Twitter?"

I nod.

"Did you see that account called Murderpalooza Next To Die?"

I freeze. Nod again. It's the one that freaked me out.

"Did you get a text this morning with someone saying as much?"

How does he know? Is it him? Am I in danger?

"I want to get out," I say, panicked, and reach for the handle like I'm going to tuck and roll into traffic.

"No, no. Listen. I got one too. So did Vicky and Davis. That account is following only the four of us. We all got a similar text. It has to do with Kristin Bailey. I think we're in a little bit of trouble. We have a connection to her, and whoever is behind this account knows what it is."

Tick tock, Motherfuckers.

I'm in more than a little bit of trouble. "Why? Who is it?" I ask.

"We don't know. But we're in danger. Did you see the last tweet?"

I shake my head and then pull out my phone and open Twitter. I read the last tweet by that account, and I'm sure I go pale. One of us is next?

"What does it mean, Mike?"

"I don't know. But the four of us have to figure it out. Right now. Before this goes any further. We obviously have something—or someone—in common. Someone who knows Kristin." He gazes out the window. "*Knew* Kristin."

"I didn't even know her! I'm not published! What could this have to do with me?"

I think back to the tons of emails I sent to Kristin. The ones I got back, first from her, then her agent, then the lawyers. A lump crawls up my throat. This can't be good. I'm going to look like a suspect. A stalker. But I'm not—I'm normal. A fan.

"I don't have any answers, Suzanne. That's why the four of us need to talk. Now."

"But why so far away?"

Another resigned sigh. "Davis thinks he's being watched."

Is someone following me too? Is that what Mike meant when he said we're in danger?

We're quiet the rest of the ride. There's a ton of afternoon traffic going across town, and the cab is stop and go, stop and go, and I use that as the excuse for why I'm getting nauseous. This cabbie must be suicidal. Fifty miles an hour for a block then BAM, brakes. Then stop and go, stop and go. Wash, rinse, repeat. We pass Columbus circle, the traffic eases up a bit, and now we're smooth sailing.

The cab stops on a corner. Mike pays with a credit card, presses the tip on the computer screen, and we get out. "Over here," he says.

I follow him to a huge wooden door, and he tugs on the wrought iron handle. Inside, it's dark but nice. There are people standing everywhere. The lights behind the bar are red and purple, and the seats are plush red velvet. Just beyond the bar are high-top tables, and Mike didn't lie—Davis Walton is sitting alone. He's gorgeous. Dark thick curls, blue eyes, and dressed so, so cool. I couldn't pull off jeans at a conference, even though I wanted to. He quirks up a corner of his lips and gives a slight smile to Mike and waves him over. We squirm through the people and make our way to him.

They shake hands, and Davis looks at me. "You're Suzanne?"

"Yeah, hi," I say. "I saw you at the bar last night."

His expression looks like I just told him he's an untalented piece of shit. Oh em gee, he hates me. He's famous, and I'm nobody.

"Well, sit down *Suzanne*." He accentuates my name. "I need to find out who the hell you are, what the hell you know about Kristin Bailey, and why the hell you're jeopardizing my life."

Uh oh.

13

VICKY OVERTON

Friday, 2:00 P.M.

I get out of the cab and stare up at the sign for Clover & Crimson, then peer through the windows. It's too dark inside, and I can't see much except for people standing everywhere. I glance over my shoulder, then down the block to see if anyone strange is following me. People are getting out of cabs everywhere. Nothing gives me immediate heebie-jeebies. What did I expect? Someone to get out wearing a sash that says *I'm @MPaloozaNxt2Die!*

I open the door and the place smells like cinnamon, probably from one of the dozen candles enclosed in smoked red glass behind the bar, and there's light eighties music playing in the background. It's jammed—wall-to-wall people. They look like young professionals, but it's two o'clock on a Friday afternoon. Doesn't anyone work anymore? Ah, I recall summer Fridays are a thing in New York, and most people have a half day. Surely not everyone is here to find out who knows their secrets and why they're being stalked. I spot Davis, Mike, and Suzanne in the corner at a table. I got here last. I wonder if they've been plotting against me.

What if they're behind the whole thing? My throat constricts, and I can't manage to swallow any saliva. I have to get out of here.

"Vicky!"

It's Mike. He waves me over. I hesitate, and then Suzanne smiles and waves at me. For some reason, that gives me comfort. Having only met her for a minute last night, I realize she can't possibly be plotting against me. She's too naïve, too *new*, to be up to anything. I go to the table and take the empty seat, hanging my purse on the back of the chair.

"Hi," I say.

"Nice to officially meet you Vicky," Davis says. Of course, the jerk is as good looking in person as I expected him to be. I hate that I think of him that way: jerk. Repeat after me: *you have nothing against Davis Walton.* It's not his fault that Penelope sucks.

"You too, Davis," I say. Of course it's the one with one leg a half inch shorter than the other three, and I feel like I'm on a ride as I try to scoot closer to the table. I eye them, from one to the next. "Why don't you guys tell me what's going on?"

Mike clears his throat. "Davis, you called this little meeting. We're all here. You start."

"We need drinks." Davis waves over a server, whose scowl shows that she clearly doesn't like having fingers snapped at her. Still, she bounces over, her blonde ponytail curled at the bottom. *Still*—delete. Her name tag reads *Krista*, and she retrieves a pen from behind her ear, then gives us a close-lipped smile.

"What can I get you?" she asks.

"Ladies first," Davis says, arms out in front of him as if he's making some grand sacrifice.

"Any Sauvignon Blanc from New Zealand, please," I say. I want to add *preferably quickly*, but I don't. Not only because they're both adverbs that I'd delete in my head anyway, but because I think the next glass is going to put me over the edge. Even though being on the edge, looking down, and throwing myself over feels like a good fucking idea right about now.

"Bloody Mary." Suzanne.

"Bud light." Mike.

Davis smiles at Krista, dazzling her, and her expression softens. "I'll have a Bloody Mary too, but not too spicy." He winks, and she giggles. He really is one charming dude. Once she leaves, he turns his attention back to us, no longer Mr. Smooth Talker. "How close was everyone with Kristin Bailey?"

Well. Right to the point. No way in hell am I speaking first about her affair with Jim. Apparently, Mike and Suzanne feel the same way because no one offers up anything. It occurs to me that Kristin must've really gotten herself into some shit. Obviously, because it got her killed. She wasn't just sleeping with my boyfriend—she's connected to them too.

"How close were *you* with her?" I ask. Screw it. I'm not giving up the goods about her and Jim.

Davis's face falls. He likes being in control, asking the questions. He ignores me.

That song from *Pretty in Pink* comes on through the speakers as we all squirm. Mike takes a deep breath, signaling he's going to be the one to get the show on the road. Again.

"She was my secret co-author for the new book," he says. "I think I'm in trouble."

Whoa.

"She was?" I say with disbelief. I didn't think they were that close. "Jesus. You must be reeling."

"Well, it's more than that." His hands wring over each other. "The book—Vita was supposed to take it to Bee Henry today. Meetings are being canceled left and right, and no one knows how the rest of the conference is going to go. Even worse, I saw Vita right before I came here, and now she doesn't want to shop it at all."

I'm still bitter about Bee fucking Banana Hammock Henry passing on my manuscript. "Why not?"

"Because . . . it's about a murder."

"Obviously," Davis says with an eye roll. "We're at Murder-palooza. We write thrillers. It's not a proper thriller if it doesn't have murder."

Mike's eyes cross, then he rubs his face with both hands. "It's about a writer being murdered. At a conference. And, it turns out, it was her co-author who did it. In the book," he adds, as if to exonerate himself.

"Holy shit, Mike. That's not good," Davis says. Then he peers hard across the table. "Do I have to ask?"

Mike scoffs. "Did I kill Kristin Bailey? No, Davis, I didn't. We were friends. I'm devastated, to be honest." His eyes are glassy, but that can be faked. His lips purse, like it's a ridiculous thing to ask.

But is it?

Poor Mike. He used to be such a huge name. I guess he still is, but this business is so *what have you done for me lately?* and he hasn't done squat. I think my debut sold more than his last book. His audience—older readers who like slow-burn political detective stories—is being replaced with the fast-paced beach read with a hundred twists and turns.

"This was supposed to be my comeback," Mike says. "She's the one that approached me. She'd been a fan for a while, apparently. Said she'd help me with a splashier thriller, and we'd leave her name a secret to get buzz. Once everyone knew I was coming out with something else and there was a huge secret around it, it got more attention. She got me outside my comfort zone, and we planned to announce her as my partner as part of the marketing campaign after it sold. And now look what's happening."

Suzanne has been quiet the entire time. Sipping water. How is she involved? She hasn't sold her debut yet. She's a total newbie, and she's so *young*, she barely looks out of college. I'm about to ask her when the waitress returns and places our drinks in front of us. We thank her, but we're silent otherwise. Staring into the glasses.

Suzanne picks hers up. "Cheers?" She says it like a question, and it's the first time she's said anything.

"To Kristin Bailey," Mike says.

"To Kristin," I say, despite my very real feelings of contempt. All I picture is her rolling around naked with my boyfriend.

We clink glasses and sip.

Davis takes a huge gulp, then spits it straight across the table and right onto Mike, causing Suzanne and I both to skid our chairs back.

"What the fuck?" Davis says, then grabs the closest full water—mine, because he finished his—and guzzles it down. "Jesus." He swivels his head until he finds the waitress. "Hey! Krista! Get over here!"

Davis's face is red, and Mike is in disbelief, wiping himself down with wet cocktail napkins. Krista rushes over, her face full of fear at Davis's anger.

"What happened?" she asks.

Davis pushes his Bloody Mary to the edge of the table like it's full of Clorox. "I said *not* spicy. This is like a glass of tabasco sauce. Fuckin A."

"Relax, Davis. It's not her fault," Mike says. He's the one that should be pissed, with red splotches all over his nice shirt and sport jacket. He looks at Krista. "Sorry." Apologizing for Davis? He's so good.

"I'm sorry," Krista says. "I swear I told him not to make it spicy. I'll get you another one." She looks at Mike. "And I'll get you a towel and some club soda. I'm so sorry."

She leaves, and no one knows what to say. But we don't have to say anything, because at the same time, our phones ding with a message. I lift my phone from the table, and there's a text from an unknown number again.

Sorry about the heat level, Davis, but do I have your attention now? Why don't you tell your drinking buddies about Jason Fleming?

We all gasp, obviously looking at the same text.

I whip my head toward the bar. The stalker from the Twitter account is here, and they were close enough to mess with Davis's drink. They're watching us. I look at my delicious, light, crispy white wine and push it away. What if someone slipped poison in it?

One of you is next.

The four of us move our drinks to the center of the table, clearly having the same thought.

We frantically look around, watching for face recognition. Another writer, an agent, an editor—anyone. All I see are men in groups, clutching bottled mircobrews with their sleeves rolled up, girls nodding along to the eighties music, and the back of a girl with a fake pink wig, wearing a sash that says something about a bachelorette party. There's no one that looks familiar to me, and there's no one skulking around alone, dumping hot sauce and God-knows-whatever-else into drinks near the bar. I look at Davis. We all do. He's white as a ghost. I'll ask.

"Okay, Davis, so who's Jason Fleming?"

14

DAVIS WALTON

Friday, 2:15 P.M.

There's no way this conversation about Jason Fleming is happening. I won't let it. *I'm Davis Walton*, and they need to remember that.

"I have to use the men's room and then I'm going to go to the bar and get us a new round of drinks. I'll watch as they're being prepared," I say.

"Come on, Davis. Sit down. Why does Murder Twitter want us to know about that guy?" Mike asks.

He checks the time, and I notice his watch. It's a limited-edition Rolex from the early nineties, one that I've been coveting, but it's a little too much to spend, even for me. It's the ice-blue Daytona and goes for well over a hundred grand now. He must've gotten that for himself when his third book was turned into a movie over a decade ago, when it was probably half the price. I'm instantly jealous of the has-been, and that irks me.

Instead of making an excuse to avoid talking about Jason, I act like a six-year-old and grab my junk. "I'm going to explode. Give me three minutes." They all nod, and I get up and lock my knees into place so no one sees my legs shaking. "Anyone else have to go?"

They shake their heads *no*. I don't want to be a pussy about it, but I wish Mike was coming with me. I don't want to be alone right now, and I have three minutes to try to double talk the Jason Fleming subject.

The space is dimly lit, and I weave around everyone to get to the back of the bar. Everyone I bump into I think is going to shank me. Squinting, I try to make sense of everything around me. I wish any sort of recognition came to me, but the fact is, I have no idea who's trying to screw with me. To out my secrets.

To attempt to kill me.

Okay, I know, *stop being dramatic, Davis*. It was extra hot sauce. This time.

The restroom sign is on the wall in the back with a painted hand pointing down. Terrific—the bathroom is in the basement. That's typical for New York, but why now?

The house I grew up in had a basement, and my parents didn't finish it into a playroom for me and Alyssa until I was ten and she was seven. Illinois winters are no joke, and for the first decade of my life, horrific clanking noises came from the basement whenever it snowed or the wind got out of control. The water heater, the house humidifier, electrical stuff—everything made creepy sounds, almost moaning, and I was always terrified to investigate. Just opening the door and seeing the gray steps that led to dank darkness and cement walls—it felt like where they locked bad little boys and girls in horror movies. Once the framing was done, the carpeting and the stainless-steel track lighting went in, and it got a coating of drywall and paint and a flat screen TV, it was bearable. Mostly because I played down there with my sister or friends from the neighborhood—I'd never go down there alone. I knew that beyond the far door in the corner was the unfinished spot with the appliances that made noises. Where the monsters lived.

I hate basements. I'm in my thirties and I'm still afraid.

Now I'm walking down the same eerie steps, descending underground, where no one will hear me scream. I let out a sigh of relief when I see two unisex restrooms, and two people are waiting on a line to use them. This means they're one-at-a-time and I won't have to worry about someone attacking me from behind while I have my dick in my hand. I can lock myself in my own private Shangri-la to take a piss.

I finish and wash up, open the door and run right into another guy, too close to the door and already pushing his way in before I exit the room. Without thinking, both of my hands mush into his chest, and I push him against the wall.

"Watch it," I say, taking a defensive stance and looking for a sign of recognition in his face. Is he the one who's after me? Was he sent by someone else? Does he have a knife? Am I going to be stabbed and shoved back into the bathroom to bleed out, alone, just like Kristin?

"Sorry, man," the guy slurs. "I've had too many and I really have to go."

He stumbles into the bathroom and slams the door. He's just a drunk idiot. Not everyone is trying to kill me.

But—I have to go back upstairs, and Mike, Vicky, and Suzanne have probably googled Jason Fleming already. I can already picture them, huddled around Mike's phone, reading up on the accident. Then again, it's a common name. They don't even know where Jason lives.

Lived.

When I'm back above ground, I exhale and make my way back toward the table, where I'm met with impatient faces. I signal that I'm going to the bar for the drinks. Finding a spot between two beautiful women, I give them the *Hi, I'm here from LA* smile, and they part to let me through to order.

The bartender is a guy, tall with the bottom half of his head shaved, and the top half, with long hair, is pulled into a slick ponytail. He's frantic, as the bar is still busy, and I do my regular move and pull out a hundred-dollar bill and wave it between my index and middle fingers, which allows me to get away with anything. Money talks, which is evident as the bartender comes right over. I place the same order as we did at the table and watch his every move. He brings over the Bloodys first.

"This one is the less spicy one," he says as he pushes one forward.

I take it in my left hand and sip it. Perfection. He grabs a clean glass and pours the white wine, then he takes a beer from a bin of ice and unscrews the cap.

"Fifty-four," he says.

I'm so grateful I plunk the bill on the bar and nod at the women who let me into the cramped space. "Thanks. Get their next round on me and keep the change."

They fawn, and I needed that to remind me that I shouldn't be shaken up. I carry all four drinks back to the table, and when I get there, they're looking at me expectantly. Which means that they googled Jason Fleming and didn't find shit. Or that they came up with some harebrained theories. I pass out the drinks.

"Don't worry, I watched him prepare everything," I say.

Vicky grabs the wine and downs it like a champ, and for a hot second, I'm jealous of her boyfriend. Mike sips his beer straight from the bottle, and Suzanne stirs her Bloody Mary with her paper straw until it looks like it's about to swirl down a drain. Then she takes out the straw and sips from the glass.

"So who's Jason Fleming?" Vicky asks for a second time. Must be liquid courage because half of that wine disappeared in record time.

I shrug. *No big deal.* "A guy I met at a Midwestern writing mini-conference a while ago. Maybe six years ago?"

"And what was his relation to Kristin Bailey?"

Fuck. "They knew each other. Lived in the same county in Iowa."

"You're from Illinois, right? Isn't that the next state over?"

I nod as I'm sipping and swallowing.

"So what did you do to him? Why would the Next To Die Twitter account nutbag mention him?"

"How would I know?"

"Because you do know, Davis," Mike interrupts, anger in his voice. "Stop screwing around. I told you about my book and Kristin being the co-author. This person obviously knows something about you and Jason, and it's obviously something you don't want out."

I continue to sip until I have to dip my head back to get the last drops and the ice hits my lips. "It's not my fault he wrapped his car around a tree."

Or maybe it was.

15

MIKE BROOKS

Friday, 2:30 P.M.

How would I know followed by *it's not my fault* and then *wrapped his car around a tree* screams of lies. What the hell is Davis involved with? Who was Jason Fleming to him? More importantly . . .

"Davis, are you trying to say that you have ties to not only one but *two* dead writers?" I ask.

He grabs Suzanne's Bloody Mary right from her hands and finishes it while she screams "Hey!" with a look of shock on her face.

His face twists, either from the extra spice he didn't want or the specific line of questioning. Something is making Davis uneasy. It's a dead giveaway.

He slams the tumbler down on the table, a little too hard. "What? You don't know two dead people?"

"Everyone knows two dead people. But two dead people who were both writers and knew each other and lived near each other? Near *you*? Unlikely."

"What are you saying, Mike?"

"How well did you know him, and Kristin, for that matter?"

"I told you, we all met at a mini-conference when we still lived in the Midwest. We were newbies and emailed about writing stuff. Look, the dude had some problems. We all know how writers are. We're tortured individuals with imposter syndrome, addicted to coffee and alcohol. Well, Jason didn't like coffee. He went for a ride one day."

Davis shrugs after the last sentence like the guy took a ten-speed and bumped into a curb. Not that he died while *wrapping himself around a tree.*

"If you weren't close, how did you hear about him dying?"

He shifts in his chair, leaning against the back of it and spreading his legs. Making himself bigger. In charge. "It was in the paper."

This isn't adding up. He's being too blasé. Was he in a secret relationship with Kristin? With Jason? "Something tells me Kristin knew about what was going on between you and Jason. And now they're both dead."

Davis rolls his eyes. "There was nothing 'going on,' and I resent the implication that we were lovers, Mike. I mean, come on."

Okay, he's right there. Davis loves the ladies. "Still. You're hiding something."

"Hey!" Suzanne interrupts the tete-a-tete. "Stop it guys. We don't even know if—"

"What's your name again? *Suzanne?*" Davis interjects. "Who the hell are you, anyway?"

Suzanne's cheeks turn the color of the pink streaks in her hair, and she shuts up. She makes herself smaller in the corner after the reprimand by the conference hero.

I remember when I first met Suzanne. Well, first "e-met" her, anyway, which is apparently how people communicate nowadays.

When Vita was interested in signing her, Suzanne asked for references, and Vita sent her my way. Suzanne emailed me, asked me all the relevant questions—what's it like to work with Vita, what's her communication style, is she editorial—and we got to chatting. E-chatting. She complimented my work over and over—Suzanne can be a little much, but she's young and that's what the kids are like nowadays. I feel so old just thinking that, but it's true.

It was nice to feel important again. The newbies have always put me on a pedestal, way more than semi-established writers who look at me as a dinosaur that can't keep up with the times and the changing market. We grabbed a drink once when she was in town to sign her papers with Vita. She lives in New Jersey, so she's in the city a lot.

Only once, though. I haven't seen her since then.

"Seriously, though, who is this girl?" Davis asks, his tone heated, looking at her. "You're no one. You haven't even sold your book yet. Why are you here?"

"That's a good question, actually," Vicky chimes in. "What happened between you and Kristin that is making the Twitter account stalk you along with us?"

"Guys! Let's not turn against each other," I say. "This is what that maniac on Twitter wants. We need to stick together. Get to the bottom of this."

"That's what I'm trying to do, Mike," Vicky says, then turns her attention back to Suzanne. "Well? What's your connection to Kristin?"

I never knew Vicky to be so pushy. She's acting like Davis right now. "What's *your* connection to Kristin?"

Vicky looks at me with fire in her eyes. "She's been fucking my boyfriend. Anything else?"

Whoa. She says it so fast, without emotion, and I'm flabbergasted.

Her eyes glass over, but she has a swift recovery. "I need more wine." Vicky tips her head back and pours the last drops of her wine in her mouth, then delicately places the glass on the table. She crosses her arms and rubs her elbows as if she's cold. Doubtful. She's pissed. She probably didn't want to blurt it out like that.

Because, man, is that a motive or what? Not that I think Vicky is a killer. Right? If this were a book, she'd be a top suspect, but this is real life. I'm so confused.

"Where were you this morning?" Davis asks her before I can.

She scoffs. "I don't have to tell you anything."

"Do you think this is a joke, Vicky? Are you not taking this seriously?" Davis waves his phone in the air, then presses the Twitter app and shoves it in her face. "This is serious."

Vicky moves her head back, then focuses. Her eyes widen, and she yanks the phone from Davis's hand.

"There's another tweet from the psycho," she says.

Davis rips his phone back while Suzanne and I grab ours and open the app.

Cheater cheater pumpkin eater, had a wife and couldn't keep her

Their eyes fly to Vicky, who laughs. I don't laugh. It's not funny.

"Sorry, Murder Twitter, too little too late," Vicky says to no one. "I already told them." She's shouting into her phone in a sing-songy voice like she expects it to answer. Like the Twitter stalker is actually Siri and she's going to say *oh, my bad*. "How does the Twitter account know what we're talking about anyway?"

Is the person behind the account still here? The stalker could be right next to us. In that group of girls at the bar. The group of guys next to us staring at them. Hell, it could be the waitress or the bartender. More likely—it could be someone I'm sitting with.

I run my hand to the underside of the table, searching for a bug. Like I'd know what one feels like. Still, it makes me feel useful, even when all I touch is decade-old chewed gum.

"Check your phones," I say. "Make sure your Bluetooth is turned off."

Everyone does, and Vicky's face goes red as she pushes buttons. "It's off."

Vicky, Davis, and Suzanne look around again frantically because we think we're being watched. However, my putting on a worried face and looking behind my shoulder is just an act for my company.

I don't think we're being watched anymore. My shoulders slump in defeat.

I know that tweet is talking about me.

16

SUZANNE SHIH

Friday, 2:45 P.M.

Sitting at this table, I feel like such a grown-up. We're all adults, but these are like *adult* adults. They have writing careers and marriages and children and movie deals. But they're acting like kids on a playground right now. Though I'm not exactly happy that some Twitter freak is listening to our conversation.

Vicky picks at her nails. Why is she being so defensive? I mean, I want to be friends with her, and I want her to like me, but all I can think about is that tweet from that agent, Meghan Morgan, wondering where Vicky was this morning. Vicky wouldn't answer the question when asked, and it's giving me pause.

Davis still looks around the bar, stone-faced—what is he hiding? I'm disgusted with myself for fangirling over him and thinking he's gorgeous and stuff because, honestly, he's kind of an asshole. Plus, he's being super shady about this Jason dude, who I fully plan on googling once I get back to my room. I certainly don't want to do it sitting here in front of these people.

Mike sits slumped, defeated—the Mike I've gotten to know in the past few months since I signed with Vita. I know him the best out of everyone, and he's the only one who started off honest. We're peers.

Except we're not. Davis might be an asshole, but he's right. I'm nobody. What am I doing here with important people?

I thought Mike contacted me this morning because of our first meeting months ago, but I was wrong. I try not to get caught up in Mike and his brilliance and chivalry, but now we know what he wrote about. A thriller conference. A dead writer. A guilty co-author. All fingers point to Mike. I suppose they can point to me too, so I try my best not to do anything suspicious or out of the ordinary. I keep my eyes focused forward, no fast blinks or dented eyebrows, no more worrisome sips of water.

Fine. I've been a Kristin Bailey fan for a while—this isn't brand new information. At least five years. I was a *teenager* when I started sending her those emails. Her prose was excellent, and I wanted to be just like her, so I sent her a message through her website. I told her that women authors of color should be bonding, that I was her biggest fan, and it was my dream to write a novel. Imagine my surprise when she wrote back! She thanked me for being a fan, gave me some advice, and told me to be persistent.

I bet she regretted that.

I printed out two copies: one that I framed and hung on my wall, another that I shoved into everyone's face senior year of high school. *Kristin Bailey knows who I am! I told you I'm going to be famous!*

I took that as the start of a friendship. I wrote to her all the time, asking for advice, giving her my own writing samples.

They went unanswered, which I didn't understand; she told me to be persistent. Maybe I became a little obsessed with her. Emails are just emails, though. It's not like I went and knocked on her door, at her apartment on Lafayette Street, unit 14B, and it didn't even take longer than a half hour to find out where she lived. It's not like I followed her here to New York. Or killed her, for God's sake. I'm here because I'm a writer, and that's the only reason.

Although . . . it won't look good if the last emails came out. When she didn't write back, I kept writing to her, growing more frustrated at the lack of two-way communication. Anyone who didn't know the nature of our relationship would think they were threats. She'd previously liked my comments on her tweets and Instagram—I hadn't misread her signal, so I was confused when she told me to stop writing to her. We were friends! I decided she didn't need to write me back, so I stopped demanding it. I just felt better each day knowing I got to tell her about mine.

It hurt when I got an email from her agent, Penelope Jacques:

> *Hi Suzanne,*
>
> *Kristin is so happy to know that you're such a big fan! However, she's been busy. Very hard at work on the next big thriller and doesn't have time to read your correspondence! Thank you for reading her previous books, and if you send us your address, I'll make sure you get a signed bookplate.*
>
> *Penelope Jacques, Literary Agent*

Clearly, Kristin cared enough to let me know she'd get back to me as soon as she could. *Oh em gee,* I got a signed bookplate! Her handwriting was exactly what I pictured—slanted (she was clearly right-handed), a few loops, mostly sharp points. The "K" and the "B" were huge, at least three times the size of the rest of the signature. It was exactly how I'd practiced mine for when I become famous—one huge "S" to share my first and last name. I was disappointed to see the return address as a New York City P.O. Box. Not that I would've gone to her apartment or anything, and as mentioned, it was ridiculously easy to find, but why didn't she trust me? She knew me.

I wrote her a thank you note. A few times. Fine, more than a few. I figured I'd keep the lines of communication open for when she was ready and basically just told her about mundane details in my life. Then I got an email from her publisher's legal department.

Dear Suzanne,

I am the retained council for HYB Publishing. We've been informed of your contact with Kristin Bailey. After Kristin and her agent made several attempts to quell your enthusiasm, we're going to have to demand that you cease and desist all contact. Any further attempts made will result in legal action on her behalf.

Best,

Irina Bottone, Esq.

That was law language—I stopped. I really did. That was six months ago.

Well . . . maybe once I sent her an email from Constantine's account. Fine. Three times, and after that, they came back as undeliverable. I just wanted to let her know how much I wanted to meet her at Murderpalooza and that I was still her number one fan.

Seeing her last night at the bar was like seeing a unicorn in all its majestic glory. And now she's dead, and this could fall on me as an obsessed fan. Especially because the surveillance tapes will show I saw her this morning. I went to her room. I mean, we were friends.

Davis and Mike have stopped bickering because we all saw the last tweet, *cheater cheater pumpkin eater,* right after Vicky's admission about her boyfriend. Which, to be honest, I think we deserve to hear more about. Maybe *he* killed her.

"How did you find out about your boyfriend and Kristin?" I ask. "Do you know where he was this morning?"

Vicky's eyes are daggers, and I feel the pierce of the blades in my skull. She doesn't have to tell me anything. I'm nobody. She looks at me with such disgust that I feel the heat on my head, and I just want to go home, back to New Jersey, back to Constantine's arms. I wish I'd never come to this conference, a stark departure from my feelings just a few short hours ago. What a hot mess today turned into.

"I don't know how he met her," Vicky says. "Probably through his editing services. Jim and I were having breakfast together when Kristin was Panel Master at one of the early panels."

"Oh. So you don't know where he was when she was murdered, then," Davis says.

"How do you know *when* she was murdered?" Vicky says to him, then looks at me. "You're the only one who hasn't talked yet. Where were you this morning? And what's your connection to Kristin?"

I hate Davis for drinking my Bloody Mary, so I sip water, which is always a sign of guilt in the books I read. I told myself not to do it, but damn, people do get thirsty.

"I had breakfast with Vita this morning." I look at Mike out of guilt, but then we share an agent so maybe he thinks I did it for camaraderie. Backup. "Then I was at panels. I met another writer, Tara Kretz, and had lunch with her. That's when Mike texted me that I needed to come here with him."

"I see," Vicky says. "And your connection to Kristin?" She's not letting it go. I swallow a lump down my throat, and I suppose the hesitation is too much because Vicky reacts and pounces on me. "Come on, Suzanne, spit it out."

My eyes don't meet hers, or anyone's. "I was a big fan, that's all."

"You expect us to believe that's it? Someone is threatening us. There's got to me more to it. What aren't you telling us?"

She sounds like the main character in her thriller that's up for the award tonight, and I fold. Might as well get ahead of it, and I pick the most non-threatening words I can think of. "I wrote her some emails that might be seen as untoward."

"What does that mean?"

The prickling sensation in my eyes activates the mucus in my nose, and I sniffle. "I thought we were friends. She didn't answer me, but I kept writing."

"And?"

"And . . . I was informed to stop."

"By whom?"

Eeeeeek. I should've kept my mouth shut. "Her publisher's legal team."

They all exhale, but not in relief.

"So you're a real-life stalker, and we're supposed to believe you're not behind this murder Twitter account *and* that you didn't kill her," Davis says.

Asshole. "I didn't. My whereabouts can be accounted for this morning. Plus, didn't someone say there's security video?" I say that even though I know I'm on it. I just want them off my back.

Vicky huffs and puffs and then her texts go off. We all freeze. Look at our own phones. Nothing. Just Vicky's.

"Oh my God," she says. "I have to go. Jim was attacked."

17

VICKY OVERTON

Friday, 3:00 P.M.

"What do you mean, attacked?" Davis asks.

"I don't have the details yet," I say, frantic on purpose, but only because it dawns on me this insanity is far from over. I grab my bag off the back of my chair and swing it over my left shoulder. "It happened on the Upper East Side. Let's meet back at the hotel bar later. We should stick together."

"Does Jim know what's going on? With the texts and the psychotic Twitter account?"

"No. I haven't told him. You said to keep it quiet."

"Good. Don't tell him. Even after this."

I wasn't going to tell him anyway. Part of me, and it's so horrible, is glad someone attacked him. It certainly saved me from splitting his head open. But of course, the rest of me is terrified because I know it's a warning to me—to all of us. Whoever this is can get to us anytime.

"Isn't everyone supposed to meet at the bar around five anyway? Let's still do that," I say. "The awards show starts at eight, so let's try to nip this in the bud before then."

"Suzanne and I are supposed to have dinner with Dustin Feeney before the ceremony," Mike says. Suzanne, who I will now affectionately call Stalkanne, straightens up at the mention of her name.

"Cancel it," I say. "I'm sure we don't want anyone else involved in this. Just the four of us tonight. Five o'clock. I have to go."

Not waiting for an answer, I exit the bar confidently—the Twitter moron isn't here; they're far away, on the east side, bopping people on the head. I think that's what they're doing, anyway. Hailing a cab, I look at the text from Jim again. The one I didn't want anyone else to see.

I don't want to worry you, but I'm receiving medical treatment. I was hit on the head while walking through a neighborhood and blacked out. Someone found me on their townhome stoop, bleeding. I'm on 81st just off Lexington. Look for the ambulance.

81st Street. Clover & Crimson is on West 81st Street. Jim is currently on East 81st Street. Basically, right across the park from the bar. *Basically*—delete. What the hell is Jim doing uptown, on the east side? I left him near Times Square when I went to meet Davis, Mike, and Stalkanne, and he was supposed to go back to the hotel. Did he follow me to the bar and then bail? Does he know about the Twitter stalker?

Is *he* the Twitter stalker?

These scenarios play through my mind as a cab pulls up. I get in and stick to the torn vinyl because of the heat. It stinks like the last passenger didn't wear deodorant and kept a diet of egg yolks and beans. I roll the window down and tell him the address as he pulls away from the curb.

Does Jim know that I know about him and his affair with Kristin? Did their pillow talk consist of her giggling secrets about Davis and that Jason Fleming guy? About her co-author, Mike? Her stalker, Stalkanne? Did Jim decide to use this against everyone? But why? And why me? What does Jim gain from any of this?

There's another question I don't want to ask myself, but I do. Did Jim kill Kristin because he thought he could keep me from finding out about the affair? Or was it a lover's quarrel gone bad?

My mind is in full fact-finding mode. If anyone can solve Kristin's murder, it's going to be thriller writers, especially once everyone finds out she had secrets. This is what we do for a living. We take something horrible happening to someone normal and create a dense backstory rife with mystery. As readers, we pick apart every breadcrumb left by the author, and nine times out of ten, we figure out the ending. The whodunnit. If I can sniff out everything about everyone, I can save the day.

The cabbie turns down 79th Street to cross through the park to the east side. The scene around me is boring, just trees and joggers, and I realize I've never been fully inside Central Park, near the famous Bethesda Fountain or any of the little ponds or boat restaurants. I start to imagine my life writing in busy coffee shops and running on the West Side Highway.

When we get to 81st Street, I spot the ambulance and tell him to stop at the corner. The back is open, and Jim is sitting on the ledge with a bag of ice on his head. There's dried blood near his left ear and a gauzy bandage near his hairline. He's not on a gurney or hooked up to fluids and machines. That's a good sign. Little man got bad boo-boo. He seems to be making small talk with two EMTs.

"What happened?" I ask as I approach the ambulance.

The two EMTs stand in front of him, almost guarding him. Ugh, *almost*—delete. They probably think I'm a reporter or a busybody.

"It's okay, this is my girlfriend, Vicky," Jim says.

They part to let me through. Jim has one arm outstretched for me since the other is holding the ice bag, and I get underneath it out of habit. He kisses my head and rubs my shoulder. Like a good, caring boyfriend does in front of other people.

"What happened? And what are you doing up here? I thought you were going back to the hotel?"

"I was, but I wanted to walk around this area. I heard it was quiet, and I just wanted to take in some of New York City while you were off doing writer things."

Liar. He's lying to me. "So you were mugged?" Jim getting randomly attacked when someone is after me? Stop me if you've heard this before, but they write books about this stuff . . .

"We don't think so," one of the EMTs says and hands me Jim's wallet and his phone. "He still had his personal effects."

I toss them in my purse. BINGO. Now I have his phone, and I have to see his texts.

This isn't the business of the EMTs, so I move to get him out of there. "Can I take him back to the hotel?"

"Yeah, that's okay," one of them says to me. "The cops already took his statement, and they're checking the street and security cameras. They have his contact info, and they'll let you know what they find."

Good. "Thanks for waiting with him," I say.

Jim jumps off the back of the ambulance, waves to the guys, and then we start walking back to the corner I just came from.

"So how was your little power meeting?" Jim asks.

That's what he wants to talk about? "Who hit you over the head? And really, what were you doing up here?" I narrow my eyes with suspicion because I don't believe him. At all.

"I told you. I wanted to check it out. Do you know those brownstones go for, like, ten million dollars? And up. Sick."

I bite my lip. He changed the subject. I write scenes better than this garbage he's trying to pass off as truth. "The meeting was fine. Just industry stuff. Let's get you back to the hotel to rest."

We get in another cab, and we're mostly quiet because he says he has a headache. I bet he does. He leans back and closes his eyes. I rummage through my purse, like I usually do. His phone is sitting on the top. I glance over at him, and he's still pseudo-sleeping. With his phone still in my bag, I hit his passcode—111222. He's so original.

The texts are there, between him and "KNB," and I know her middle name is Noelle because I saw it in an interview and that's my mother's name so I always remembered. They're from a month ago and they're unmistakable.

Her: *Guess what color panties I'm wearing* and *Do you think Vicky knows? Are you going to tell her what's going on?*

And him: *I'll tear those panties right off* and *I told her I was visiting my parents in West Palm for three days, she has no idea I flew to NYC to see you.*

Tears sting my eyes and I press my lips together. Did he love her? I need to be careful. I can't just throw his phone at his face and run away screaming. There's a dead body to deal with. I need to be rational, if that's at all possible. I can deal with it for one more day.

Once trust is gone, it's completely gone. I look through the rest of his messages. There's one from a blocked number.

I know you were with Kristin last night. Meet me on 81st and Lexington, now, or I tell the cops about your fight this morning.

Well, well, well . . . what do we have here?

KRISTIN BAILEY
THE NIGHT BEFORE THE MURDER

Like most people, Kristin never turned on her sound on her phone, leaving it a little vibrating rectangle that took her forever to find when she misplaced it. Usually, it was nonchalantly tossed on her couch, her bed, or a pile of laundry. This time, it was on the hotel's concrete nightstand, so it pulsed in a small circle, waking her with a barrage of text messages. She adjusted to the darkness, and the clock read two-thirty A.M. It could only be one person.

Open the door

Hurry up, I'm here. I don't know how long I have

I need to see you

She answered back *Give me two minutes*

Unfortunately, she never "woke up like this." She rose from the king-sized bed in the hotel and shivered. Her pale-blue silk nightgown wasn't going to cut it. What if someone saw her answering the door at this hour wearing that? She ran into the bathroom and grabbed the hotel-provided bathrobe and slipped it on, tying it tightly at the waist. It was one of those luxurious ones, thin but heavy, softer on the inside than the outside, and she instantly felt like she was at a spa, waiting for her massage. After fumbling with the touchscreen on the wall, the lights came on as a soft amber glow, in nighttime mode. Peering at herself in the mirror, she knew she couldn't answer the door with her head wrapped in a silk scarf, so she took it off and fluffed up what she could of her curls. The silk *did* keep them shiny.

After gargling mouthwash, she rubbed her eyes to make sure no crusties were visible. That's what her mama always called them. Crusties. Kristin was almost forty and still used the term. She caught a glance of the emerald-green dress she planned to wear at the awards ceremony in the mirror and smiled. She kept it hanging on the back of the bathroom door so the steam from the shower everyday would relax any kinks. She adored the jeweled color, even had a headband dyed to match, both stunning against her dark hair and skin. The ceremony was going to be the highlight of the conference.

Well, the next half hour would also do.

She floated over to the door and checked through the peephole. Jim Russell. She cracked the door open, chain still attached.

"Did anyone see you come up here?" Kristin asked.

"No," he whispered. "Hurry up and let me in before someone does, though."

She closed the door, detached the chain, and let him in. He smirked.

"What?"

"Nothing. You look cute. I'm so sorry for the late hour, but Vicky wouldn't leave earlier. I tried to get her to go to the bar as soon as we got here so you and I could get some alone time. She's out like a light right now, but I don't think I have more than a half hour. We can't risk getting caught."

She nodded. "Well then, let's stop wasting time."

18

DAVIS WALTON

Friday, 3:15 P.M.

We decided to leave Clover & Crimson strategically. Suzanne went first while Mike stayed behind with me. I told him I wanted to go next, five minutes later. If a stalker is watching us, they might go after Suzanne, then realize she's alone and come back for us. By then, I'll be long gone. Sorry, Mike. I'm more important—I'm the bigger name right now. Whoever is doing this must think so too. The others offered up their information—cowriting, stalking, affairs—but the Twitter stalker had to text everyone about my business and Jason Fleming. Shit.

I walk a couple blocks and park myself at the opening to the Central Park traverse by 79th Street. There are too many people around here for me to be a target. No one is going to attack in broad daylight.

Then again, I wonder what happened to Vicky's boyfriend. He probably got mugged because he looks like a tourist. I don't wear socks with my sandals.

I punch in my passcode on my phone and open my emails—Good Lord, there are over a hundred, just in the last hour while I was trying to stay alive. So many moving pieces for me right now—books, film, interviews—I'm everywhere. I spot one from my editor, Bee Henry. I wonder if anyone knows her real name is Banana. I open it.

Hey Davis. I'm sure you've heard that most things are canceled with this whole Kristin Bailey thing. I'm still willing to have dinner tonight before the ceremony if you are . . .

I pause reading for a moment of pride. The biggest editor of the biggest publisher in the biggest writer's town in the world still wants to see me, despite a real live murder of one of our own. Everything's canceled, but not me, and I let that sink in. To hell with Vicky and Mike and the little girl. I'm not meeting them at five; I'm seeing Bee instead.

Then I finish reading.

. . . Also, I'm still waiting for your full outline and the first three chapters of Book Two. Did you print them out for me to read or are you going to email the electric copy? You know I prefer paper so I can handwrite the notes. Hopefully I'll get them tonight. Let me know what time is good for you.

Fuck.

No, I have no outline and I have no pages, and one day I'm going to have to sit down and actually do it. Not only do I not have an outline, but I don't have as much as a pitch paragraph. I don't have comps. I can't even come up with two catchy lines for this one. Writer's block? Mine is a grid.

A crazy person is after me and my past is haunting me. And Bee Henry wants dinner. Of course, I can't let her know what's happening. I have to keep my LA-cool. I write her back.

> *Bee,*
>
> *Gosh. I'm flattered but I really don't think clinking glasses is the best idea today. Let's adopt a wait-and-see approach for the rest of the conference. So far, nothing is canceled tomorrow. Maybe we can circle back then. I'll keep you posted on my schedule and let you know if I can squeeze you in—I have a lot set up already.*
>
> *Davis*

There. The word I'm looking for is s-h-a-m-e, and hopefully I've shamed her into feeling like a selfish ass for thinking about dinner instead of the dead girl. Of course, it's an act on my part, but I had to go with something. I didn't mention the pages. She won't now either. She needs to know I'm in demand and that she's not the first on my to-do list even if I'm first on hers.

With a trembling finger, I open the Twitter app, and there's nothing else from that psychopath. I don't want to walk through the park alone, and I don't want to be in a bar alone, and I don't want to go back to the hotel where it's apparently stalker central, but I decide that's the best move. I can hole up in my penthouse until it's time to go down to the bar. There are worse places to be. I have a private terrace. Unless the stalker is Spiderman flying from rooftop to rooftop, I should be safe there.

From the cab, I call Penelope, and of course she answers immediately.

"Davis! Where are you?"

"Almost back to the hotel. Where are you?"

"At the office right now. I have to comb through Kristin's contracts for her estate. I'm just trying to get ahead of it because I know the request will be coming."

I take a deep breath. "I have to ask you something, and I want you to keep this private."

"Oh?" Her voice rises. She's intrigued.

"What do you remember about a Kristin superfan named Suzanne Shih?"

"Oh yes. Wow. She sent some really messed up stuff to Kristin."

Now I'm the one who's intrigued. Of course Suzanne played it down, but what kind of shit was she sending? "Messed up how?"

There are papers rustling and sounds are muffled, so I know Penelope is frantic at her desk, looking for the evidence of the past. "From what I remember, first she started talking about her writing, then the emails turned into soliloquies, to be honest. She'd clearly done research on Kristin and knew personal details that I don't even know. You'd think she was in love with her."

"Can you gather up whatever you can and email it to me immediately?"

"Yes. Why? Is something wrong? You don't think—"

"I don't know what I think, I'm just playing detective. But I think whatever happened between Suzanne and Kristin isn't good. Promise you'll send it my way ASAP?" I say it like that too. A-sap.

"Yes, I promise. Should I come back to the hotel?"

"I'm not sure what sense it makes right now. Take care of your paperwork, and I'll text you if I need you."

"Okay. Be careful. Just in case someone is targeting writers."

Just in case. If she only knew. "I will."

I disconnect and feel satisfied. If this Suzanne girl is going to be a threat to me and all that I've built, I'm nipping it in the bud. Tonight.

When the cab stops at the hotel, the police fanfare appears to be gone—just the normal New York City sirens and horns. Heading to the elevators, I feel the magnetic pull of the bar for a drink, but I keep going. I turn the corner and—

"Davis! I've been looking for you!"

Shit. It's . . . not Janie. Jamie? Julie!

"Oh, hi. What's up?" Still I avoid saying her name. Just in case.

"I lost my favorite lipstick. I thought maybe it rolled out of my bag last night. I stuck a note under your door. Because I don't have your phone number."

I saw it earlier, but I don't want to give this girl any more ammo.

"Okay. I'm on my way up now. I'll check."

"Great! Can I come?"

Her voice drips with such sexual innuendo that Old Davis—Davis from this morning—would've said yes, in a heartbeat. But not now. This Davis is wise. Ha. Sure.

"I'm pretty busy at the moment. I have some work to do. You understand? I'll check around for the lipstick." The look in her eyes is too hopeful. "You left your contact info on the note, right?" I add, just to give her some optimism.

She smiles. She's cute, but too young. It's unfortunate that she's a romance writer. Self-published? No way. I just can't.

"I did. But you can just call me now, so you'll have my number and I'll have yours."

I run my hand through my hair to disarm her—girls usually swoon when I do that—and I see her soften and know she's going to back off. Right after I tell her this. "Actually, I'm planning on meeting some people at the bar in a few hours. Why don't we meet up there?" I wink. "I really have to go."

I don't wait for an answer; I just turn and leave and pray she doesn't follow.

When I get to my room, I see the note on the floor with Julie's phone number. Housekeeping came, and my freshly fucked bed is prim and proper and tightly tucked in, there are new towels in the bathroom, and yes, there's that damn lipstick standing upright on the desk. I open the mini bar and that too is newly stocked. I grab a glass and a Jack Daniels and decide to forego the ice because the ice machine is on the other side of the hallway and I'm too lazy—I need a break. I open the terrace door and place the drink on the table and sit down, staring at the sky.

Kristin Bailey.

Jason Fleming.

Tommy Johnson.

Wait until everyone finds out about the third long-departed writer I'm connected to.

19

MIKE BROOKS

Friday, 3:15 P.M.

I can't stop myself from shaking. Davis just left the bar *("Come on, I've got to be the next to go!"* he said) because of course—he's Davis Walton, after all. I'm alone, but am I really? Am I ever going to feel alone again, with prying eyes coming at me from all angles? Inside, outside, online . . .

As soon as Vicky got that text, I thought about my kids. And of course Nicole. If someone was able to get to Jim, how do I know my kids are safe? I check my watch and it's just past three. They aren't due home from camp until five-thirty, and Nicole should be back from lunch with Donna by now. I call her.

One ring.

Two rings.

Three rings.

I think the worst. My mind immediately goes to a scene I'd have in one of my books. She got a phone call that the kids were missing, and she didn't even have time to call or text me in a panic as she ran out the door. Or worse, maybe they were slaughtered and found hanging from a tree in the park, the killer taping a note to their swinging bodies saying it was Dad's fault.

I need to get out of the thriller game.

Four rings. Five rings.

I'm about to go ballistic when she answers.

"Hey."

Super casual. Nothing happened. The kids are fine.

"Hey, Nicole. Are you okay? Are the kids?"

"Why would you ask me that? Are you having me followed?"

I hear the apprehension in her voice. Why is that the first thing that jumps to the front of the conversation? What is she doing right now that she's so worried about me knowing?

"Where are you?" I ask suspiciously.

"Saks," she says matter-of-factly.

Shopping. "Everything on schedule for Taylor and Tyler?"

They're six, and I'm still not used to saying their names. It was Nicole's idea, down to dressing them alike. She has custom dresses made for Taylor with the same pattern turned into pants or a button down for Tyler. I hate to admit she's *that* Upper East Side mother—she loves them with everything she is and cares for them, of course—but she also has the summer camps and the nanny picking them up at private school so she can shop or go to lunch or get massages and manicures.

"I told you, the kids are fine. What happened with the writer? The one who died?"

I look at my watch again. I have an hour and a half before I have to go to the bar to meet Vicky, Davis, and Suzanne. I need to tell Nicole what's going on—she needs to be more aware of her surroundings in case someone tries to get to me through her. This is my family.

"I'm coming by you. I need to talk to you. Meet at the bar in the Waldorf in twenty minutes."

"Mike, why do you always do this to me with no notice? I need more than twenty minutes."

I look at the phone suspiciously, even though she can't see me. "It's less than two blocks away from Saks."

"I have an armful of clothes. I was about to go into the dressing room."

"So? Put them down. Go back to it later. It's important."

She's silent.

She's not at Saks.

"How much time do you need to get to the Waldorf?" I'm such a pussy. I know where she is.

"I guess I can be there in forty-five minutes or so. But the kids will—"

I cut her off. "I'll see you then."

I disconnect. The kids will be fine with Janina after camp. I bet Nicole canceled on Donna for lunch as soon as I left. I curse at myself, because God damn, I should've known when I saw the keynote speakers for this afternoon. Maybe I brushed it out of my mind on purpose.

Nicole's old crush—the professor she studied under a hundred years ago when *she* wanted to be a writer, before he promptly moved out to Providence for a cushy writing job at Brown for MFAs—is in town for Murderpalooza. The same professor she ran into five years after she graduated and had an intense summer-long affair with—and I say *affair* because Matthew Payne is very fucking married and older than me. It was way before she and I met, and I don't get jealous over ex-lovers, but ahem, I prefer them to be *ex*-lovers. He was a keynote speaker earlier this afternoon, and once that panel finished, I bet he went right to his old contacts in New York City. Why waste the trip?

He's supposed to be talking about how to improve writing technique. Not banging my wife.

I'll know she was with him if she's wearing a different outfit when she meets me. She'd go skintight or super short if she were going to meet him. I wonder how long they've been in touch. Is it casual check-ins? Or phone sex while I spent nights writing my manuscript with Kristin?

That's all I did with Kristin—write the manuscript. My heart squeezes again at her loss. She was an awesome writer and a better person, and I sadly think of the exciting plans we had for the promo, how we were going to introduce her. Everything, over. Just like that.

I leave Clover & Crimson in a huff, not caring if anyone is watching me. I hail a cab and tell him to take me to the Waldorf. With any luck, there will be zero traffic and I can get there in ten minutes. That's the thing about New York City. Across town and thirty blocks south could take ten minutes; it could also take an hour. I just want to knock back two fingers—four fingers—hell, six—of scotch to calm my nerves. This day has been a mess, from the murder to my new posse, to the Twitter Murder Stalker Person.

I think back to the last tweet that came in from that account.

Cheater cheater pumpkin eater had a wife and couldn't keep her.

It was talking about me. I *thought* it was talking about *me.*

I can't be trusted either. Which indiscretion does the Twitter stalker know about?

Nicole's or mine?

20

SUZANNE SHIH

Friday, 3:30 P.M.

I try to speed through the lobby to the elevator bank—I just want to hole up in my room, alone. I want to talk to Constantine. I want to google Jason Fleming. I have to figure out how I'm going to explain seeing Kristin this morning. Someone investigating will ask, I'm sure of it.

Of course, my new friend Tara spots me and beelines over. Great.

I smile as she approaches. "Hey!" Way too enthusiastic. But I can't let her know that I'm scared. It could be her. What if she befriended me only to kill me? I can't trust anyone. What if she's the stalker?

"Where have you been?" she asks, her eyes wide. "You have to hear what people around here are saying about Kristin."

Here we go. She's pumping me for information because it's her. I have to think this about everyone I come in contact with right now. Instead of telling her where I was, I dive right into her news. Authors like being the center of attention, so I let her do the talking, thinking she's got some great gossip bomb to drop in my lap.

"What have they been saying?"

Her eyes shift. "One agent tweeted out earlier that she thinks Vicky Overton had something to do with it. Okay, not so much that *exactly*, but she mentioned her name in connection with it. A lot of people got on her case, and she deleted it after that, but you know, screenshots are forever."

Vicky is going to be eviscerated because of that tweet. Better Vicky than me. I'm sweet, innocent little newbie Suzanne. On the outside, anyway.

"Oh man. That's rough. Have the cops talked to anyone yet? Or have they reviewed the video footage?"

"I don't know anything about video footage. There's some guy running around. Pearson, I think is his name. He's talking to everyone. Nothing super official, and he hasn't asked me any-thing, but I don't really know anything anyway. I didn't know Kristin. I think he was hired by the hotel. They're still trying to keep it quiet. I've been totally stalking Twitter for news since I can't find anything on the normal news outlets."

And someone from Twitter is stalking me.

"Do you want to have a drink?" she asks. "I've been sitting with Bethany Walter and Erik Nelson. Did you know he's been friends with Kevin Candela since childhood? Kevin came by and talked about being nominated for the award, and—"

She name-drops authors who I'd normally drool over, but I tune her out because I want to be alone. Alone in my room, with the door closed and bolt locked. Fame can wait this time because my life is in danger. As much as I want some of this insider info from the more established authors, I think Tara has a point.

Twitter is fact as far as writers go. One author can complain about another and then everyone jumps on a side, and one will undoubtedly get dropped by their agent and the publisher will cancel their contract. I've seen it happen—the cancel culture that Twitterverse authors love. They're worse than the mob, and Twitter is Tony Soprano. I need time to research. I have to be the main character in my own real-life thriller.

We say goodbye, and I head to the elevators. Despite there being eight of them in a row, no one is here in a line, and the one on the far left opens immediately to take me to the tenth floor—it's not my floor, but curiosity gets the best of me. The carriage is empty as I step in, which I'm thankful for, but it also scares me as the doors zip quietly closed.

Hummmmmmmm. Up, up, and away.

The elevator stops at the mezzanine level, which is where the bar is located. *Crap.* The doors swing open and a man steps in. He stands around five feet ten, probably in his mid-fifties as there are a few errant gray strands in what's left of his dark mop of hair puffed out on each side above his ears. I think of Danny DeVito from *It's Always Sunny in Philadelphia*, which my parents love to watch on reruns, then I suppress a laugh. It's hard to picture Danny DeVito this tall.

He hits the button for the twelfth floor and stands back, his hands folded in front of him. He nods at me. Hanging around his neck is a badge for the conference, but I don't want to look down and stare at his name. Part of me wants to fangirl over who it may be (famous author!?); the other part wants evidence of who did this to me so I can write his name on the walls of the elevator with my own blood after he stabs me and leaves me to bleed out. That thought skirts me closer to the corner of the box, which has halved in size and not because of the guy. It's closing in on me. My phone is clutched in my hands, so I glue my eyes to it to avoid talking to him. It's a bad habit of mine, talking to strangers. I'm the one who becomes Instagram friends with my Uber drivers.

This little trip to Murderpalooza will certainly put that in perspective for me.

The elevator stops at the tenth floor, and I exhale loudly as I make my way to the exit. He says something like *See ya*. I make a left down the hall and don't look back, practically running. When I hear the doors close, I turn around and go right. He doesn't need to know what wing of the floor I'm going to. I'm in enough trouble.

But there are no footfalls behind me. I'm being paranoid.

Kristin's closed door is at the end of the hall, and it's covered with DO NOT CROSS police tape. I glance left and right to make sure no one else is around me. The scene was probably cleared hours ago. Tip-toeing down the hall, I don't know what my game plan is. I'm not going to try for the handle—fingerprints—and I feel like I'm getting myself into more trouble, but dammit, I have to. It's my nature.

When I get there, I press my ear against the door, and I'm stunned when I hear a male voice talking low. It sounds one-sided, like someone on the phone. I plug my index finger into my other ear and strain to listen to the broken conversation as I pick out some phrases.

I know . . . don't worry . . . everyone knows she's dead, so we have to think about the ceremony . . .

I gasp louder than I mean to, and then the voice halts and there's movement inside. I freeze like a deer in headlights, and my instinct tells me someone is approaching the door. The breathing is loud enough for me to hear, and I know the guy on the other side is doing the same thing I am: pressing his ear to the door.

I take off like a bat out of hell, head to the stairwell, and run down five flights of steps to the fifth floor where my room is. I hold my keycard at the door, three green lights flash, and the familiar click of the lock releasing blares. I push my way in and slam the door, then peer into the bathroom, behind the shower curtain, and in the closet just to make sure there's no boogeyman waiting for me. My heart is going at twice its normal rate, and I berate myself internally. What exactly did I think was going to happen?

Who is in her room, and who are they working with? Are they looking for me?

There are no messages on the hotel's phone, and while leaning against the minibar, I text Constantine to see if he's available to talk. He never answers immediately, usually elbow deep in amps and rhythms, but just the act of texting him, feeling normal, makes me let my guard down a teeny bit. Once my heart rate returns to normal, it's time to get to work.

I google Jason Fleming. There are too many people with that name, so I narrow it to "Jason Fleming Iowa" and "Jason Fleming Iowa car accident," and I have to scroll through two pages of Google hits before I find a blurb from a small newspaper.

Jason David Fleming, 26, was killed in a car accident on May 11, 2016. His car was found by another driver on Long- fellow Road, crushed into a tree. Preliminary reports show no foul play or drug/alcohol use.

Arrangements will be held at Hawthorne Funeral Home May 17th. He is survived by his parents Judy and Jason Fleming Sr., his stepmother Carla Fleming, and his half-sister Diana, 16. In lieu of flowers, the family asks for donations to the local library, Heimer Public; Jason's favorite place.

There's a picture of the family. It's grainy and in black and white, but I can make out his face a little. Something about it is familiar, but I can't put my finger on it. Still, I got Heimer, Iowa. It's a place to start.

The comments on the article are mostly solemn, but of course, the trolls come out at night. One comment stands out in particular.

KooKoo4: I heard it was suicide. There was a note in his pocket.

LisaPease1999: You don't know shit. Your name says it all @KooKoo4

KooKoo4: @LisaPease1999: I have cops in my family. One was at the scene.

LisaPease1999: Sure he was. File that under "things that never happened." Go fuck yourself @KooKoo4

Welcome to the internet, friends, where this behavior has been normalized. Even celebrated. Retweets and going viral—that's what counts. Not the truth.

Still, it's not a total bust. Suicide? A note?

I continue my Google search for "Jason Fleming suicide," but I only get a few more hits on comments sections of articles. Nothing concrete. My stomach sinks as I type in "Jason Fleming Kristin Bailey." Davis said they all knew each other. An article pops up—she was interviewed. I scan the article until I get to it.

> *"Jason and I were in a critique group together," Kristin Bailey, a local author and friend, says. "We exchanged pages between ourselves and other writers. He was talented but insecure, as most writers tend to be. I didn't know he was so depressed. I wonder what put him over the edge."*
>
> *"What edge? The autopsy showed no alcohol in his system. Do you have reason to think he was suicidal?"*
>
> *"No, but we've talked about the twists on Longfellow Road before. He mentioned he didn't like driving there. I'm afraid someone gave him a bad critique, and he subconsciously knew what would happen if he drove fast. I feel so bad for his parents and his sister."*

I wonder if Kristin heard about the note as well. It's not like anyone can ask her.

Do I contact his family and see if I can get more information on what Davis Walton has to do with this?

I sit on the bed to contemplate.

Then a hand grabs my ankle.

21

VICKY OVERTON

Friday, 3:45 P.M.

Jim and I get out of the cab and head into the hotel through the sea of people. I wave at a few as we pass in the lobby, but I don't think many people are in the mood to stop and talk, as most look the other way after they spot me. Then again, the boisterous roar coming from the bar up the stairs tells me differently. The coffee shop in the lobby has conference-goers huddled around tables in their regular cliques, the ones who share publishers or release dates or started out in the business together as newbies. They're easy to spot. I know most of them by face because of Twitter and Instagram. How did authors get to know each other before social media? There are clearly still many people who are eager to discuss theories. *Clearly*—delete.

Speaking of, I wonder which theories are being thrown around by now? Did anyone else witness this alleged fight between Kristin and my boyfriend? I can't wait to get into my room and read Twitter.

We're almost to the elevators when a mammoth man cuts me off and holds up his hand. *Stop.* He stands about six feet three, his dark hair buzzed almost completely off. *Completely*—delete. I'm getting worse with my crutch words. His thick, dark eyebrows sit above deep-set brown eyes, and his cheeks are round, making him look younger than what I assume is mid-thirties. He's wearing a sport jacket over a polo shirt and dark pants, and there's a shield on his belt.

A small gasp escapes because I'm afraid.

"Vicky Overton?" he asks.

"Yes?" He knows me. He was looking for me.

"Name's Pearson. I'm an investigator hired by the hotel. Can we talk?"

Well, here it is, the moment I've been waiting for. I look at Jim. "Go ahead. I'll catch up with you."

Pearson eyes him up and down. "You Jim Russell?"

"Yeah," Jim says, not meeting his eyes. Of course he isn't; he doesn't want to talk about his bleeding head and the rando texts sitting on his phone that he doesn't know I know about. Oh, also that *sleeping-with-the-dead-girl* thing.

"Together?" he asks, stabbing a finger between Jim and I. Okay, stabbing isn't the best word, but he's insistent.

"Yeah." Jim is sheepish. His cheeks are flushed. "Vicky's my girlfriend."

For now.

"You should stay," Pearson says. "I want to talk to both of you."

Jim's shoulders wilt, as I expect them to. Caught.

I regard my surroundings. I don't want to go to the bar where everyone will see us talking to the investigator. I haven't done anything wrong.

Still . . .

Why has everyone around me stopped to stare? Why am I the center of attention in all this? I can't be the first one Pearson has spoken to. Any good investigator would've talked to half the organizers and authors here.

"Do you want to come up to our room for privacy?" I ask.

Pearson's thick neck propels his head with a flick. "No. Over there," he says, nudging to a quiet corner of the lobby, one with velvet benches that normally hold check-ins waiting for their rooms to be ready. By now, almost everyone has checked in, and the space is empty.

"Sure," I say, because what else am I going to say? I'm not going to be combative with someone who probably knows that my boyfriend had a relationship with Kristin and thinks I'm a suspect.

I lead the way, and through my side-eye, I see Jim lagging behind me, and I know Pearson is behind him. It's unsettling. I feel like I'm walking a plank and a one-eyed pirate is inching me forward with a sword, ready to stab me in the back and propel me into shark-infested waters.

I want to plop myself down on a bench, but I stay upright when I turn to Pearson. "What can I help you with, sir?" *Sir.* Because cooperation.

He exhales a deep breath and yanks a notepad from his left breast pocket and flips a few pages. His dark eyes scan a few, slowly, making me wish I *were* at the bar. Like I need another wine—it's a miracle I remember my own name at this point. I've had too many for an afternoon, and Penelope canceled lunch. All I had was a bite of Jim's dirty water dog in Times Square. I'm a bit hammered. My ability to process wine is legendary, but still.

"Vicky," he starts. "How well did—" He pauses, scratches his head with the pencil in his hand, and changes tactics. He looks at Jim. "Jim Russell, how well did you know Kristin Bailey?"

Oh, you're *good*, Pearson. So, so good, I almost want to high five you right here in front of everyone—they're all still staring, by the way. Make him say it. Wait, how does *he* know about Kristin and Jim? Shit. Security found evidence of their affair in her room, didn't they? They know she was sleeping with my boyfriend. I'll be wearing cuffs in a half hour. *Revenge murder!* It's a perfect book plot.

I make my shocked face—dented brows, half duck lips, as I whip my head in Jim's direction. *How well did you know Kristin Bailey?*

"Uh, she's a writer. Like my girlfriend." He moves closer to me. I stifle a chuckle.

Pearson nods. Then smiles, shows no teeth. "So you know her from seeing her book at Barnes & Noble, then?"

Jim looks at me, then back at Pearson. "I'm just here with my girlfriend. For support." He's said *girlfriend* three times in the last two minutes. The guilt is eating at him. "I'm not a writer, I'm a developmental editor. It's not the same thing."

Pearson holds his stare. Point made. Then he looks at me. "How well did you know Kristin Bailey?"

I'm prepared for this. I knew it was coming. "Pretty well through social. We share an agent, so we've had a lot of contact. She's a brilliant writer. *Was.* Was a brilliant writer." My mouth curves down. "Honestly, such a tragedy what happened."

"Right. And where were you this morning at approximately ten A.M.?"

I hesitate, and I know I'm sunk. But it's not like this information is going to be in Publisher's Lunch and emailed to half the industry. I'm talking to an investigator. "I was meeting with another agent."

Fine. Penelope sucks. At least she does for me. She was amazing for Kristin, but honestly, it wouldn't shock me if Kristin planned on dropping her too. She's been all Davis Walton, all the time, for the past six months, and yes, I'm so sick of her not answering my emails or taking my calls. I have stuff going on too. It's taboo for the author, as well as the new interested agent, to meet and discuss representation while still under contract with someone else.

Do I care right now? No. Fuck it. Wine.

"I was meeting with another agent because I'm not happy with my current one. She hasn't been giving me the attention that I need to propel my career." I say it with confidence. It's true. "It's kind of in bad taste to do that in my industry, so I'd appreciate if this stays here."

He jots down a few notes. "And someone can verify this?"

"Yes. I was with Gina Farrant. She'll back me up."

"Huh." That's all he says.

"Huh, what?" Down, girl.

"According to some tweets, people seem to think you had it out for Kristin. Competition, you see."

"What tweets?" My breath catches. More damn Twitter. People are talking about me? Is that why everyone is looking-not-looking at me? I immediately take my phone from my purse and pull up the stalker account. Nothing new from that nutbag. "What are you talking about?"

Typing like a maniac, I hashtag my name. Well holy mother hell, what is this?

My glassy eyes see my name, over and over. There's a tweet from an agent, Meghan Morgan, screen-capped by half the industry—a thinly veiled accusation. That it was me, little ole' Vicky Overton, who wanted to take out Kristin Bailey. What? Why? Because of a stupid made-up award by a made-up committee about made-up scenarios. Are you fucking kidding me? This isn't a thriller book; this is real life. I lift my head from my phone and scan around us, looking for Meghan.

"I'll kill her," escapes my mouth.

Oops. *Use your words,* Jim always says to me when I can't form a thought. Well, I formed that thought and coughed it up at the worst possible time.

"Sorry, you know what I mean," I say.

Pearson's lip twitches. Suspect number one, here! "I'm afraid I'm not one for jokes right now, ma'am."

Please—you're older than me, don't call me ma'am. "Why were you asking Jim about Kristin?" Might as well find out what he knows. Does he know about the affair, or does he think they were just acquaintances?

He snaps the pad closed. "Someone saw them fighting this morning."

"What?" I say it too loudly, and I direct my attention to Jim. He needs to think I don't already know this tidbit of information. "That's a lie."

But truth time—I wasn't with Jim the entire morning.

Which, again, makes me wonder—while I was with Gina, where was Jim?

22

DAVIS WALTON

Friday, 3:45 P.M.

After two glasses of Jack Daniels, I say fuck it, I can scrape together an elevator pitch for Bee Henry. I am a writer, after all. The only reason I haven't is because I've been too distracted. Not that today helps, but maybe I can channel my inner fear and push something out.

The truth is, I've tried to come up with something as meaningful and excellent as the first novel I turned in for publication. It's hard living up to your own hype. Everyone in the industry always talks about the sophomore novel slump, how it's so much harder to write than the first one.

No shit.

I rise from my super comfy chaise lounge on the terrace and go inside. My closed laptop sits on the desk, mocking me. For the past month, it's been an accessory, something to hold, something to make me feel secure. *I'm a writer.* When people see me carrying it around, do they know who I am? Do I scream *famous author?*

My laptop is super thin and weighs less than a pound, so it takes no effort for me to slide it to the center of the desk and flip it open. I press the button and the screen comes to life—my background being the cover to *Memories Gone Wrong*, my first published thriller that comes out this fall—the one that got the movie deal. I'll be a frontrunner for the M-TOTY next year.

If I can make it through this year. What do I write about now?

I open Microsoft Word and hope the inspiration will come to me. The only thriller-related thing I have experience in right now is four writers being stalked at a conference. And I guess Mike has that kind of story locked up from his manuscript with Kristin. No one likes a copycat.

One of the last conversations I had with Kristin runs through my mind—the one after she told me what she knew about me.

"You know what you're going to do? You're going to use all your special newfound fame to make sure I get the votes to win the Murderpalooza Thriller of the Year award. I don't care how you do it. I honestly don't care what you have to do, but I better be on that stage with the attention on me."

"Be reasonable, Kristin. What do you expect me to do?"

"Well you're Davis Walton, aren't you? You'll find a way. Figure it out, or else."

I did it, though. I got Jonathan DeLuca, the head of this whole shebang, to promise he'd wrangle votes. In return, I promised him I'd do everything Murderpalooza wanted for the next two years. It'll make the conference more popular than it already is, giving him leverage to double the registration fees to attend. As it is, it's already five hundred bucks for just a few days of panels, and that doesn't include the hotel room or airfare for people who aren't local. I think back to the text he sent me earlier today.

Kristin being dead doesn't change anything between us

How do I get myself into these messes? I'm in the middle of so many messes, I should walk around with a sponge and a bucket.

Time to write. I look at the blank page and just decide to go for it and I type *The* . . .

My mind goes blank. I have nothing to say. The *what?*

I remember a piece of advice Jason Fleming always said in our writing group—which also included Kristin and Tommy Johnson. One group, three writers who are no longer with us. *Write what you know.* That's what Jason used to say. Write what you know. It makes me think of our hierarchy. Kristin Bailey ended up making it big. Jason Fleming would've eventually, had he not died—he was that good. Tommy Johnson, however, was so untalented, it was unreal. That guy's pages were always full of the worst writing clichés—starting with a character waking up, telling instead of showing, and stupid rudimentary metaphors. One time, when everyone passed around their work, his pages actually said "Brrrr. I'm very cold. It must be winter out. I see clouds and the sky is gray."

To authors, it's just bad form. Everything about it. It's telling, it's passive, it's beyond basic, and who the hell uses the word *very?*

Now, Kristin, Jason, and Tommy are all gone.

Write what you know.

Fuck it, I know a good thriller and suspense story. A great whodunnit too. People with secrets. Things they'll do to keep them hidden.

I erase *The* and start with *His talent was supposed to take him places, but not to an early grave.* I lean back and reread it. Huh. Not a bad start. Before I know it, I have a page. Then two. The more I type, the easier it is to write about a *was-it-really-a-suicide* mystery. Of course, my characters aren't writers; they're something basic like finance guys. And friends. And my book will involve a friendship gone wrong, and who really knows what's going on, and red herrings, and the good stuff. I can do this. I can make it seem easy. I'm Davis Walton.

After a quick session, I have a whole chapter. The opening has Character A driving in his car with his buddy, Character B. Character B gaslights the Character A about stock purchases that didn't pan out until a fight starts, causing Character A to speed around a steep curve. The car skids and hit driver's side first into a tree, which deploys the airbag, which snaps Character A's neck. For Character B, it was a head gash and a sore neck but mostly just trauma. He didn't want anyone to know he was with Character A that night (more on that later, obviously, I mean, it's a suspense novel, I can't give away the farm in chapter one), so he scribbled *I'm sorry* on a piece of paper and shoved it in Character A's pocket before he slipped out of the car, undetected. He made it look like a suicide. It wasn't Character B's fault what happened—it wasn't. It wasn't murder. He just didn't want to be involved with the aftermath. He had other plans for his life.

Write what you know.

The note I wrote and shoved in Jason Fleming's pocket said *I'll never make it as an author.* Then I walked for fifteen miles, until it was light out, across state lines. I lived in Illinois on the border of Iowa, and Jason Fleming, the opposite. I tended to myself alone for almost two weeks. As my bruises healed and I was able to turn my head again, I threw myself into writing and editing. It took years before the masterpiece *Memories Gone Wrong* was finished enough to shop around.

The only person who knew I was in the car that night was Tommy Johnson, and thankfully, he's dead too.

But now, other people know about Jason Fleming, and I'm afraid of Tommy Johnson's disappearance coming out.

Penelope better bring the goods on that kid Suzanne stalking Kristin. Everyone needs to focus on her instead.

If they dig on me any further, they'll find out I killed Tommy Johnson.

23

MIKE BROOKS

Friday, 3:45 P.M.

My second scotch is on its way while I wait for Nicole. She better pull up her panties and show up in the next fifteen minutes.

The Waldorf has a lobby bar that is one of my favorites in New York City. The décor screams old New York, with a thick, oak bar, bookended by onyx and gold columns that run throughout the open space. It's warm and inviting, and the tables have brightly colored flowers—today, hot pink—to contrast the prim and proper feel. People mill about—businessmen handshaking deals and tourists looking at the gold ceiling with wide eyes.

My jacket hangs over a chair that I'm saving for Nicole. Not that the place is so crowded that I have to save her a seat, but as the husband, it's what I do. My hands wring over themselves as I think about my wife rolling around with Matthew Payne. Pawning the kids off to camp, and then Janina, just so she can wrestle around with that jerk.

Then there's the declaration from the Twitter account. *Cheater cheater.*

My fingers tap nervously on the table—*rat-a-tat, rat-a-tat*—until the server finally returns with my second drink. She places a new cocktail napkin on the table and then my drink on top of it, and clears away the old glass, condensation on the outside making the old napkin stick. The single large ice cube melts for a minute or so before I pick up the new drink and sip. I look like a damn alcoholic, sitting here alone. A decade ago, someone might've spotted me. *New York Times Bestselling Author Mike Brooks Sits Alone at Bar, Gets Hammered.* I couldn't make the paper now unless I donated half my earnings to children with cancer. Maybe my upcoming divorce will make the paper. Maybe. Hell, maybe I'll be an eligible bachelor again. I inadvertently touch my paunchy stomach—it's not what it was in my thirties, that's for sure. My almost-fifty self-esteem is equivalent to wearing a shirt in the pool.

I'm getting way ahead of myself. I have no proof Nicole is with Matthew Payne. Just a gut feeling.

I'm swallowing a rather large gulp of scotch when Nicole walks in, her hair still blowing from the door closing behind her. She's not wearing anything skintight or short like I suspected, but she's not in the same outfit I zipped her into this morning. So she did change. Why? Supposedly she was having lunch with Donna, then went shopping at Saks. Supposedly.

She spots me and waves, and I try to read her face. She has one for every occasion. Proud of the kids? Her eyes twinkle. Too much wine? Her right eye droops. Spent five grand at Saks? Her lips purse. Right now, she's smiling. There's nothing there. She's neutral.

She's guilty. She's doing it on purpose.

"Hi," she says as she reaches me and bends down for a kiss. I normally stand to greet her, but I can't muster the desire to do so right now. "What's the emergency? Did they find out what happened to that dead author?"

That's the second or third time she's been so casual about it. She's not a *dead author*; Kristin was my friend. I study Nicole as she places her huge Louis Vuitton bag on the seat beside her—God forbid it touches the floor—and smooths her cotton sundress under her ass before she sits.

"The dead author has a name. Kristin Bailey," I say. "She was murdered."

The color drains from her face. "At the conference?"

"Well the hotel where the conference is held, yes."

"Yikes. Do they know who did it?"

She's very cool in her questioning, waving over the server to order a club soda with a lime wedge. She doesn't like to drink during the day. Something about "drinky wrinkles."

"Not that I know of. I haven't been to the hotel since early this afternoon, it was chaos there."

"Mmhmm. So where have you been?"

Where have *you* been?

"Just out with some other authors. Vicky Overton. Suzanne Shih. Davis." No last name needed. Madonna. Cher. Prince Harry.

"Wow, he spent the afternoon with you?" she asks, eyes wide.

Right. Because I'm no longer the toast of the town. I haven't told her that Vita doesn't want to shop my manuscript anymore because it's about exactly what's happening. And oops, in the book, *I* did it. So instead of letting her make me feel like shit, I turn on her.

"Were you with Matthew Payne this afternoon?"

Her face changes, and I immediately know I'm wrong about her having an affair with him because she doesn't look guilty; she looks hurt.

"What? He's here?"

Forty hit Nicole hard, mentally. She still looks great even if some of her is enhanced, but the number itself, the *middle age* of it all, didn't go down well. Now she's forty-one, and she just learned her ex-lover, whom she had a passionate affair with, didn't call her when he came to town. She's pissed off because she's not young anymore, and I know she's picturing him chasing the twenty-somethings like he did when he pursued her at that age.

"He was a keynote speaker at the conference. And then with everything that happened this morning . . ." I shrug. "I assume his afternoon was free."

"And what? You assumed he called me? And worse, that I lied to you and ran over to sleep with him?"

"You're wearing a different outfit."

"I changed after lunch. It's hot out and I was sweaty."

I kind of feel like an asshole, and I should. I blow out a breath. "I'm sorry, Nic. I've had a stressful day."

I lean forward and rub my temples. That *cheater cheater* tweet was definitely about me, then. Jesus, it was one time. I didn't mean to. I'm not making excuses because what happened was dead wrong. It wasn't even sex, it was just some rough kissing and hand-roaming, not that that makes it better. For me, it started with a hard day, and I'd had a huge disagreement with Kristin and left angry. I began drinking, and there she was, all over me—not physically at first, but so flattering about my earlier work. I was weak. She told me I was brilliant, and I hadn't heard that in so long. When she put her hand on my leg and nodded toward the bathroom, I broke.

It's one hundred percent my fault, and no one will ever make me feel worse about it than I've made myself feel.

She obviously talked to someone, but I haven't told a soul. Shame will do that to you. And now the Twitter stalker knows. I question everything now. Everything, and everyone I've seen today.

I place my hand on Nicole's knee. It's time to come clean.

"There's something else I should tell you."

She sips her club soda and raises her eyebrows as much as the Botox allows. It's not done in the curious way, but rather the *what-are-you-about-to-tell-me* way. Like the coward I am, I chicken out. Even though I want to get ahead of it in case this whole thing blows up, I decide I'll burn that bridge if it comes to it. So I tell her the other thing.

"Kristin Bailey—she was my co-author."

"What?" Nicole yelps. Now I can read her face. Shock and awe. "Are you in danger?"

"I'm not sure. But there's more."

"I bet. Are you allowed to sell the manuscript now?"

I take a deep breath. "Well that's the least of my concern. Vita already told me she doesn't want to shop it."

"Great," she slams her hand on the table. "For a year, you've been gone almost every night working on this thing. And now I find out that the co-author is dead and the work was for nothing?" She finishes the club soda and stabs the lime with her cocktail straw, not looking at me. "This was supposed to be your big comeback, Mike."

"I know, but—"

"Maybe you can use this. The publicity. Posthumously and all. Don't authors love that stuff?"

"Jesus, Nic. Stop and think about what you're saying. The body isn't cold yet."

"What's the book about, anyway?"

"Well that's what I've been trying to tell you. It's about secret co-authors, and one gets killed at a conference. And in the book, the co-author did it."

She stops talking over me and stares. Now her head is in her hands. "What are we going to do, Mike? If you can't sell this book, then what are we going to do for money?"

"Money? We have plenty of money." How many times does she need reminding that once upon a time, I was the next Michael Connelly? My advances have always earned out, and I'm still getting royalties from Book One. Come on, wifey, who do you think pays your store credit cards and your plastic surgeon bills?

"We need a bigger place," she says.

How could I forget? It's the talk I get every month about the bells and whistles of a full-service building with a gym and an entertainment roof deck.

"I told you, I like where we live. It's hardly the inconvenience you make it out to be."

"Not that," she says, like a teenager accused of cheating on an exam. "Mike—" There are tears in her eyes before she speaks again. "I'm pregnant. I wasn't shopping at Saks. I was at the doctor getting confirmation. This isn't exactly how I wanted to tell you."

Whoa.

I feel like someone hit me across the chest with a bat, and then a calm settles over me. Of course, I'm happy. My wife and

I made another baby. But at forty-one and forty-seven, I can't help but think how much harder this is going to be. I wasn't planning on potty training in my fifties.

I stand and lift her out of her seat and wrap my arms around her. "That's great news." I kiss her on her forehead, then kiss the tip of her perfect nose.

She has tears in her eyes. "Is it, though? I'm high risk at my age anyway, and it's still so early. Plus, I wasn't planning on potty training in my mid-forties."

Just like that, I know whatever happens with this whole thing, it'll be okay. At least in the book of life, we're on the same page.

Speaking of pages, I have to find a way to get this book out—even if it makes me a suspect. And I have to do whatever I have to do to make sure that my messing around doesn't come out.

Whatever I have to do.

Which means, if I have to sacrifice someone in my newfound posse, so be it.

24

SUZANNE SHIH

Friday, 3:45 P.M.

I'm on the floor, leaning against the closet door, shaking. Constantine doesn't understand why I won't speak to him. He didn't live the past few hours that I did, and he doesn't know how much danger I'm in. Sneaking into my room to scare me by hiding under the bed and grabbing my ankle is normally something I'd shake off, but today, I'm just . . . I can't.

"It was just a joke," he says. "I thought it would be funny."

"It wasn't," I say. "How did you get in here?"

He rolls his big doe eyes. He's wearing eyeliner again, and his too-long, razor-chopped hair swings with his laughter. "Remember I told you about that time me and my ex snuck into a hotel room? I did the same thing. I waited for housekeeping, and when she was leaving, I just walked in like I owned the place. Perception becomes reality, you know."

Constantine is so much more confident than me. He's a few years older—twenty-six, and he's been urging me to become more independent and take more control over my life. Not just with my traditional parents—his divorced when he was five and both remarried shortly after. He has half-siblings and step-siblings and lives this carefree band lifestyle with zero structure. One day could be spent jamming and smoking pot, the next a full day stocking shelves at Target (where he gets his paycheck), and the following at the beach day drinking. He doesn't get it.

"You almost gave me a heart attack. Someone was murdered here today!"

"What? Oh my God, that's terrible. Why didn't you tell me?"

I shake my head. "I've been busy. It was another writer, so everything has been a mess here. When you grabbed me like that, I thought I was next."

"Oh please, why would you think you're next?"

If he only knew. It's not his fault that I haven't told him anything. And I still can't. I need him separate from what's going on here. Compartmentalization.

He crawls toward me and hangs an arm around my shoulder. I think he senses my shaking, or maybe feels it, because he strokes my head and kisses my temple. "I'm sorry." My arms are wrapped around my shins, my knees under my chin. He pulls my ball-shaped body toward him and holds me. "Aren't you at least glad to see me? The guys bailed because someone's girlfriend or boyfriend gave attitude over something. I wanted to surprise you, so I hopped the train."

I am glad to see him. With him here, we're just a young couple in a hotel, exploring New York, like we did when we first started dating a couple months ago. Still, part of me stings at him. I told him I had to be at this conference for work and that Vita set up meetings to try to sell my novel. I got here last night, and I'm due to be home in less than two days. The awards ceremony is tonight. I need to be networking. Why couldn't he let me have this time to do what I need to do? I'm busy into the evening. What was his plan, to stay under the bed until midnight if I didn't just stop here right now?

I lean into him to ease his mind, then give him a quick kiss before I stand. My head swivels, looking for the phone that I dropped—maybe threw—as I screamed when he grabbed me.

"Looking for this?" he asks as he pulls it out from underneath him, then reads the screen. "Who's Jason Fleming?"

I tear the phone from his hands, not wanting to explain the ins and outs of my day. Not quite yet.

"He was a friend of one of my new writer friends."

"Oh. You're making a lot of new friends?"

Constantine isn't clingy; in fact, he's a bit aloof. He might be realizing how different our worlds are. I'm hoping mine takes me in the direction of book tours and panels and movie premieres. I'll walk a red carpet under the spotlight if it's the last damn thing I do. While he thinks his band is the next Panic at the Disco, they don't even get real gigs—they play at bars and county fairs. I mean, I have an *agent*. For now, he has to let me grow my brand so my name will be recognized. I want everyone to know the name Suzanne Shih as if I'm a Kardashian.

"Yes, I've met a ton of people." I hesitate. This morning, I was so excited to post all over social about hanging out with Vicky, Davis, and Mike. But now . . . shit, Vicky is half a murderer as far as the Twitter mob is concerned, Davis turned out to be a complete douche nozzle, and Mike . . . well . . .

"I know sometimes you think I don't support your new career, so I did what you wanted me to do."

Huh? "What do you mean?"

He crawls to the bed, where underneath he has a satchel hiding. He opens it and rummages through. I see clothes, and holy moly, is he planning to stay the night? That's going to cause so much trouble for me, but how do I tell him to go home? He can't stay. He can't.

I glance at the clock and realize I have less than an hour before I have to meet the gang at the bar. He finally gets to the bottom of the bag and tugs out his phone, then presses a few buttons. He smiles and hands it to me. *Just Breathe* is tattooed across the inside of his forearm, and I try to heed the advice.

"What am I looking at?" I peer at the screen.

No.

No, no, no, no, no, no, no . . .

"It's the interview you wanted me to do for you for the 'Next To Die' series for Murderpalooza. I filled it out when I was on the train and sent it back already."

What is he talking about? I never agreed to anything like that. My hands are shaking, but I somehow manage to get to the bathroom and pull a hairclip from the counter and twist my hair off my neck. I take a small bottle of water from the mini fridge, even though they're going to charge me six dollars for it, and I sit on the bed. The email came from MPaloozaNxt2Die@gmail.com.

Of course it did.

Hi Constantine Walker! We're doing a limited series on a few of the lesser-known authors to boost their profiles, and Suzanne Shih gave us your contact info. If you wouldn't mind answering these questions ASAP, we can put together her Murderpalooza profile. Thanks, and have a k i l l e r day!

No, no, no, no, no, no, no . . .

I begin to read, and I'm not happy.

Q1: How well do you know Suzanne Shih, and how did you meet?

A1: We met at the tattoo parlor. I was getting some ink added to my sleeve, and she was browsing for something small that her parents wouldn't see. She was easy to talk to and we had a lot in common, and she's just so damn cute. So one thing led to another!

Q2: Suzanne is a thriller writer. What is her biggest fear?

A2: Without question, being locked in the dark. We saw a movie once where someone was locked alone in a cage and couldn't see anything, and she mentioned how that would be the worst thing ever.

Q3: What was the biggest motivator for Suzanne to come to Murderpalooza?

A3: Definitely to hobnob with other authors. She gets kind of obsessed. Some people freak out over seeing Tony Hawke or David Grohl, she freaks out over people like Kristin Bailey.

Q4: Have you read her writing, and what did you think?

A4: I think she's super talented but I'm biased.

Q5: Last question: has she told you who her favorite writer is, or could you guess?

A5: Definitely Kristin Bailey. She told me they've interacted on social media in the past and that they're good
friends. She's very excited to meet her in person.

I drop the phone on the bed and look at him. "Why?"

He's smiling. He doesn't know how bad he's made things
for me.

"It's going to go on some profile page for new writers on
the Murderpalooza website. You said that Kristin girl was up
for the big award. Wait until she sees this profile. She'll know
how much you admire her. Imagine what she could do for your
career, promotion wise! Could you imagine if she gives you a
blurb for your book?"

I'm dizzy. The room swirls before me, then blackout.

KRISTIN BAILEY

THE MORNING OF THE MURDER

Kristin was all thumbs trying to clasp her earring into her ear. She was tired as hell, and her middle-of-the-night visitor only made things worse. She didn't get enough of her beauty sleep. It sounded like a cliché, but her mama was in her sixties and could pass for at least a decade younger. Always attributed it to getting her beauty sleep.

It was just before seven A.M., and Bethany Walter had texted that she'd come and pick Kristin up since they were on the early panel together. They planned to stop for the cold buffet since Kristin couldn't function without breakfast. The most important meal of the day, according to Mama. Although, at this point, she'd probably only have time to stuff half a bagel in her mouth and wash it down with coffee. She needed her coffee, at least three every morning. Authors ran on caffeine and self-doubt.

She admired herself in the mirror. With her almond eyes and dark skin, she looked so much like Mama. While she had her daddy's lithe build, she had her mama's most beautiful features. Great hair, even when relaxed, just because that made it more manageable. Great smile. Great skin. She missed her parents and her two younger brothers like crazy since she'd moved from Iowa to New York City. She'd spent over three decades there, and Mama always told her to hold her queen head high.

New York was much more accepting. It was a better place to grow her career, and well, she had to get away from the Midwest after her friend Jason Fleming died. She needed to start anew.

There was a knock on the door, and Kristin knew it was Bethany. She grabbed her blue headband and slid her hair back. Today she wore all black, but her accessories—earrings, necklace, bracelets, scarf, belt, and headband—were all turquoise, which stood out against the bland.

"Coming!"

Without looking through the peephole, she unchained the lock and opened the door and—

No way. It was that crazy little bitch, Suzanne Shih. The one who'd been stalking her for years. She panicked, and just as she tried to push the door closed, Suzanne shoved her arm between the hall and Kristin's room, a violation even worse than showing up unannounced.

"I just want to talk to you," Suzanne said. "I won't even come in. I have something for you."

She wondered if she should slam the door shut anyway and break her arm. "I'm either going to call security or scream until someone else calls."

Suzanne's eyes pleaded, but Kristin saw the crazy behind them.

"Please, Kristin, you've misunderstood me. I just want our friendship to go back to how it used to be."

"I don't even know you. I'm going to count to three before I scream."

That meant serious business in Kristin's world. Mama always counted to three. It was a warning to her and her brothers that that was all the time they had until she flipped out or they got the *wait-till-your-father-gets-home* speech.

"One." Should she break her arm? "Two." Where was Bethany? Please let those damn elevator doors open.

"Fine," Suzanne said. Her right arm was still in the door, and she grabbed something out of her bag with her left hand. "It's just a card. I just wanted you to know how much you mean to me and how you've helped me in my career." She dropped it on the floor inside the room. "I'll go now. Hopefully, this will change your mind about me."

She withdrew her arm from the doorway, and Kristin couldn't slam it closed fast enough. Then she locked it, bolted it, and chained it, her heart going a mile a minute. The sweat beading at her hairline and the shaking of her hands told her she needed a Xanax. She couldn't though . . . she was Panel Master in thirty minutes.

The envelope on the ground mocked her. She didn't even want to touch it. That crazy bitch probably got her hands on some Anthrax, but she opened it anyway.

It was a poem. A poem that in Suzanne's warped mind was innocent, but Kristin saw it as the threat it was.

She threw it out, sat on the bed, and waited for Bethany. She didn't want to be alone for the rest of the conference. She wanted to talk to Jim as soon as possible.

25

VICKY OVERTON

Friday, 4:00 P.M.

We finish answering Pearson's questions—the "fight" according to Jim was that Kristin ran into him and didn't apologize and he said something nasty to her, and her back to him. Sure. I'm thankful that Pearson doesn't want to bring us "downtown" or whatever they say on TV.

Back in the room, I close the door behind us and throw my purse on the desk next to my laptop, then move swiftly past Jim, who's standing awkwardly and always in my way, into the bathroom.

I turn on the faucet—one of the only things you don't have to push a button for—and stick my middle finger under the water until it runs warm, then pull my hair into a ponytail and splash the water on my face. I find my tube of cleanser and foam it up in my hands, then rub it on my face as if I'm a parent trying to erase a child's marker squiggles from the walls. After my final rinse, I blot dry and stare at myself in the mirror.

My whole life, I was a pretty good student—*pretty good*—delete. I ran with the middle of the pack, not a band geek nor a cheerleader. Straight B student. Never got in trouble, and that was by design. My parents were stricter than others, and to be honest, I was afraid of them. They had a lot of money and always held it over my head. Subconsciously, it's why I went into a field that pays garbage. They would've much preferred I was a plastic surgeon like him or a lawyer like her. Point is—I was boring, if you will. Now, I'm getting interrogated, someone I know was murdered, and my boyfriend was having an affair with her, and oh my God, is there a killer in the next room? In just a few hours, my life stopped being vanilla.

"Are you okay in there?" Jim the psychotic murderer asks, knocking on the door.

I startle, just now realizing I don't want to be alone with him. What if I'm right?

Then again, there's that text that came into his phone, saying to meet on upper Lexington. And he was attacked. Unless that was staged? Could he have sent that text to himself from the same burner phone he's been using to torture the rest of us, knowing I'd look at his phone after the text I got this morning told me to? Could he have given himself the head injury to throw me off?

It's all so confusing, and now I'm making things up. It's the author in me. But when you lose trust in someone, you'll doubt everything they do. I have to ask him about Kristin. I deserve the truth.

"I'm fine. Be right out," I say.

Inching my head toward the door, I wait silently, holding my breath. I hear nothing. No movement, no TV. I yank the door open, and Jim is there and jumps back. He was doing the same thing I was doing. Listening. Face pressed against the glass, if you will.

"What were you doing?" I ask. "Why were you so close to the door?"

"I just wanted to make sure you were alright." His phone is in his hand.

I lower my eyes suspiciously. "Why?"

"Nothing. Just what they're saying about you online."

I pull the door open and brush past him. Bypassing my purse, which holds my phone, I go straight to my laptop and open it and log onto Twitter like a damn dinosaur. No one uses the desktop version. I hashtag my name again, and it's not exactly trending but there are tons of posts when I click "latest." They're still coming in every few minutes.

JUSTICE FOR KRISTIN @Murderpalooza #murderpalooza
Where was @VickyOvertonWriter?
One female left @Murderpalooza. You know they aren't giving that award to a man. Certainly makes @VickyOvertonWriter a shoo-in JUST SAYING

Can you say guilty, @Murderpalooza? Just saw @VickyO-vertonWriter in the lobby being grilled by a detective or whatever #murderpalooza

Wasn't it the best friend in her book? Vicky and Kristin were friendly if social is anything to go by. @VickyOvertonWriter life is playing out in real time @Murderpalooza #murderpalooza

One after the other after the other. My mouth hangs open, and I rise from the chair. Jim puts a hand on my shoulder, and I brush him off, even though my hands are tingling. So are my feet. So is my face. My eyes find the cabinet that houses the minibar, and I head over and open it, then open the fridge.

There's no Sauvy B, but a mini bottle of her big sister Chardonnay stares at me with a smile.

"When Pearson asked you about Kristin Bailey—why did you stutter?"

It's funny when I actually see the blood drain from his face. *Actually*—delete. "I guess he was covering his bases. You know, questioning everyone. Isn't that his job?"

"Are you telling me you weren't sleeping with her?" Might as well come out with it.

"No, that's insane." He says it without hesitation, like he was waiting for me to ask the question. "Why would you ask that?"

I swig some liquid courage. "You've been sleeping with her." I say it with trepidation. "Now she's dead."

His eyes aren't on mine, and he moves to the window. Puts his hands on his hips like a fancy little secretary from the eighties and stares at the street below. Thank God we don't have a balcony because I'd push the liar right off. Nah—I'm not a character in a book. As previously mentioned, normal people don't kill for stupid reasons.

"You lied, Jim."

"Why do you think that?"

Round and round we go. He's been answering every question with another question. A sign of guilt. "Well for starters, I saw your text messages from a few weeks ago. How long has it been going on?"

He shakes his head. "You're misunderstanding the situation."

"Then explain it to me." It's hardly fair to say I was misunderstanding the situation when he talked about ripping her panties off. I mean, come on.

He flinches. "I don't have to explain anything." There's an edge to his voice now.

"You were with her this morning. People saw you. What were you really fighting about?"

He pauses. "Don't believe it just because Pearson said it."

Busted. "So are you denying it?"

We're locked in a heated stare.

"Say it. You think I killed her." His hands are up defensively, like I'm coming at him with a knife. Or like I'm going to pick up the lamp that's right next to me on the desk and hurl it at the other side of his head for a matching bruise, which is a much more likely scenario. Normal people *do* tend to let passion get the best of them.

"Get out." It's the only thing I have left to say.

At first, he doesn't move. Then he scrunches up his face—*I don't care!*—and turns toward the door and opens it. He mutters a curse and pulls the handle hard, but these damn hotel room doors are soft-close and it won't slam behind him. The soft click tells me I'm alone. Now I can cry in peace, and it's not over him. Mostly.

I grab tissues from the bathroom and sit back down at the desk and turn my attention to the computer again. I click "top" to see what the most popular comments are on Twitter, and a bunch of them are that screen-grab from Meghan Morgan. I read the comments from the one with six hundred twenty-eight likes and over a hundred retweets. Terrific. It's spreading like wildfire.

Is anyone coming to my defense?

Sure, of course. The other nominees, Kevin Candela, Larry Kuo, and Marco Crimmins, have all stepped up, scolding the insufferable Twitter crowd, saying that real feminism isn't throwing a female under the bus without evidence. *Thank you.*

While there are a handful on my side, I see a comment from the most unlikely ally.

@MPaloozaNxt2Die Has anyone at @Murderpalooza #murderpalooza ever heard of Jason Fleming? Maybe you should look into him before making accusations about @VickyOvertonWriter #kristinbailey

Well, shit. Do I love the Twitter stalker now?

No, I don't, but after seeing my name blasted over and over, and the stuff with Jim and the detective weighing on me, I forgot about Davis's connection to that other dead writer, Jason Fleming.

Not anymore.

I open Google.

26

DAVIS WALTON

Friday, 4:15 P.M.

Forty-five minutes until I have to meet the gang at the bar. I lean back from the desk chair and stretch my hands over my head in an exaggerated manner. My button-down creeps up and exposes my abs, and I pat them for no reason, still nice and hard. I catch a glimpse of myself in the mirror and see the makeup stain that Penelope left on my Versace shirt. Shit, I've been running around with this on all day. Christ. I get up and walk to the closet. My shirts are lined up meticulously. I grab a navy UnTuckit, because I want to portray that I can hang with the plebs. I don't need everything to be designer.

Still satisfied with my newly written Chapter One, I begin a light sketch of an outline for the rest of the novel, or at least for the first three chapters. Maybe I can *wow* Bee tomorrow with a surprise, like, *of course I have your outline and first three chapters, this shit is second nature to me!*

Where exactly do I want this story to go? I can't make it close to what really happened *after* the car accident, because I'm not stupid like Mike. I won't write something that makes me look guilty of murder. Even though what happened to Jason wasn't murder.

I decide to let Chapter Two start five years before the car accident and show how Character A met Character B and so on, building the tension of them working together and moving up in their hedge fund and how they came to be in that car, arguing, before Character A wrapped it around a tree.

Publishing is slow as shit. By the time this book comes out, it'll probably be almost two years from now. Jason Fleming will be long forgotten by then. People fake rage online, but they also have short memories. What these people attempt to cancel when they come with the pitchforks and the fire one day gets glossed over for new rage over something else a few days later.

Back to the desk, I go through my emails. First, I look at the ones that come in through my website. So, so many fans, even though the first book isn't out yet. My publisher sent out advance reader copies to about five hundred bookstagrammers. The reviews have been amazing. Bee said my preorders are through the roof, but I guess having David Fincher attached to direct your maiden project will do that too.

David Fincher. One day soon, people will know my name better than his.

I answer about ten emails. I'm satisfied with myself and check Twitter again.

Oh no. There's a new tweet from @MPaloozaNxt2Die.

By this point, y'all are probably doing my job for me. What did you find out about each other?

At the end, there were a few emojis. A computer. A detective with a magnifying glass.

A car. An explosion. Handcuffs.

Son of a bitch, the Twitter stalker knows it's struck a nerve between all of us. Yes, we're looking into each other. In fact, the first thing I did was press Penelope for details about Suzanne. Has she sent them to me yet?

I set aside my fan email and open my regular email. There's one from Penelope with an attachment. The subject line says *Suzanne.*

Here we go. I clasp my hands together and dig in.

I read through it all. It started out innocently enough—she was a fan. Big deal, I have tons of fans. Her emails, forwarded from Kristin to Penelope, and now to me, tell a story of obsession.

This chick is crazy. Absolutely, one hundred percent batshit crazy.

One of the emails went through every single thing she did that day, like she was writing to a lover at war. What dreams woke her, what flavor her toothpaste was, what she bought at the grocery store, what her Intro to Humanities professor talked about—every little detail. She talked about living with her strict parents a lot—really, still? What a little girl.

Then they got dark, of the *why-don't-you-write-me-back* and the *do-you-want-to-be-responsible-for-what-happens-if-you-don't* variety. That's when the lawyers got involved. And it stopped.

Crazy bitches gonna crazy, and I don't believe for a second that she just stopped cold. Did she come here to talk to Kristin? To show her what happens if she's ignored?

To murder her?

I look on Twitter again, this time at Suzanne's profile. Scrolling through, it seems innocent enough. She acts like a little kid, with cat video retweets and ridiculous quotes pondering life. Lots of pictures of food, pictures of her with friends clinking White Claws. A picture of her and some skinny dude with dyed platinum hair and a bunch of piercings and tattoos with a little heart above it. What exactly am I looking for? I don't really know.

Until I find something from many months ago that hits me hard and fast. What the bloody hell is going on here?

@AuthorSuzanneShih
  I'll always remember last night <3 This slipped off, LOL
Don't worry I'll get it back to you

No one is tagged, but below the tweet is a picture of what appears to be a watch on a nightstand. I've seen that watch before. It's one I covet.

It's a limited-edition ice-blue Daytona Rolex from the early '90s.

27

MIKE BROOKS

Friday, 4:30 P.M.

I check the time—four-thirty. I feel terrible leaving Nicole right now, but in order to protect her, my kids, and my career, I have to go. I grab her hands and kiss them, left to right, right to left. Her perfect tiny hands that fit so well inside mine, hands that didn't dial up Matthew Payne and touch his body. That was me projecting my guilt. Shit.

My own indiscretion.

It was over the winter, after a long, grueling writing session with Kristin, and I lied to Nicole and said it was going well into the night. What I needed was a drink and not to walk into the third degree, the kids screaming about school, shoving construction paper doodles at me, wanting me to smile and pay attention. It sounds shitty, I know, but sometimes, for my sanity, and the sake of keeping my marriage together, I need to be selfish.

Kristin lives—lived—on Lafayette Street in NoHo, a funky neighborhood with lots of restaurants and bars, just south of Union Square. After we tackled Chapter Thirty-Two—the one where the reader discovers that the co-author is guilty of murder—I needed an escape, because we butted heads on how it was going to be revealed. I remember I had just let her win and I stormed out, slamming the door behind me.

I walked north to The Strand bookstore to escape. Being surrounded by books has always calmed me. The smell, the feel, the people standing around, browsing, some with open books in their hands, reading. It's heaven.

Bypassing the "must read" and "new thriller" section, I went to the rows of fiction. I turned the corner to where "B" was located, and there, on the second shelf from the bottom, were my eight books. One of each. Forgotten. At least my third—the most popular that became a Hollywood blockbuster—was face-out like a headstone.

Here lies Mike Brooks.

The depression was real.

Right at that moment, an email came in from Suzanne Shih. She was in town to sign representation papers with Vita and wanted to know if I had time to grab a drink and meet in person. We'd been chatting via email for a few weeks, and she was so complimentary every single time she wrote me. I needed an ego boost, so I gave her the name and address of a lesser-known bar in the neighborhood.

It was a good twenty-minute walk from Vita's office, so I sat on a barstool and placed my light coat on the one beside me, saving it. I had a one-two-three shot special of tequila. Three shots in five minutes. I hadn't done that since Nicole and I were in Cabo for our honeymoon. At the time, I was in my mid-thirties and processed it way better than now, in my upper forties. Five minutes after I drank the shots, I didn't care about what had transpired between Kristin and I.

I was numb.

I blankly stared at a basketball game on the TV mounted above the bar until Suzanne showed up. She held a Strand polybag, and inside were all eight of my books. She cleaned out their entire Mike Brooks inventory, which meant they'd have to order more. It felt good.

She asked me to sign them. It felt better. She gushed and gushed and gushed, for well over an hour, while I sipped a bourbon, her a Bloody Mary. Then I had another, as did she. My vision had long gone blurry when she touched my inner thigh. She wanted me. Maybe not me, but Mike Brooks. I just wanted to feel like *Mike Brooks* again.

We went to the vestibule by the bathrooms, and she grabbed my shirt and pulled me toward her, where we made out like teenagers, roaming hands and all. Then she shoved her hand between my legs, and I snapped out of it.

I was married. She was young and starstruck. I jumped back and wiped my face, told her it was a mistake, and apologized. She held my wrist and said it was okay and that she understood. It was a lapse in judgment, though I doubt Nicole would feel the same.

Still, I was a bit hammered, and she said she'd help me into a cab to go home.

She held my wrist the whole time. I was so out of it, I didn't remember her slipping my forty-thousand-dollar watch off.

The next day, she emailed me a picture. She said it "fell off," and she grabbed it and had it in her room for safekeeping. She also said that she'd be in the city the following week and we should meet up to get it. That day, I made up an excuse—a horrible one—about my father having a heart attack and asked her to leave it with my doorman. She did.

And I hadn't seen her again until today. My how things have changed in just a few short months. Now Twitter Murder Stalker Person is trying to kill us, and my wife just told me we're having another baby. I don't want to leave Nicole and go back to see the three other possible victims, one of which is Suzanne. But I have to do it, to keep my family safe. If one of us is really the next to die, I need to make damn sure it isn't me.

"Baby, I'm so sorry, but I have to leave. I have a big meeting back at the hotel at five," I say to Nicole. Kiss her hands again. "The ceremony is at eight, and I have to be there. I'll come home as soon as it's over. No bar scene tonight. I promise."

Her eyes deceive her when she says, "Okay, do what you must." She sips the rest of her club soda. "Who are you meeting with? I thought you said Vita didn't want to sell the manuscript?"

Uhhh. "Davis again. Earlier, he said he'd bring some people he knows who have connections." It's a white lie, something I'm getting good at. I'm not proud. "Maybe someone else will want to sell it."

"You're going to leave Vita?"

No, I'm never going to leave Vita. I've been with her for two decades. We started our careers together, and I really hope she's as loyal to me as I am to her. "Maybe. That's why I want to have this discussion."

Another lie. I have no fear that I'll be able to talk Vita into selling the manuscript. Eventually.

"Hang on one sec," I say as I grab my phone.

I pretend to check emails, but I'm really opening Twitter to see if it's safe to leave Nicole. There's another tweet from that murderous stalker account.

By this point, y'all are probably doing my job for me. What did you find out about each other?

I hope no one dug up anything on me and Suzanne. And shit . . . wasn't I supposed to be finding out who Jason Fleming was? And what Davis is hiding? Hopefully, I'll find out soon enough.

I take another glance at the watch that now turns my stomach. "I have to go. Are you going to be okay?" On second thought, "I'm going to put you in a cab." I don't want her walking unattended.

We exit the Waldorf, and I have my arm around her protectively as I hail a cab. She turns around and smiles, and I land another little kiss on her perfect nose. I close the door and the cab takes off. I stand and watch until my old eyes can't see it anymore.

Now I have to hail my own cab back to the hotel, and while inside, google Jason Fleming.

28

SUZANNE SHIH

Friday, 4:45 P.M.

I come to when Constantine throws a glass of water on my face. The confusion sets in. Why am I wet and why am I on the floor?

"Did I pass out?" I ask.

"Jesus, Suzanne, you scared the shit out of me!"

"Sorry."

I look around the room. I know where I am, and I see my laptop on the desk. Constantine's knapsack is still on the ground in front of me. Why, then, do I feel disoriented?

Oh, right. My boyfriend gave an interview about me to the Twitter stalker. Now they know that I'm afraid of the dark and enclosed spaces.

"Drink this," he says. "I caught you before you hit the ground. Thank God. You could've split your head open."

It's water. I need something stronger, but I drink it anyway. When I stand, my legs wobble and I kick off my shoes, opting to go flat-footed in case it happens again. As much as I want to yell and kick and scream, it's not Constantine's fault. He thought he was doing me a favor, and I almost love him for that.

"I really wish you hadn't filled that out. I wish you'd asked me first."

"Why?"

"Because I never approved it."

"Oh." His face falls, confused. "What's the big deal? They said you gave them my email. How was I supposed to know?"

"Well I didn't. And after reading that, I think you should know that the person who was murdered here today was none other than Kristin Bailey."

His hand flies to his open mouth. "Oh shit. Are you serious? You, like, totally loved her." It stings coming from Constantine. "I'll email them back and see if I can withdraw it. I really doubt the conference would publish this now anyway."

"The conference didn't—" I stop myself. The four of us agreed to keep this between ourselves for the time being. Though, right now, I have no idea where my loyalties lie.

Davis Walton is involved in something messed up with Jason Fleming, I just don't know what it is. Vicky's boyfriend was sleeping with Kristin. Mike wrote a book with her.

Mike.

I acted so cool when I saw him this afternoon. I didn't run to him when he first texted, saying he wanted to see me, and instead said I was at lunch with Tara, which was true. I'm still kind of embarrassed about what happened this past winter. He didn't bring it up, so I didn't either. He probably wants to forget about it, and so do I. What was I thinking coming on to him like that? I'm a nobody. Did I think it was going to get a blurb from him or procure his contacts at the *New York Times*? It happened after the email from Kristin's lawyer, and I guess I wanted to hitch myself to someone famous again so I could be famous by association. I've been pondering bringing it up to him, but we haven't been alone. Only in the cab to Clover & Crimson, but by then I was terrified of the rando text and the stalker Twitter account. It wasn't the time.

Stalker. Now they think I'm a goddamn stalker, even though I'm not. Kristin just wasn't ready for my friendship. Mike probably feels lucky that he got out when he did, and I didn't go all *Misery* on him. Imagine if I'd stayed besotted and did to him what I did to Kristin? Or worse?

Constantine can't know. It was before he and I started dating, but I don't want him to know I shamelessly threw myself at an author who was twice my age. He'll look at me differently. I don't want him to think I'm some climber. No matter what I am, there's still a way I want people to see me, which might be deceptive, but hey—that's fame. Show me one person in Hollywood who *really* takes two-minute showers and turns off the water while brushing their teeth because of the environment. I don't buy it. No one should. But that's the price of fame and one I'm willing to pay.

"I don't think that questionnaire was conference-related. Maybe it was part of her PR stuff that was timed to go out. I did fill out a form and gave emails for interviews," I lie. "The conference wouldn't have sent that out after this morning. I bet someone gets fired today, regardless," I say with a shrug. I don't want him to feel bad.

He stares at me, his face a mixture of happiness and regret. "Well, do you have time to grab a drink or something?"

I look at the clock on the nightstand. Shit! I have to be downstairs in five minutes, and Constantine can't come. "I have to meet some authors. Like, now."

"Oh." His shoulders slump. "Can I come?"

"It's not for me. It's an industry thing. I told you I'd be busy the whole time I'm here. But I promise I'll come right back up here when I'm done. I swear." I put my hand over my heart as some sort of pact. It doesn't matter that I swear—Constantine doesn't believe in God; he's Wiccan, which is honestly kind of cool the more I read up on it. It's not what movies make it out to be. "I swear on Hecate."

After a couple months, I've picked up some Wiccan lingo. That's his goddess. He smiles because I've made the effort.

"Okay. I'll keep the bed warm. How long do you think you'll be?"

"A couple hours, max. I promise." I kiss him on the lips. "I have to go."

I run into the bathroom to drag a brush through my hair and reapply my lip gloss. A spray of perfume and I'm out the door with a wave.

On my way to the elevator, I check the Murderpalooza hashtag again to see if there's anything new going on.

There is. Vicky's sort of been exonerated, because now the Twitter mob has a new suspect.

29

VICKY OVERTON

Friday, 4:45 P.M.

Either I don't understand what the big deal is or I'm missing something about Jason Fleming in my search. All I can put together at this point is that Kristin, Jason, and Davis were in a writing group over half a decade ago when they were in the Midwest. Davis told us as much. Then Jason died in a car accident, which may or may not have been suicide—that was only conjecture online. And now Kristin is dead.

Twitter Stalker said it was connected, and also that one of us is the next to die, so given all this, my betting money is on Davis being next. That'll certainly take him down a peg. Being dead and stuff. With his luck, it'll immortalize him. *The* Davis Walton, dead at the start of his fame, Golden Boy Never To Be. They'll probably erect a statue. Rename tonight's show the *Davis Walton Thriller Book of the Year Award*. We already have The Lefties, The Agatha, The Anthony . . . might as well add The Davis. All hail.

I'm about to slam my laptop shut, but the self-preservation side of me needs to defend myself. I mean, really. Since Meghan

Morgan—that coward—deleted her tweet, I find the one that was most retweeted and Quote Tweet that. It's been retweeted over a thousand times. I'm going to sue that bitch for defamation when this is over. I start it with a row of "laughing so hard I'm crying" emojis.

@VickyOvertonWriter

Sorry I've been out of touch on the topic, I was cleaning my knives and lying to cops! (eye roll emoji) If anyone believes this nonsense, I really hope you seek help. And my lawyers are coming for you when this is over @AgentMegaMorgs #murderpalooza @Murderpalooza

I click the button and send it out into the Twitterverse and wait. Within seconds, my little blue bell lights up with the numbers one, two, three, twenty, thirty . . . it's being well received. Or I'm being accused of being a lying murderess. Either/or.

I have a few minutes before I have to head downstairs to my little meeting, so I splash water on my face again and reapply my makeup. I decide to forego the full face and apply a tinted moisturizer, a shiny lip gloss, and curled lashes with mascara. That'll be good enough.

Exiting the bathroom, I head to check the computer once more before I leave when I hear a noise coming from outside the door. I tip-toe over and look out the peephole, and Jim is standing there, white keycard in hand, pressing it against the magnetic keypad. Nothing is happening. Just *click, click, click*. My hand hovers over the door handle to open it, but I'm not positive I want to let him in. Why is he back after only ten minutes?

I'm about to find out when he stops pressing it against the door and slides his hand into his back pocket and retrieves his wallet. He slides the keycard in and takes another identical one out. He presses that one to the keypad and the dials turn, so I jump back. He opens the door, and I'm standing too close in the entryway. His eyes go wide.

"I thought you left. I thought you had a big meeting," he says.

"I'm leaving now," I say. We're locked in another heated stare. "Why are you back?"

And whose keycard were you just using?

"I just wanted to grab my stuff. I thought you needed space, so I got another room for the night."

You don't say? In midtown Manhattan, in the middle of the summer, which is the height of tourist season (after Christmas, obvs), where this hotel has been sold out for months because of the conference? Just like that, in less than ten minutes, he was able to go downstairs, wait in line, check into a new room, and get back up here?

Whose key is that? Kristin's? Wouldn't the cops love to find that on him.

"Bullshit."

His eyes roll as he pushes past me. "Text me if you change your mind and want me to come back tonight." He opens a drawer and throws his boxers, socks, and a couple pairs of shorts in his bag as I stand there silently. If he's waiting for a mea culpa, he better get used to disappointment. Once he zips his bag, he looks at me, his mouth downturned, his eyes begging for forgiveness. "I never lied to you."

"I saw the text messages, Jim. You didn't go to your parents' place last month. You were here. With her. And her panties."

This time, the guilt registers. He swallows heavily, and I see the sweat on his forehead. "I guess we'll have to have a talk when we get back to Florida."

He waits for me to say something, but I don't. I step aside and gesture my hands toward the door, inviting him to leave. He picks up his bag and walks out.

My eyes sting, and I'm thankful I didn't reapply my shadow as I blink away tears. I'd been planning a strategic breakup. But of course, now I think of the good times. The way I fit in the nook of his armpit, the way he drove us around up and down the west coast of Florida to every Barnes & Noble and indie bookstore so I could sign books, and how damn proud he was when it came out. Could that really have been faked? Why did he flush it down the toilet?

I grab a tissue and dab the corners of my eyes so my mascara doesn't run and make me look like the quintessential jilted lover. One more check to the computer to see how my tweet is faring, and I'm out of here. I refresh the Twitter page and yes, it's doing well. Over sixty retweets, four hundred likes. I want to read the quote tweets and what they're saying, but I really am out of time. For good measure, I click on the Murderpalooza hashtag and . . . what?

I squint. Holy shit.

This is like a movie! What say you, @AuthorMBrooks1234 #murderpalooza #killer #guilty

    Well, I bet @AuthorMBrooks1234 regrets the fuck out of this #murderpalooza

    WHERE THE FUCK ARE THE COPS ARREST @ AuthorMBrooks1234 #murderpalooza

Career suicide, did @AuthorMBooks1234 think no one would find out? #murderpalooza #justiceforkristin #murderer

OMG @AuthorMBrooks1234 killed his co-author, it was #KristinBailey someone find him! #murderpalooza

It's everywhere.

What happened?

I check my watch. It's time to go, but shit . . . one more minute. I scroll through until I see it. @MPaloozaNxt2Die tweeted a picture and hashtagged #murderpalooza and #KristinBailey. I click on it and expand it.

Oh no. It's the one-page synopsis of his new book, with the giveaway murderous whodunnit ending and all. With his name and Kristin Bailey's name on it as co-authors.

Whodunnit? Mikedunnit.

It's been retweeted over a thousand times.

30

DAVIS WALTON

Friday, 5:00 P.M.

I can't wipe the smile off my face. No, I lied. This is a smirk, and one that eclipses my looks. The information I received about Suzanne from Penelope is too good. And to top it off, Mike Brooks had a fling with that kid? When I questioned him early this afternoon and told him about the Twitter stalker, he was all "Oh, sure, I know Suzanne, we share an agent." Ha! It's so, so, so much more than that. His watch on her nightstand is undeniable proof.

They've been lying to us. I have the evidence now, and I bet they've been playing me and Vicky. They're doing this together. Between Suzanne being a stalker and Mike clearly penning the story with Kristin, he probably got the infatuated young girl to do his killing. He wanted Kristin dead, and to have the fame for the story that she probably wrote 90 percent of, all to himself. I wonder how long he's been planning this? Looks like at least six months. Suzanne is young and impressionable, and apparently crazy, so I can barely blame her for doing Mike's bidding. Mike is old and married. He has kids for God's sake.

He's a former success. He knew what he was doing from the beginning. Grooming.

In addition to all of that, someone leaked the synopsis of the book he wrote with Kristin online. The one with all the secrets and the ending, and both of their names were on it. People in general will forget if it ever gets published, because it won't hit shelves for at least two years. But now everyone thinks Mike killed Kristin. I personally don't think he did—I think he got Suzanne to do it—but whoever *did* do it had access to Kristin's computer and put it out to the Twitterverse. Whatever. As long as it kept the accusations and secrets away from me.

And now that I have this fodder about Suzanne and Mike having an affair and probably being co-killers, plus the new online accusations pointing to Mike, I can keep questions about Jason Fleming at bay. Anyone asks, I shove Suzanne's tweet of Mike's watch in front of them. You bet I screen-shotted it, saved it, and emailed it to myself. The internet is forever, my friends.

I'm the first at the bar, and that's both good and bad. Good, because I'm able to command a bar table for four and no one will ask questions. Bad, because despite knowing that Mike and Suzanne are probably behind this murder, I'm still looking over my shoulder. I'm still scared of the basement monsters.

Evident by how I scream like a girl when someone's hand lands on my arm. Heads twist my way to see where the high-pitched shriek came from, and when I turn, I see Janie. No, it's Julie. Why can't I remember her name? Anyway, I told her I'd meet her *later tonight*. Only people who are eighty think five o'clock is *later tonight*. Why does she always find me when I'm alone and vulnerable? Suddenly, I want to take my chances with the potential murderers and not have to make small talk with her.

"Hey you. Did you find my lipstick?" she asks.

Shit. "Yes, I did. I left it upstairs by mistake. I'm a very busy man." I say it, nodding, agreeing with myself. My time is important, and this isn't. Can't I give her a dollar and tell her to buy a new one? "I'll bring it back later. I'm waiting for some people. Can we talk some other time?"

"Oh. Can I wait with you?"

Can this chick not take a hint? She smiles and sits down at the table before I can answer, and plunks down a drink she's been holding. It's amber but foamy and has a maraschino cherry floating on top. Is that an Amaretto sour? Man, she's young, but I didn't think she was that young. Penelope mentioned twenty-one. That'll only work for me when I'm in my forties. Why is she always around? Doesn't she have any friends with her? She's always alone, always after me. A stalker?

A gruesome thought comes to mind. Oh my God, could the self-published romance writer be using murder as research on how to get into thrillers?

She sucks the rest of her drink through the straw until it makes that horrific air-tunnel sound that I hate.

"What are you doing before the ceremony?" she asks.

So desperate, but still, I don't want to piss off another possible murderer who has it out for me. I need all the support I can get right now. "Working." I give her a knowing ho-hum nod.

I've never been so happy to see Vicky Overton in my life. Thank God for that new dark purple hair she's sporting that I'm able to spot out of the sea of people conglomerating at the stairs near the bar entrance. I smile and wave my hand way high in the air. *Come now.* "Sorry. One of my attendees is here." Might as well make it sound like I'm running shit, and I will be as soon as those other two liars get here.

Vicky approaches the table, and I see something different behind her eyes. Is it fear or sadness? This afternoon, she was indignant. Oh shit—I forgot about when she ran out of the bar. I wonder if her cheating boyfriend is okay. I wonder if she cares. And a half hour ago, I wondered if *he* killed his lover. Now I know better. Mike and Suzanne have the proverbial *K for killer* tattooed on their chests.

However, presently I'm considering Julie too.

"Hey, have a seat," I say to Vicky, then feign concern. "How's Jim? What happened earlier?"

She's silent, then presses her lips together, and I swear she's stifling a smirk. Then she turns to Julie. "Do you mind?"

"Oh," Julie says, then sticks out her hand. "Hi, I'm Julie Keane. I met Davis last night."

She says it with a knowing look that sinks me. Terrific, Vicky knows I slept with a self-published romance writer.

Vicky shakes her hand limply. "Can we have some privacy?"

I give Julie a wink and a nod. *There, there, little girl. Vicky and I have to start the big boy thriller business, so see yourself out.*

"I'll see you later, Davis," she says. With her almost empty drink in her hand, she walks away.

"Really, Davis? Julie Keane?" Vicky asks, one eyebrow raised.

I wave a hand in front of my face to avoid detail. "What happened to Jim?"

She shrugs. "Idiot got mugged and it wasn't related to this or didn't have anything to do with us." She strings those sentences together so quickly, I know she's got to be hiding something.

Now isn't the time. I couldn't care less about her boyfriend getting attacked when someone could be after me. "Anyway, have you seen Twitter?"

She nods. "Yes, and I'm surprised you still want to be seen in public with me after that lashing. But you know the Twitter mob, their narrative is the gold standard until enough of them jump on something else. Short memories."

It would be sad if it wasn't true. "Yep. Have you seen the latest?"

Another nod. "What do you think? Who was able to get a hold of Mike's synopsis?"

Well his agent, Vita Gallo, and anyone she submitted it to, but he'd mentioned earlier that she wasn't subbing it to editors because of the storyline. Vita looks guilty, but is this her way of dumping Mike after two decades? *You saw the synopsis, and Kristin Bailey was stabbed, I had to drop him!*

I lower my voice. "I think Suzanne and Mike have been playing us from the start. They're in this together." I tap my index finger on the table twice to indicate that my words are law.

"Stalkanne? Hardly. She's just a starry-eyed kid. Fan emails don't equate to murder conspiracy."

Vicky calls herself a thriller writer after a statement like that? "Well take a look at this, then."

I pick my phone up off the table. It's full of texts—of course it is—and I quickly make sure none of them are from an unknown number. I tap the photo app and scroll to the screen cap I took of Suzanne's Twitter page, the one with the incriminating photo. Vicky takes the phone and squints at the image, then blows it up and looks again. Shrugs. Hands it back to me.

"So?"

"That's Mike's watch."

"Oh come on," she says with flair.

Do I tell her I know because I'm jealous? How would that make me look? "He's wearing it today. I noticed it earlier. A guy I know had the same one in a collection he was preparing for me. I picked a different one, but I still know what it looks like. It's vintage." That sounds much better. *I'm* the one who rejected the watch.

"There's no way they wouldn't have told us about this if it were true, after everything that went on today."

"Think about it," I say, then lower my voice more. "Mike wants the fame again. Suzanne is nuts. They did this together, and they've been playing us."

"Why?"

I didn't graduate from an Ivy League school, so I don't have all the answers. I throw my hands up in the air. "Where are they, then? Why are me and you the only ones here? The four of us were supposed to be here at five. This is important. We have to find out what's going on. Remember the movie *Scream*? Two killers. One playing off the other. They always had an alibi. These two are in it together. Wouldn't shock me if Mike was halfway to Panama by now."

"No extradition there," Vicky says, eyes wide. "My character in Book Two—he researched that."

We're quiet. It's just the two of us. I never would've seen me partnering with Vicky through this whole thing. She probably feels the same way, though I don't know why. Running with me should be a plus in anyone's book, but she knows what I'm saying makes sense.

Then Mike walks in. Thank God someone who looks like a cop gets to him before he gets to us.

31.

MIKE BROOKS

Friday, 5:05 P.M.

Just when I thought I had it figured out, Twitter Stalker Murder Person comes for me.

I don't read Book Twitter; it's ridiculous. It's a bunch of people puffed up on their own opinions who literally bully people into thinking like them and cancel everyone who doesn't, instantly. They complain about people bullying others, yet don't see the hypocrisy. I can't keep up with what I'm supposed to know from one day to the next.

Well, if anyone forgot my name, they know it now. Even the young 'uns. I'm all over Twitter. My name, connected to Kristin's name. Our fucking book synopsis is on there. The only one who had that was us and Vita. While I really don't think Vita had anything to do with this, I'll admit I'm suspicious. Something else that passes through my mind is that maybe Kristin sent it to someone that I don't know about. I don't know why she would, and it goes against everything we'd discussed, but someone killed her. Maybe she was in a pile of trouble that I never knew about. Then again, whoever murdered Kristin has access to a treasure trove of shit that she knew. The synopsis is small potatoes.

Due to a massive amount of crosstown traffic, I have the cab let me off a couple blocks away, and I duck into a bodega and call Vita.

One, two, three, four, five rings. Voicemail. Of course. She's avoiding the murderer.

"Vita, it's Mike. I need to talk to you. I know you know what's going on." I swallow hard. "Online. With Twitter. I'm sure you know what they're saying isn't true, but I need to know who else you gave that synopsis to. Call me immediately."

I hang up the phone and put it in my jacket pocket, then decide it's time to face the music with the rest of my new posse. Though this time, I have something to say when they try to gang up on me, if they're reading Twitter, which I'm sure they are. I walk around the corner and pause at the door, then take a deep breath and walk in.

Someone who looks like a cop stands near the door, and my heartbeat races. Why, though? I haven't done anything. But perception is reality in this new online world, evidenced by this large man stepping in front of me in a swift move.

"Mike Brooks?"

"Yes?" I need to clear my throat, but I can't, not in front of him. I need to show zero signs of being uncomfortable, even though I feel like I'm a living voodoo doll, being stabbed everywhere with pins. *Stabbed*. Oops. Pricked?

"Pearson. I'm investigating for the hotel." He pulls some sort of badge from his jacket pocket and waves it in front of me before returning it to its original spot. I didn't get a good look at it, but it had some sort of official looking seal. "Follow me."

I DIDN'T DO IT

He turns and walks in long strides, and I have no choice but to follow. What am I supposed to do, run in the other direction and not cooperate? If anything, I want to be an asset. Kristin was my friend. If answering his questions helps find who murdered her, all the better.

As we walk to the corner of the downstairs lobby, everyone is staring. Whispering. Pointing. At least everyone knows who I am again. Doubt it'll translate to sales, unless I get arrested and write a book from jail about being wrongfully accused. Not exactly what I had dreamed for my memoir.

Pearson stops at the corner and turns around, pulls out a pad and a pen. God, I'm thirsty. My tongue feels heavy and sticky.

"Mr. Brooks, I'm sure you've heard about Kristin Bailey."

"I did," I say with a sad nod.

"We have it on good authority that you two recently completed a project together."

"Correct." I want water. I can't swallow.

"Some recent information has come to light regarding said project."

"Yes, I saw online. Someone leaked the synopsis."

Pearson writes, head down. Shifts his eyes up to me. "I read it. Rather incriminating, don't you agree?"

"I was home this morning. With my wife. All morning."

"Right. Your wife will corroborate this story, I'm sure. Did anyone else see you there?"

He thinks Nicole is going to cover for me? "My nanny, Janina, came and picked up the kids around nine-thirty. For camp."

"Ah. Nine-thirty. And she didn't see you again after that?"

I *need* to swallow, but I can't. I have no saliva. "No. I spent the morning answering emails, then I got ready to meet my agent for lunch. And that's when she called me with the news. I was still at home when she called. I rushed right over."

He's jotting down every word in shorthand. "People said you were here last night. Did you interact with Kristin at all?"

"Not last night, no. I saw her at the bar, but I was with another group." Fucking Davis. Maybe if Kristin and I interacted like normal people, I could've saved her. She was the one who'd said she didn't want people to see us too chummy.

"Some people mentioned Kristin was a bit . . . tense . . . last night. Did you notice anything out of the ordinary?"

Who noticed that? Who else has he been talking to? Shit, probably everyone who had a drink at the bar last night. Probably even regular hotel guests who wouldn't recognize Kristin. That's the thing, only authors and avid readers would be able to recognize an author by face. Unless, you know, you're Stephen King.

"No, nothing out of the ordinary. I was with Davis Walton and some other guys. I remember seeing her with her agent, Penelope Jacques, and a couple other writers, but I honestly don't remember exactly when. I left early and went home. I live uptown, so I'm not staying here at the hotel."

"And at the time, no one knew you were co-authors on the new project?"

"Not that I know of."

"Well, Mr. Brooks, you understand why this looks bad for you."

I find the saliva to gulp. It's heavy, and I feel like I swallowed glue. "It wasn't me." Shaggy's "It Wasn't Me" replays in my head. A song I liked from when I used to be cool.

I've finally had enough and decide to break the pact. I open my mouth to say it, but what good would that really do?

Mr. Pearson, sir, someone sent me and three other authors a threatening text message and a stalker Twitter account said bad things! It reeks of deflection, which I don't need to do because I'm not guilty of anything surrounding Kristin's death. Let me talk to the others before I get Pearson involved.

"Did she suffer?" I ask, my eyes glassy because my feelings are real.

Pearson blows out a breath. "Stabbing is not the best way to die, Mr. Brooks. But you know that, right? Didn't you write about that in your book?"

I'm shocked into silence but wipe my forehead in frustration. Poor Kristin. It's not fair.

Pearson takes a card out of his pocket and hands it to me. "If you can think of anything last night that sticks out as strange, please call me."

I nod. "I didn't do it. She was my friend. I'll help in whatever way I can."

Shit.

Shit.

Shit.

Why did that come to me so easily? It was the exact lines the co-author in the book used when he was accused. And we know how that ended.

Pearson leaves, and I'm left alone while everyone stares. I want to scream at the top of my lungs *I'm not in cuffs, move along!* But instead, I hunch my shoulders to make myself smaller, less noticeable if that's possible, and slink away.

As soon as I get to the bottom of the steps that lead to the bar, I spot Suzanne taking a seat with Davis and Vicky.

32

SUZANNE SHIH

Friday, 5:10 P.M.

The bar is still packed, and people are clinking glasses and laughing. Like Kristin didn't mean anything to them. Like a wonderful woman wasn't murdered here this morning. Once her body was shipped into the waiting van, all memories of her went with it, to most people, because hey, it's happy hour.

I'm not most people. I still can't believe she's gone. I can't believe I've held it together as long as I have today.

I spy Vicky and Davis at a bar table in the corner and apprehensively walk over. They both look at me blankly when I get to the table—there's something different about their expressions. They look like they don't care about Kristin either.

"Hi," I say as I pull back a chair and take a seat at the square table next to Vicky, facing Davis. "How's Jim?" I ask her.

Vicky blows out a puff of air. "He's fine. How's *Mike?*"

She italicizes his name when she says it.

"Mike?" My breath catches when I realize he's not here. "Where is he? Did something happen to him?" *One of you is the next to die.*

Davis's eyes match his mouth. They narrow just like his pursed lips, and I feel like I'm about to get yelled at by my parents. Then his gaze trains over my head, and he lifts an arm and waves it. "Over here!"

I swivel on my chair and see Mike on his way. I release a breath as he approaches. The Twitter stalker didn't get to him.

Yet.

"Hey. Sorry, I got held up. Some investigator guy wanted to talk to me." He takes the last seat between me and Davis. "I'm sure you've seen the interwebs."

He uses air quotes and says it the way old people say it, and I'm sure it's meant to be funny. Gallows humor. He's making fun of himself because he's in serious trouble. Now everyone knows about him and Kristin being co-authors, thanks to that Twitter account. That's when I notice the music in the background, one of the slower jams by Bruno Mars. Why did it come into my head so fast? Because the chatter has slowed to a whisper, and everyone is staring at our table. When any of us look toward the crowd, eyes avert and heads dip down. Halted conversations resume.

We're all outcasts. First it was Vicky, now it's Mike.

Me and Davis are next. Twitter will come for us, and it leaves no one standing.

As soon as I think that, the investigator who's been hovering around approaches our table and points his finger between them.

"Vicky Overton. Mike Brooks . . . you guys know each other well?" he asks without so much as a hello.

"Yeah. So?" Vicky answers.

"I wasn't aware you were so chummy." He raises his eyebrows. "I wanted to talk to your other company here anyway," Pearson says and looks at Davis. "Davis Walton, correct? Would you mind stepping away for a word. Privately?"

Davis freezes, and all of a sudden, he looks ten years younger than he is. A scared little boy. I'm glad I'm off the hook.

"Actually," Davis says, turning on the charm for the detective. It's something I can pick out in his voice now, after only knowing him for a few hours. "Maybe you should talk to Suzanne here first." He gestures toward me. "Turns out, Kristin Bailey had to file a restraining order against her."

"That's not true!" I shout.

Vicky doesn't come to my defense. Neither does Mike.

"Come on, Suzanne. You told us about it earlier. You said lawyers got involved. Are you going to lie to this guy, right in front of us?"

"You don't know what you're talking about!"

My heartbeat skyrockets, and I think of Constantine sitting upstairs in my room, waiting for me. He doesn't know the extent of what happened. It was a friendship that Kristin was too busy for at the time, and I should've given her the space she needed. But come on, they can't arrest me for something stupid like that, from *emails*, from six months ago. They can try all they want to pin Kristin's murder on me. The fact of the matter is, I didn't do it.

"Go ahead, detective. Ask her. She's a stalker." Davis is really drilling it home, and I have no defense.

"Stop it!" My raised voice has gained attention, and people have stopped to stare again, this time not minding if they get caught. They don't bother looking away when I make eye contact. Vicky sips water and looks away, and Mike is a deer in headlights. Pearson's head swings left to right between me and

Davis like a tennis match. "I'm not a stalker. We were friends. We knew each other." I feel so small, so insignificant with all these adults, so I go for broke, because why not? "You should ask Davis about Jason Fleming."

Pearson looks at Davis. "Who?"

"Jason Fleming. He's dead too. Davis and Kristin both knew him. They all used to live near each other, and now they're both dead."

The look Davis gives me puts a bullet right between my eyes, and my head snaps back from the hit. It wouldn't shock me if blood dripped into my eye. I should've kept my mouth shut. He's going to kill me.

Kill me next.

"It's Davis," I say. "Davis did it. He had to."

No matter what the mob on Twitter said, I don't think Vicky did it. I don't think Mike did it. And I didn't do it. Davis is probably behind the whole thing. Davis could very well be the Twitter account. It was his idea for us to meet up. How do we know his Bloody Mary was spicy? He made a huge deal about being targeted because he knew there was no way for us to check. He's setting us up. He made Vicky a suspect, and then Mike. Of course he'd turn on me!

"Enough," Pearson says. "I don't understand what's going on here between all of you, but sort it out. Davis, I'll be waiting right there—" He points to the couch at the bottom of the stairs, "—for when you're done with your meeting. We'll talk alone."

Pearson heads toward the steps, and there's no other way out of this area unless Davis wants to jump out the window.

And *ha ha ha*. Pearson doesn't want to talk to me yet. Only Davis.

"You're finished in this industry, little girl," Davis says, jamming an index finger across the table at my face. "You'll get no author support. And if you ever had a dream of Bee Henry buying your book, well I can tell you that'll never—"

"Jesus Christ, Davis, enough of your smug shit," Mike says.

Davis calmly turns his head to Mike and chuckles. "Well this doesn't surprise me. You coming to her defense. Does it surprise you, Vicky?"

"Nope," she chimes in.

"What are you both talking about?" Mike asks.

Davis pulls out his phone, taps a few buttons, and turns it toward Mike, who looks, then turns red. Then Davis points it toward me.

Oh. Em. Gee.

Oops. It's Mike's watch on my nightstand.

Mike quickly closes, then opens his eyes and looks at me with disgust. "I can't believe you put that on Twitter."

"I—" I what? I have no idea what I'm supposed to say. I'm twenty-three and I like attention. Someone old like Mike wouldn't understand. "It's generational." It's the best I can come up with. "We put everything online."

Mike slams his hand on the table, Vicky is stifling laughter, and Davis is grinning like a circus clown. I swivel my head and see Pearson documenting everything.

"Guys, Pearson is watching," I say, my voice high-pitched to hold down my crying. I don't want to have to explain the tweet.

"So what?" Vicky says. "Let him watch. If one of you assholes is up to no good, I hope he catches you. I'm clean as a whistle. My boyfriend cheats. Big deal." She sucks the last of her water up through the straw.

"You never told us where you were this morning," I say, still trying to keep the heat off me. I don't think Vicky did anything, but I want to cast doubt on her for the others. Not me. Her.

She stabs the leftover ice cubes with her straw, and I picture her using that motion to stab Kristin again. "I don't have to tell you anything. Fact of the matter is, I told Pearson where I was. Do you see me wearing cuffs? No? So stay the hell off me."

Tears brim in my eyes, then spill over. I grab a cocktail napkin from under my water and blot, but it's no use. I'm blubbering. Vicky decides to play with her phone, and Davis is still staring death rays at me. Mike won't look at me. I don't owe anything to Vicky and Davis, but I feel terrible that Mike hates me.

"Guys," Vicky says. "There's another tweet."

@MPaloozaNxt2Die

I see you at the table next to the sunflowers. Order drinks, or else. Davis better tell you about Jason. Both must happen, or someone dies

33

VICKY OVERTON

Friday, 5:15 P.M.

I look to my right. Against the wall next to Davis is a planter
filled with sunflowers. We're being watched; it's not the first
time, and something tells me it won't be the last. Who was
around when I got here? I can't remember. Fearing for my life
kind of takes precedence.

"I'm not thirsty," I say. Ha. That'll be a first.

"I'm not getting a drink. It'll be poisoned," Davis says, his
palms forward.

He's been awfully twitchy since he got out of speaking with
Pearson. How did he get away with that? Him and his Davis-
ness. Everyone falls for it.

"I'm scared," Stalkanne says.

Then it's quiet. We all look at Mike.

"We have to do what it says."

I know he's right. But I also wonder what happens if I stand
up, grab my purse, pack my shit, and leave. Do the three of them
get slaughtered for staying? Or is that what the Twitter stalker
wants? Do they expect someone to leave, and the murderer is

waiting under a bed? At this point, I miss Jim. I don't want to be alone. Davis's ego is so big, he's never alone, and Stalkanne can just shack up with Mike, it seems, but I threw Jim out and now I'm on my own. That's not comforting. Even if I think it could still be him.

A cocktail waitress comes over, and I study her. She's smiling that smile that only a divorced single mother slinging drinks can have. Tired, resigned, but hopeful. *I need these tips to pay rent, so please don't torture me.*

"Can I take your order?"

"Yes, three house cabernets and a sauvignon blanc from New Zealand, please," I say, taking charge, making it easy. For us. For her.

She nods and gestures toward the menu encased in hard plastic standing in the center of the table. "That's our happy hour menu from four to seven, but we have the full kitchen available too, and I can—"

"Just the drinks for now, thank you," I interrupt.

"Okay, I'll grab them and bring over a couple of menus in case you change your mind." She turns on her heels and scuttles to the serving area at the end of the bar.

"House?" Davis says, and I roll my eyes.

"I don't like red wine," Stalkanne says.

"I don't care. Drink it," I say. I've about had enough of her. Jesus, first she obsesses over Kristin Bailey, and now we find out about Mike too? "What exactly went on between you two?" *Exactly*—delete. The gossipy part of me wants to know what the hell happened with Stalkanne and Mike before the Twitter stalker kills me. We'll get to Jason Fleming. Davis must have a full wet diaper.

Stalkanne looks down, and Mike's face is pained. He looks like he aged a decade today.

"Nothing happened," Mike says. Davis opens his mouth to object, and Mike puts up his hand. "I know what it looks like. We were out one night, and I had a few too many drinks. Suzanne helped me into a cab, and it slipped off."

"*I'll never forget last night, heart emoji,*" Davis says in a high-pitched, sing-songy voice, making fun of what Stalkanne tweeted with the picture.

"It also says it slipped off," Stalkanne says.

"Why didn't you guys tell us something like this happened? You acted like you just met."

"Do you think I'm proud?" Mike says. "That I got so drunk in front of a young girl that *she* had to help *me*?"

"I'm young and got over excited," Stalkanne says. "I mean, I just signed my agent papers and then all of a sudden, I was having a drink with Mike Brooks. That's why I said I'll never forget it." Her eyes shift to him, then back to me. "Nothing happened. I guess by now you guys know that I make things out to be a bit bigger than they are."

It makes sense. I can't see Mike hooking up with this kid who's half his age. He's not Davis.

"You've beaten around the bush about Jason long enough, Davis," Mike says. "We aren't your agent or your fans or your publicist. We're still in trouble here." He sighs. "Maybe we should tell Pearson what's going on. With the Twitter Murder Stalker Person account."

The waitress comes back and places the drinks in the center of the table. "Okay, we have a sauvignon blanc and three house cabernets. Anything else?"

"Not yet. Thank you," I say instead of shooing her away. After she leaves, I take a sip—ah, sweet relief!—press my lips together, and agree with Mike. "It's time. We need to tell Pearson what we know. About the Twitter account and what it's been doing to us."

"I can't have my life ruined because of a Twitter account," Davis says.

"Ha, like yours would be the first." I mean, come on. Twitter ruins one life a day, minimally.

"We can't tell him yet. We don't know the repercussions. This person murdered Kristin."

"Are we sure about that?" Mike asks. "I think we have to tell Pearson. Maybe he can find out who's behind the account. Those guys usually have inside people at the police. They have departments specializing in that stuff."

"Easy for you to say," Davis hisses. "Your huge secret is out, Mike. Everyone knows that Kristin was your co-author. We know you and Suzanne messed around. And I'm sure it's about to come out that Suzanne stalked her." He looks at me. "Your boyfriend was screwing around with Kristin. It's probably him doing this to us. Fuck, Jim probably killed her."

I hate that I agree with Davis, again. I don't know where Jim was this morning when I was meeting with Gina Farrant. I don't know what him and Kristin fought about. It doesn't look good. It really, really, doesn't, and I'm not going to censor two identical crutch words—and adverbs—in a row there. Knowing that he left after I told him I saw the texts, and him saying we'll have to have a talk when we get home—it upset me more than I thought it would.

I was ready to say goodbye, but I'm heartbroken. I don't want to believe it was Jim. So I deflect. "Now that you bring it up, what's *your* secret, and what does it have to do with Jason?" I ask. "Do you think this is a joke?"

"Oh come on, this isn't a book, Vicky. Do you really think someone is going to try to take us out right here?" He grabs a glass of wine and takes a swig, his face turning red. "This is gross. I told you that house wine—" He stops. He swallows heavily multiple times. His eyes bulge.

Then he grabs his throat.

34

DAVIS WALTON

Friday, 5:30 P.M.

What's happening to me? Oh my God, am I dying? This isn't how it ends for me. How do I die right here, with all these people around? If I fall off my chair, people will know what's wrong. They'll stand around and watch my face contort. People will take video of it. That's not how I'm going to be immortalized. Worse, if I survive—people will have seen that side of me. How do I die gracefully? I can't exactly excuse myself and walk down the stairs and pass out like Snow White on one of the lobby couches. It's all going to happen, right here, in the lobby bar.

That's what I think as I clutch my throat. My legacy. Then . . . then it goes away.

Why am I so extra?

My eyes water, sure, but whatever I felt happening in my throat—the burning, feeling like it was trapped in a vice, is gone. I swallow a few more times. What is that taste? Was it spiked with *gin?* Imagine taking a gulp of red wine and gin mixed together. Disgusting.

But hardly poisonous. I'm not going to die.

"What's happening?" Mike asks. "Are you okay?"

I nod. Pass off my drama. No big deal. "I think someone put gin in it."

Mike picks up the glass and smells it. "Gross." Then he smells the other two, looks at the three of us, and takes a baby sip out of one of the glasses. Nothing. Then the other. Nada. "These two are fine."

"The waitress tried to kill me! She's got to be in on it."

"Kill you? It's gin. Plus, she didn't know which one you were going to pick up."

I look at Vicky. "Well at least you knew you weren't going to drink it. Why did you get something completely different? You ordered for us. Where's Jim? Are you in this together? Remember *Husband's Double Life* by Kevin Candela? The husband and wife were in on killing the mistress together." I string together the accusations because I know what's coming.

"Yes, you caught me," Vicky says. "I told Jim, who's nowhere to be found, by the way, to make sure that gin goes into a glass of wine. I'm so sneaky and bad. Now, Davis, start talking about Jason Fleming."

She shifts in her chair. Have I touched a nerve?

If it's not them working as a team, then whoever is behind the stalker Twitter account knows we're here and is within viewing distance, because they know I'm sitting next to the sunflowers. Fine, maybe it's not *directly* someone I'm with, but one of them is working with Kristin's murderer. I'm sure of it. And whoever doesn't die narrows it down.

But I can't die. I'll tell them what they need to hear. Hopefully it'll be enough to get the Twitter stalker off my back.

"Okay. Twitter Stalker probably wants me to tell you what I didn't tell you before." The three of them look at me intently.

They aren't getting the whole truth. I'll never let another soul know I was in the car with Jason when he died. No one knows. I don't even think Twitter Stalker knows or they would've just come out and said it. They want me to tell these three how I treated Jason. How maybe I'm not such a good guy after all.

"Well?" Vicky asks.

I take a deep breath, ready to let it out. "I wasn't nice to him. He was a good writer, and I was jealous. I used to put him down. One particular scathing email I sent him . . . was on the day he wrapped his car around the tree. I've always been afraid that I had something to do with his accident." I swallow. "It could've been suicide. There were rumors that there was a note in his pocket. But it was never confirmed."

I know for a fact I made it look that way, but no one other than his family and the cops had that information. Sure, there was speculation because some people can't keep their mouths shut, but you know what they say about speculation and the internet. Anyone who ever said a thing about it being suicide, I told them they were wearing a tin foil hat. No one wants to be labeled as a conspiracy theorist, even if they know they're right.

Plus, by me vehemently denying that it was a suicide means *I don't know about any note.*

"Jesus," Mike says. "Now I know why you don't want this out. I'm sure if Paramount knew you were involved in a bullying incident that led to suicide, your whole film deal would go bye-bye."

"I was young."

"You were twenty-five, Davis."

Twenty-seven, but semantics. "I have no excuse." I shrug sympathetically, mouth downturned. "I guess I used to be kind of a douche."

Vicky scoffs, or chokes on her wine. Either way, she has no right to judge me. We used to be pretty cool over social and stuff, but I don't think she likes me much after today. I'm waiting for them to pile onto me, tell me what a jerk I am, threaten to tell other authors, but then I see my lifeline. I squint because, before I make the accusation, I need to be sure I'm seeing what I'm really seeing.

I knew it. I fucking knew it.

That's Vicky's boyfriend Jim. Right?

I squint further because I can't make a mistake here. Yeah, it's him all right. He's got a stupid hat on . . . what is that? The Tampa hockey team? What a loser. I don't care if they're playing in their third straight Stanley Cup, you're in New York, dude. He's leaning over, elbows on the bar . . . enthralled with his phone. Texting? His thumbs are moving a mile a minute.

It's him. The Twitter stalker is him. I grab my phone off the table and pull up Twitter and yes, there's another tweet.

Are you paying attention now, @TheDavisWalton? I saw their reactions when you told them about Jason. Make sure you're all at the awards ceremony together tonight. You won't want to miss it.

I know it's Jim. The rest of them are saying something, but I tune it out. My gaze is across the bar, watching him like a hawk on a field mouse. No way. No way in hell am I going to let him fuck around with me. I'm going to find out what he knows, right now. I stand up.

"Where are you going?" Mike asks.

I don't answer. I move around the table and walk and—

"Mr. Walton. Going somewhere?"

It's Pearson. Shit. I forgot he's watching me. I can't exactly shake him off. I can't tell him about Jim being the Twitter stalker. I can't tell these three that I see him. I'll talk to him man to man.

"No, I—I just needed to stretch."

"Well now that you're up, maybe you can answer some questions for me."

"Right. Sure." I smooth down my shirt even though I know it's not wrinkled. My company stares at me, at him. They expect me to be rattled. I'm not. I didn't do it. "After you?" I gesture for him to lead.

Okay, so maybe I'm sweating a bit as I follow him down the stairs. Once there, he places his hands on me and pulls me off to the side, within sight of the table upstairs. On purpose? Probably. He wants them to know he's not harming me.

"Mr. . . . Walton, correct?"

Obviously not much of a reader or he wouldn't be asking that question. "Yes. Davis Walton, sir." I add the *sir* to be compliant. Hiding nothing. Cooperating with your investigation.

"Mmm." He tips his head to his notepad. "Just a few quick questions about Kristin Bailey. You don't mind, right?"

I put my hands in my pockets. Casual. Nothing to hide. "Fire away, sir."

"When was the last time you spoke to Kristin?"

Well he's trying to catch me in a lie. "About two weeks ago." I swear, that was the last time I *spoke* with her. Not our last contact. If he wants to hang on semantics, so will I.

"Huh. Really?"

"Really. Have you spoken to Suzanne Shih yet? The two of them had some problems."

He doesn't say anything, and his investigative brain must know I'm deflecting. He wants me to hang myself. I've done enough book research to know not to speak unless spoken to. Don't give any more information than asked. This is a steadfast rule. I'm not stupid.

"Did you share an email account?"

"What? That's silly." God, I'm so fucking caught. Why don't I just tell the truth? I'm going to look guilty now either way. Me and my short temper and mouth. "Well, by share, what exactly did you mean?"

"Her laptop was open on her desk. There was an email account called 'OurLittleSecret1234@gmail.' There was something from that account sent to Kristin Bailey's email address."

I'm dead. So fucking dead.

"What was it?" Why, Davis? Why are you playing dumb? You're caught.

"It went back a few months. It looked like a rough draft. Messages back and forth from two different people. Something about the awards tonight. One blackmailing the other for votes to win the award that's coming out tonight. The second making promises, secured a deal with someone named Jonathan DeLuca. Apparently, the first person was blackmailing the second person about information regarding a . . ." Pearson flips a few pages. "A Jason Fleming. And a Tommy Johnson. Do you know anything about either of them?"

I'm sure my face goes alabaster. I can tell him the same thing I told the others about Jason. It's all pretty much true. But how the hell am I supposed to explain Tommy Johnson being gone?

I look behind me. Vicky, Mike, and Suzanne are staring.

"Is this in confidence?" I ask.

"For now."

He'll understand. I can convince him of the repercussions.

I'll pay him if I have to. It's *me* on the line. I won't say anything about the Twitter stalker . . . for now.

"Ok, Pearson. I'll tell you about Jason Fleming. And Tommy Johnson."

35

MIKE BROOKS

Friday, 5:45 P.M.

Am I in danger? Sure. Are Nicole or my kids in danger? Doubtful. But I'll do anything to protect them, and right now, that's all I care about. I look at the Twitter account and reread the last tweet.

> *Are you paying attention now, @TheDavisWalton? I saw their reactions when you told them about Jason. Make sure you're all at the awards ceremony together tonight. You won't want to miss it.*

I hate to admit Davis has a point. What if it is Jim?

When Vicky got attacked online, it was because of that agent Meghan Morgan. Twitter Murder Person didn't come for her. In fact, Twitter Murder Person came to her defense once, by redirecting the issue back to Davis.

If Jim was having an affair with Kristin, he one hundred percent could've gotten the synopsis. God only knows the last time he saw Kristin. The synopsis has been done for about four months, so it could've been anytime between early spring and now. Maybe he was with her last night. Maybe he killed her this morning and got a copy to post.

Now Twitter Murder Person is after me. Making me look guilty. Suzanne is next, I'm sure of it.

While I try to wrap my head around what's going on, one thing keeps coming back. Every. Single. Time.

"Hey," I say to the girls, now that we're alone, "why does this Twitter account, and whoever is texting us, keep talking about Jason Fleming? Over and over and over. I have a feeling we still haven't heard the whole story." I exhale loudly, my belt tight against my waistband. I need to go on a diet if I'm going to be chasing around a toddler again. "Davis is hiding something. I know it. Have you guys found out anything about Jason?"

"Just basic stuff," Vicky says. "I'll admit, I didn't get too deep into it. I was kind of in the middle of throwing Jim out of our room and reading the vitriol about myself." Her eyes water and she blinks quickly, then grabs the wine and takes a long sip. It's her second, and she doesn't have an immediate reaction like Davis, so I assume hers is good and not laced with gin. Or something worse.

I nod in solidarity with Vicky because I know what it feels like to have Twitter accuse you of being a murderer. I look at Suzanne. Hell, she's a stalker. She probably has Jason Fleming's social security number by now. "What did you find on Jason?"

She grabs her phone, thumbs scrolling. "I did find one article that's kind of interesting. Kristin was interviewed. And I found out where he lived: Heimer, Iowa. His parents and sister Diana were still there when this happened a long time ago."

My interest is piqued, and for some reason that I'm sure only I feel, I think solving the Jason/Davis connection will get the rest of us off the hook. Now I think we need to use our strengths to get to the bottom of this.

Suzanne's strength is stalking.

She scrolls through her phone and finds the article—it's short, so I read through it and then hand the phone over to Vicky, who reads it with interest, her chin resting on a fist as she scrolls with her other hand. She tosses the phone back to Suzanne.

"Okay, so what do we do now?" Vicky asks.

I look at Suzanne. "No offense, but we're going to need you to do what you apparently do best. Did you find out anything else?"

"The obituary said the family was taking donations for his favorite place, which was the Heimer Public Library. That's how I found out about Heimer," Suzanne says.

This is good. This is exactly what we need. "And you said his family still lived there?" She nods. "What can you find out about his sister, Diana Fleming?"

Now she looks terrified. "What am I supposed to do? Call her up and ask her about her dead brother and Davis Walton? Come on. I can't do that."

"I'll do it," Vicky says. "Get me the number."

"Wait, wait," I say. "Let's not do anything insane or rash. Right now, we just need more information. Suzanne, can you—" I gesture toward her cell phone. She nods and picks it up to start research on Diana. I look at the time. "The awards show is in just over two hours. We have to be there by seven-thirty, right?"

"Yes. I have to shower and change. I have a nice dress for the ceremony. Just in case," Vicky says.

With the commotion of the day, I almost forgot about her nomination, and I feel like a shit. "Hey. How are you doing? Are you nervous for tonight?"

She shakes her head. "Not really. It's just an honor to be nominated. I thought Kevin Candela was a shoo-in, but now I think it's going to Kristin Bailey."

"Those votes had to be finalized weeks ago. I doubt anything will change it just because . . . because of today's events." I rub my face, still shocked and sad that Kristin is gone. "She was really looking forward to this. And I know you have your issues with her, Vicky, but if you win, can you do me a personal favor and just mention her in your acceptance speech? She was my friend. And I think before today, she was yours too."

Her face twitches. "I mentioned all of the nominees in the video short that they'll play before the winner is announced." She takes another sip of wine. "Friends don't sleep with other friends' boyfriends. And it wasn't just Jim being a douche and going behind my back. She knew we were together. She mentioned me in some of the texts she sent him."

I don't want to make Vicky upset, so I ask Suzanne how her research is coming along.

"Good. Parents are still in Heimer. Working on more info." She looks behind her, down the stairs, to where Davis is speaking intently to the detective. "How do I know you're not going to gang up on me like we're doing to Davis now?"

I laugh. "You don't. You're going to have to trust us. Davis is lying."

Like he knew we were talking about him, Davis barrels back up the stairs, two at a time. I shush everyone before he reaches us, and he takes his seat. He looks nervous and starts tearing at a paper cocktail napkin as soon as he sits down.

"How'd it go?" I ask. "You clear everything up with Pearson?"

"Well, like Vicky said earlier, you don't see me in cuffs, do you?"

He keeps peering over my head and looks distressed. It's in the eyes, and I've seen it all day on him. I turn around and scan. "Looking for someone?"

"Thought I saw someone I knew." He trains his gaze on Suzanne. "Pearson wants to talk to you now."

36

SUZANNE SHIH

Friday, 6:00 P.M.

"Me? What did I do?"

Oh no. Everyone at the hotel knows. They looked at the footage, which will hang me and exonerate me at the same time. How embarrassing.

"Come on, Suzanne, I'm sure they have proof about you stalking her," Davis says.

"I wasn't—" I was about to argue, but a kick hits my left shin from under the table. Mike.

He widens his eyes at me and gives a little head shake, which I read as *Don't engage with Davis, he's guilty.* Right. It's me, Mike, and Vicky against Davis. Still, I'm afraid to leave this table and have them turn on me. Davis has had it out for me since the first time I saw him this afternoon, and he's going to smooth talk his way into their heads. *Suzanne is a stalker stalker stalker!*

Fine. I'll talk to Pearson, and then I'll make sure I get Diana Fleming's number for Vicky. If Davis thinks he's taking me down, I'll beat him at his own game. But do I tell them about what I heard through Kristin's door? A man talking and something about the ceremony tonight?

No. I can't. *Stalker stalker stalker*! What was I even doing there anyway?

"I have to run. Time to shower and change for tonight," Vicky says. "Good luck." She doesn't finish her wine before she moves past me without another word.

"Well, I'll go talk to the detective, then I'm going to go back to my room," I say. I have to figure out what to do with Constantine tonight, assuming I'm still alive before the ceremony begins. "I guess I'll see you guys in the ballroom later."

Mike places his hand on my forearm and gives it a good shake, and Davis gives me a peace sign and a smirk. What a jerk!

My legs are unsteady as I descend the stairs to where Pearson waits for me. I think I'm having a quarter-life crisis at only twenty-three. I felt like such a little girl yesterday—bubble gum happy—and today I just feel worn out. Old. Tired.

Still. I'm being questioned in a murder case. Famous. I can't help having some stars in my eyes.

My hands are in my dress pockets so Pearson can't see my clenched fists. Technically, I wonder if he can arrest me. He's not even a real cop, and Kristin isn't alive to press charges. Unless they found that note in her room with my name on it.

He's standing in the corner where he's been talking to everyone, and I give him a close-lipped smile as I approach. "Hi. I'm Suzanne. You wanted to speak to me?" I extend a hand and he shakes it, and I wish I wiped my palm on the inside of the pocket. I feel the clamminess. Gross.

"I'm Pearson. How well did you know Kristin Bailey?"

Right to the point. I know this is a trick question. "Pretty well. We hadn't met in person, but we corresponded a lot online."

He raises an eyebrow at me. "Corresponded? Really?" He flips a bunch of pages in his little notebook before he settles on one. "No. I confirmed with her agent that you wouldn't leave her alone and that her publisher's legal team had to get involved." He pauses, waiting for me to admit it, but I don't. "We were able to get some footage from the security cameras in the halls. You went to her room this morning, didn't you?"

I knew it. I knew they were going to find it. "It's not what you think."

"You tried to shove your way in and gave her an envelope. Her door opened and closed immediately, as if she wasn't expecting you, as if she wanted as much distance between the two of you as possible. We found something in her room. Presumably, it's the same thing."

Crap. "Where?"

"The garbage in the bathroom."

I don't know why this disappoints me. It's not like I thought she'd be clutching it in her dead hands while zipped in the body bag that wheeled past me six hours ago. I thought maybe she'd read it and reconsider her treatment of me. Maybe she'd press it between some books, maybe pack it up to bring home with her. Once she realized I was sincere.

"So, Ms. Shih, anything else you want to tell me?"

I shake my head. "If you saw the tapes, you know I wasn't there when she was killed. I saw her in the bar last night and heard what floor she was staying on. When I went up there to try to find her, I saw her room number. It was too late to knock by then; even I wouldn't cross that line. She needed her rest for the ceremony tonight. But I just thought—I thought I was doing something nice."

"A creepy poem and flower petals stuffed in an envelope? She repeatedly told you not to have any more contact with her."

"I—I just wanted to wish her luck."

"Then why did you end it with a threat?"

"It wasn't a threat!"

"Oh, no?" He whips out his cell phone and produces a picture of it.

Tonight's the night for all the thrills
Tonight's the night for all the kills
When you become the Murderpalooza winner
Maybe you'll accept my invite to dinner
It won't even be a formal date
Just a way to celebrate
What is it you keep saying, though?
I won't accept another no

He scratches the side of his head with the pencil tip. "This is classic stalker material, Suzanne. And just so you know, the hallway cameras were malfunctioning at the time she was murdered. Did you go back?"

"No!"

How is anything I said in that note stalker material? Why doesn't anyone understand me? I cut off contact six months ago. I'm not allowed to wish my friend luck when she's up for an award?

Pearson's cell phone rings, and he looks at it, then back at me. "Hang on, it's my boss." He slides his finger across the screen to accept the call, never taking his eyes off me. "Pearson . . . uh huh . . . why . . . give me the four names . . . really, those four? Got it." He disconnects the call and studies me the way only a detective can. Whatever he just found out, he's planning to coerce out of me. "Do you know anything about a strange Twitter account?"

37

VICKY OVERTON

Friday, 6:15 P.M.

I take a deep breath before I press the keycard to the door. The lights turn green, it clicks open, and I step in and close it behind me. The closet is open to my left, and I get a pang of sadness at the empty hangers—not that I expected Jim to come back, but I don't know where he is. Somewhere in the hotel, I suppose.

That is, if I choose to believe him. Liar's gonna lie.

Like the heroine in a horror movie, I check all hiding spots, besides the closet: under the bed, the bathroom, and the wardrobe. Anyplace that someone could be, ready to jump out and scare the shit out of me. Or worse. When I'm confident I'm alone, I deadbolt the door and use the metal lock for additional protection. I don't need any *Psycho* murder shower scenes happening to me today. I've heard enough about stabbing as it is.

I undress and attempt to get the shower on. Jim turned it on this morning, and I got in as soon as he got out. These fancy modern hotels have buttons with unrecognizable icons to push. I don't need steam or eucalyptus; I need hot water. Why does everything have to be more complicated than turning a knob?

After pressing most buttons several times, the water finally comes out, and I step in and dunk my hair under the shower-head. I shampoo aggressively, trying to scrub the events of the day out of my own brain. And I hate myself for the horrible thoughts I've had all day. I'm *not* glad Kristin is dead. She was a brilliant writer, and her career has spanned about a decade by this point. I've read all her books, and she was considered an auto-buy author for me.

Isn't it funny when your idols never live up to your expectations in real life?

Plus, its nagging at me. Could Jim really be a killer? Jim might want to fuck with everyone for some reason, but would he really kill someone?

After I rinse the shampoo, I use a huge glob of the color-depositing conditioner so my hair will be freshly violet-ish and shiny should I get called up for that award tonight. Of course, my mind travels again. The thought of standing up there by myself, all eyes on me, is a terrific way to have me killed with an audience. Like *Carrie*, clutching my bloody flowers. Isn't that what psychotic murderers love? Adulation? I'm sure the murderer won't care how my hair looks when a shotgun blasts me between my eyes right after I say *thank you for—*

Jim wouldn't do that. But someone else might.

The only button I recognized in the shower was the red octagon, and that one turns it off. I grab the hotel's robe off the hook behind the bathroom door and put it on, then make my way to the coffee machine. It's not real coffee, it's the plastic pods, but I need the caffeine to replace the alcohol that's been on a steady stream today. Besides dying in front of everyone, imagine tripping up the podium to accept an award? Jeez, that might be more embarrassing than bleeding out in front of my peers.

I pour water into the top of the machine and scan the choices. I have to go for a super dark roast right now—*super*, delete—and my heart squeezes seeing the French vanilla option. Jim's favorite. I need to stop thinking about him. I pop the pod into place and turn it on.

I sit at the desk and turn on Twitter because I'm a sadomasochist today, and of course, most of the mob has turned to poor Mike as a suspect. Only a few hangers-on are still saying it's me. Good grief, to be accused of murder by a bunch of strangers who don't know anything, just to follow the herd, is something else. I search the hashtag for Murderpalooza along with Mike's name, and these people are brutal. They don't know what they're agreeing with, just that they want to be on the "right side" of the outcome. *See! I knew it was him all along!*

An hour ago, they were agreeing that *I* was a killer. I shake my head as I read.

#murderpalooza knows that #MikeBrooks @AuthorM-Brooks1234 is a killer and he's still allowed to walk free! I just saw him in the bar for fucks sake! #DontAcceptADrinkFromMike
Do your job NYPD! Ugh this is why you're defunded. Fucking hacks, arrest the man! #murderpalooza
Holy shit do my eyes deceive me @VickyOvertonWriter and @AuthorMBrooks1234 are sitting together with @TheDavisWalton and some other chick. Who is that? #murderpalooza

Then, ones with pictures attached follow. Blurry, out of focus, far away pictures of the four of us sitting at a table in the bar.

Taken by people desperate for likes and comments and retweets because go algorithm.

> *It's a table full of killers! #murderpalooza*
> *Who is that other chick #murderpalooza*
> *How is @TheDavisWalton involved in this? Please say this is a joke #murderpalooza*

Then . . .

That son of a bitch.

After that bitch Meghan Morgan sent the rest of Twitter into a frenzy about me, I set the record straight as much as I could. Poor Mike . . . he's not a social wizard so he's just taking the lumps. Stalkanne is probably still talking to Pearson, so she won't know what's going on.

But fucking Davis Walton has started answering individual tweets.

> *@TheDavisWalton*
> *Didn't anyone see me show up alone? Then Vicky joined me, then that newbie girl, then Mike. What was I supposed to do? Throw them out? I guess sometimes I'm too good of a guy*

He didn't have the nerve to tag us. He doesn't think we're reading this. He's throwing us under the bus to save himself. Pretending he's not with us.

He's the one with the biggest secret. We just have to figure it out.

And just like fate, because I deserve a little bit of that today, I get a text. It's from Stalkanne.

Pearson mentioned the Twitter account. I played dumb. I don't know if anything is going to come of it, but he knows it's following the four of us.

Diana Fleming's number is 319-555-8112. Are you going to call her?

You bet your ass I am.

38

DAVIS WALTON

Friday, 6:15 P.M.

Vicky's gone, Suzanne is talking to Pearson, and Mike won't leave. People are staring at him because he's the one currently being accused of murder. Why is he still sitting next to me, making me guilty by association? He has nowhere to go. If he goes home, he'll have to turn right back around to be here for the ceremony. Why won't he just go to a bar down the block? Why does he have to tarnish my brass? I pull my phone from my pocket.

"Hang on, I have to answer a few emails," I say to him.

But I don't. I go straight to Twitter to see if I'm right, which of course I am.

Holy shit. I can't have this. I'll be ruined. If Twitter cancels me, it'll take more than good press and apologies to bring me back from the dead. People love headlines, not retractions. If the headline on Twitter reads *Leo DiCaprio starts fistfight, injures eighty-year-old bystander*, then that's what happened. Fact. End of story. If the retraction the next day says *Correction: Leo DiCaprio intervenes in fistfight, saves eighty-year-old bystander*, people won't care.

The sensationalized headline will get all the likes and retweets and comments.

These people think admitting they were wrong about what they vehemently retweeted is worse than actually being wrong. So they leave it up. And they repeat it. And then it's reality.

Because of this, I answer a few tweets. I say I barely know Vicky, Mike, and Suzanne. That I feel bad for them, and hey, what's a good guy like me supposed to do? Kick them out?

Still. I can't take the stares, and I want to be alone so I can look for Jim Russell. I know that was him I saw earlier at the end of the bar. Watching us. Stalking. Tweeting. And I'm going to get to the bottom of this. I mean, he was screwing Kristin for God's sake. That's way worse than what I did. And I didn't really do anything! Jason crashed the car by himself. Honestly, I should be the one who's upset. I still have a scar on my head from that crash.

That's why I don't feel so bad about the thing I did to Tommy Johnson.

"Mike, I've got to take a few calls and stuff. I might go back to my room for a bit. I have to talk to Bee Henry. Sales stuff." *Sales, sales, sales, which you don't have.* "I guess I'll see you at the ceremony later?"

He looks at his watch, and man oh man, I really want to ask him how much he paid for it, but that's bad taste even for me. "Okay. I think I'm going to get out of here for a little while anyway. Change of scenery."

"Yeah, I think that'll be good for you."

I say nothing else, just train my face toward my cell so he'll get the hint and get up and leave. This is *my* table. I was here first. He finally ambles up—he's got to have bad knees at his age. He makes some sort of *see ya* noise, and I really want to watch as everyone looks at him disgustedly, but instead, I glue my eyes to Twitter.

There's another tweet from @MPaloozaNxt2Die:

Let's tally them up! 1 dead writer, 2 dead writers, 3 dead writers . . . maybe Davis makes four? Nah. I have someone else in mind #murderpalooza

My mouth drops open. I'm mentioned in that post.

I'm the next to die. Or . . . I'm not? Why is this account fucking with me?

The Twitter stalker only has eleven followers—likely from hashtagging Murderpalooza all day—none of whom are us. We'd agreed not to follow it back because it looks bad. I doubt anyone outside of our little square will pay attention to that tweet, but that doesn't make it any less real.

It takes all of three seconds before that Julie character is back.

"Hey. I saw everyone leave," she says and sits down, uninvited again, with an Amaretto sour again. "What's going on? Is what they're saying about Mike Brooks on Twitter true?" Her eyes are hopeful. Not that it's true about Mike, but hopeful that I'll give her my company and insider information.

"Oh, hey you," I say. "Yeah, I don't know much about what's going on with that whole thing." It could still be her.

"Mike was just here. You all looked like you were having a tense conversation. And I saw that detective looking guy talk to you and that other girl."

"Yes. I'm trying to help with the investigation." See, I'm important, not a suspect, no matter what you're trying to set up behind the scenes. I didn't do anything wrong.

"Mmm." *Slurp, slurp, slurp* on that plastic straw. "I'm hoping to get an agent. I started writing about six years ago. It's so hard to make the right connections, especially when you suck at writing." She stops and speaks quietly. "I guess we all feel like that until we have some success."

My peripheral vison detects my subconscious. "I'm sure you're a fine writer," I say blandly, not looking at her. As my head swivels, I see it again. That hat—that stupid Tampa Lightning hat, and I know it's Jim Russell.

He's talking to Pearson alone. No Vicky. My thoughts instantly drift back to him as the sole suspect. He has more connections and he was screwing Kristin. This Julie person doesn't know about people's deep dark pasts—she's a romance writer. I smother a chuckle at the thought of Jim shitting his pants without his girlfriend there to be his alibi. Fucking murderer is probably tripping over his words, and man, I realize I'm just as bad as the Twitter mob: my opinions become fact from one minute to the next.

Julie is talking. I hear her deep voice, but I'm not paying attention anymore. I'm waiting to see if Pearson slams Jim against the wall and slaps cuffs on his wrists.

But he doesn't. They shake hands, smile even, and Jim walks toward the exit.

"I'm sorry, Jules, I have to go. I'll see you later."

I use the stupid nickname because she'll think it's charming. I stand and realize that we haven't gotten the check yet. What the fuck, how do I always get stuck with the bill? My eyes roll. Reaching into my pocket, I feel the wad of hundred dollar bills I like to keep and peel one off so it looks like I miraculously produce high-ranking bills like a magician. I leave it and take the customer receipt for my taxes. It's way more than the cost of four glasses of wine, one being half gin, and I leave Julie in a rush to get down the stairs to the double doors.

"Hey!" I shout when I get there. Jim turns around. "You Jim Russell? Vicky's boyfriend?"

His eyes glaze. "I'm Jim, yeah. Not so sure about the second part."

I stick out a hand. "Davis Walton. Let's chat."

39

MIKE BROOKS

Friday, 6:15 P.M.

I've had it with this place anyway. I really do need to get out of here for a little while. With my tail between my legs, I skulk past the people who've been alternating between staring at me and staring at their phones while reading about me. I need to be alone when I see what they're saying.

At the bottom of the stairs, I turn a corner and run right into Dustin Feeney. He's about my age, maybe a few years younger. He has that "Indiana Jones when he was a professor" look about him. Round metal glasses, a pocket watch, and a deep side part in his sandy hair.

Crap! Suzanne and I were supposed to have dinner with him tonight, and we never canceled. Nope, just left him high and dry. Everyone must think I'm such a garbage human being, myself included.

"Dustin." We shake hands as his eyes shift around, looking for a witness to his murder because *OMG Mike Brooks is a killer, didn't you hear!?* "Jesus, I'm so sorry I forgot to call you about dinner," I say.

"Hey there, Mike. It's not a problem. I ended up having something come up anyway. You know how these things get."

Every conference I've ever been to for the last two decades were the same—I've never made all the meetings I'd scheduled. Things run over, people get caught up, and time becomes convoluted. I get it. But I know Dustin left me high and dry too, with better reason. He didn't want to be around me and a steak knife.

He's holding an armful of books, and they look like they're about to come crashing down. I extend and arm out for him. "You need a hand?"

"No, I got it," he says quickly and withdraws at my attempted touch.

Got it.

I nod and decide to relieve him of his embarrassment. Why make him uncomfortable? "Okay, well it was great to see you. I'm on my way out. Maybe I'll catch up with you at the ceremony tonight."

He gives me a captain's salute with his free hand and practically runs away.

My life is over, I think as I push my way out the door. If—no, *when*—this ridiculous murder thing is cleared up, what's next? I can't write a splashy beach thriller on my own. I often wonder why Kristin came to me and wanted my name attached to it, with her being the secret co-author. Why didn't she want the immediate accolades? Why wouldn't she let her own agent, Penelope Jacques, shop it? Why would she do this for me?

The only thing I can come up with is that she was a selfless person. She'd been cranking out a book about every eighteen months and has five total under her belt. This project with me would've been her sixth. Unless she wrote another novel in the interim, which if she did, she was more talented that I knew. No one writes that fast.

I find a dark bar about five blocks south of the hotel. It's not fancy, which is exactly what I'm looking for. A dive bar. Being this late on a Friday in mid-summer, it's kind of empty, which is perfect. Most of the companies here let employees take full days or half days off on Fridays between Memorial Day and Labor Day, and half the city leaves for the Hamptons or the Jersey shore to drink tequila shots and screw strangers. Ah, to be young again.

I sit on the stool, a regular twirly stool with a chrome bottom and no back, like I'm at the counter of a fifties diner, and order a beer. When the bartender brings it, I take a sip. I don't look over my shoulder to see who's following me or who could be watching. No one I know would be here. And the conference people are obsessed with staying at the hotel for gossip. And the show starts in just over an hour, so no one is leaving.

I haven't eaten a thing today. I forgot lunch with Vita was canceled, and I didn't eat at Clover & Crimson. Not even a handful of nuts at the lobby bar.

"Can I grab a menu?" I ask the bartender.

He takes one from under the counter and slides it my way. It's only page, laminated and sticky, but what did I expect? At my age, I tend to eat on the healthier side, but there are no orders of broccoli and asparagus to compliment my expensive steak at this place. I shy away from the garden salad with grilled chicken because experience says it'll be wilted and slimy. I go with what dive bars are best known for: an order of wings and a side of fries, promising myself I'll do two extra miles on the treadmill tomorrow.

Time to face the music: I open Twitter.

When I first became well-known, there was no social media. Email wasn't even around for a decade at that point, and most still had AOL accounts. I became famous because of good reviews and interviews in magazines, appearances on local TV and radio, and book tours. People still read the newspaper. Whoever your publisher knew at any of these media outlets determined how much publicity you'd get. Now everyone self-promotes and shows their abs and their butts, and it's about followers. It's all foreign to me. When my name was all over the place, it was because of my books and the one that became a movie. Then it was because of my bad trade reviews, and the headlines were suddenly *Has Mike Brooks Lost His Edge?*

I didn't like to see that.

I like to see this less. A tweet from the Twitter Murder Stalker Person.

> *@MPaloozaNxt2Die Let's tally them up! 1 dead writer, 2 dead writers, 3 dead writers . . . maybe Davis makes four? Nah. I have someone else in mind.*

Terrific. It's after Davis, but maybe not. Which means there's a one-quarter chance it's me.

I read on to the rest, where Twitter proves it's the cesspool of life. The worst of the worst go and hide behind their avatars, or whatever they're called, and just gang up on people. Unless you're some egomaniac like Davis who charms his haters (the few he has), you probably have a love/hate relationship with it. Right now, for me, it's all hate.

Fuck you and die @AuthorMBrooks1234 #JusticeForKristin #murderpalooza

They'd probably need 2 knives to stab you in your fat gut you fucking pig #MikeBrooks

They should let @WriterVickyOverton kill him. He probably started the hate against her

And then, my friends, the cream of the crop.

It was a matter of time before @AuthorMBrooks1234 snapped. His books suck anyway

That hurt more than the others.

As I wait for my wings, I dial Vita. One, two, three, four, five rings and voicemail again. I shouldn't be shocked, but this time I am. Come on, really? She won't talk to me? I finish my beer as her voicemail message rolls to a close.

"Vita, it's Mike. I can't believe you aren't calling me back. Where are you?" I pause because I don't want to say it, but to hell with it. "How do I know you didn't leak that synopsis? You're setting me up. You were the only one that had it."

I say that even though I know whoever killed Kristin had full access to her papers, her files, her computer—everything. But maybe that'll put a small fire under Vita's ass and make her call me back.

I hang up just as my heart attack on a plate arrives, and I dig in like a ten-year-old, getting hot sauce all over my fingers and my face. Toward the end of my meal, the bartender brings the check and five moist towelettes so I can clean myself up enough to go to the bathroom and wash properly like a grown adult.

When I'm lemony fresh and smooth as the skin of an apple, I head back to the bar and throw two twenties down for my twenty-five-dollar meal. It's almost seven P.M. now, and I have to meet the last three standing at the awards ceremony. First, I pick up my phone to torture myself some more.

Holy shit. People on Twitter are freaking out. There's news of another murder in the hotel. Female.

Where's Vita?

40

SUZANNE SHIH

Friday, 6:30 P.M.

After lying to Pearson about the Twitter account, I quickly skipped away to the elevator to get away from him. I'm so embarrassed he read the poem I wrote to Kristin. It was private. And for someone who doesn't know anything, he certainly thinks I'm a stalker.

Whoever made that Twitter account is the stalker and a murderer. Not me. But Vicky was right—we need to find out what Davis is hiding, and maybe this will work out and I'll be alive to see tomorrow. I open my email, and the information I ordered is there. I figure my life is worth $59.95, so I requested a background report on Diana Fleming.

There are leather couches on the landing outside of the elevators, so I sit and read. I can't do this in front of Constantine because I don't want to have to explain why I'm doing it. Time to get comfy. I settle into the supple brown leather.

Diana Fleming, twenty-two, still lives in the Midwest, though she moved out of Heimer and attended college at the University of Iowa in Iowa City. She majored in English and recently completed her degree. She still lives in Iowa City and is currently employed at the college as a TA. The report has her current address, her email address, and her phone number.

I text the phone number to Vicky. She said she'd call.

Satisfied, I plop my phone into my bag and head to the elevator bank. It's eerily empty, but I guess that's to be expected with happy hour in full swing upstairs. I press the call button, wearing a smile I haven't used since I was happy this morning. We're going to get to the bottom of this, I'm going to be off the hook, my book is going to sell, I'm going to be famous, and everything is going to work out. I step into the empty elevator to go to Constantine. I already feel the pressure dissipating as the doors close and it begins to ascend.

Clunk.

There's a noise and something halts the elevator. I'm thrown off balance, dropping my bag and spilling its contents onto the floor. I use my arms to steady myself against the walls. On the panel to the right of the door, the light for the fifth floor, where my room is located, is still lit. For no reason, I hit it again. Nothing.

My heart pounds in my chest—I actually feel it—and my breathing gets shorter. Within seconds, I'm unable to gulp air at all and my throat constricts. The lights on the floor indicator at the top of the door keep blinking with "3" and "4." I'm stuck.

Stuck. In a box.

I press the call button, but nothing happens, so I bang on the door. "Help!"

My nails jam into the crack as I try to pry apart the heavy doors like I'm Captain America. I'm not, and I don't know what I think I can accomplish. I pound with my fists again.

"Help!"

How long until I run out of air?

For a quick second, I think *at least I'm not in the dark*, but of course, the lights go out.

I'm stuck between floors, in a small box, in the dark. This isn't by coincidence. The temperature begins to rise, though my teeth chatter like I'm in an igloo. Fear paralyzes me as I slide down the wall and huddle into a corner, gripping my knees into my chest.

"Help," I whisper.

My brain isn't functioning correctly. One part of me, the rational part, knows that my phone is somewhere here on the floor, but I'm terrified to move. I know I'm alone. The irrational part of me thinks if I reach a hand out, another one will grab it. Another hand, of another person in this dark elevator. No, not another *person*. It's the stalker. This isn't random.

I sit in the corner, vibrating with fear, praying for something, anything, to happen. All the adulting of the past few hours disappears, and right now, I'm a little girl who wants her mommy and daddy, and I want to be at home in my twin bed with the purple-and-white-striped comforter. I make end-of-life promises. *I swear, Mom and Dad, I'll do anything you want me to do. You can set me up with someone you deem "proper." I'll stop seeing the rocker Constantine. I'll help out with the dishes more. Just please, come and rescue me and take me out of New York City. I can't make it here. Not for the rest of the weekend. I want to go home.*

Over my teeth clanking against each other, I listen for any other sounds. There's a whirring noise coming from above me, above the elevator shaft. Is that the broken part that stopped the movement, and is someone trying to fix it? Or is someone up there cutting the wires so I drop? I hear no people on the other side of the door, pressing the buttons over and over, cursing the delay. I'm utterly alone.

Just me, my teeth, my heartbeat, my breath, and whatever is going on outside of this dangling box.

Am I moving? Is someone pushing the box?

My cell phone lights up. Oh my God, I have service! I just need to grab it. Which means I have to move from my little fort in the corner. I have to unwrap my knees and propel myself to that little light on the floor before it goes out and I'm bathed in darkness again.

Move. Move! I will myself to do it, and I finally can. I grab the cell phone like it's my lifeline, which it kind of is, and press the home button.

Oh God, help me.

It's a text message from an unknown number.

Scary in there, isn't it?

I scream, and the sound reverberates in the small space. Tears flow as I bang on the doors again, still not fully erect. If I stand, I'll fall right back down again. My knees can't support the panic.

My phone lights up again.

> *If I let you out, you better be a good little girl and comply. You try to leave before the awards show, well . . . 6051 Sunshine Boulevard. I don't fuck around.*

If the lights were on, if I was able to find my compact and open it and look at myself, I know there'd be no color left in my face. That's my address. They know where I live.

I'll do anything, I swear, please let me out, I type back, but it immediately comes back as undelivered. I don't know if that's because I'm trapped or because it's being sent from some crypto phone.

"I'll do anything you say!" I scream. Irrational me. "Please!"

Then I wait. I raise my fist to bang on the door again, but rational me kicks in. Comply. In the dark. I wipe the tears from my face and stand, even though they can't see me. I flatten out the front and back of my dress with my hands in case it wrinkled while I was crouched in the corner or banging on the door from my knees. I force out normal talk.

"I'm ready to comply," I say in a lower pitch, though my voice cracks at the end. "Please let me out."

It's about ten seconds before the light goes on, and I don't dare move. Light as a feather, stiff as a board. My text goes off again.

Pick up your shit and act normal when the door opens. Sunshine Boulevard!

Looking down, I see everything else from my bag is still splayed on the ground. I shove everything back in at once in an arm swipe, not caring if things are in the right pockets. I place the bag on my shoulder and fold my hands in front of me like a good little girl.

The elevator moves up. Five seconds later, it opens to the fifth floor.

No one is here.

On my way out, I notice the mirror in the top left corner. Everyone knows there's a security camera behind there.

Someone at the hotel is involved.

41

VICKY OVERTON

Friday, 6:30 P.M.

Do I have enough time to call Diana Fleming? I have forty-five minutes before I have to leave to get downstairs. I still have to dry my hair, do my makeup, and get dressed. Maybe go over my "I'd like to thank the Academy" speech once more, just in case.

Screw it. If I don't find out what Davis is hiding, this will never end. It's not like Diana is going to pick up anyway. If memory serves, she's kind of young, maybe still in college. She's either out wasted somewhere or napping to prepare for another epic Friday night. I remember being that age when all I did was party and upload pictures of food to Instagram. God, I miss Instagram. I've been so preoccupied with Twitter today.

I punch in Diana's number and hit the green button to connect the call.

Two rings.

"Hello?"

My breath catches in my throat, and I don't know what to say. Did I think this was going to magically come to me? *You're a writer, use your words*, as Jim always said.

I miss Jim.

Focus.

"Hi, I'm looking for Diana Fleming?" I say it with a tilt at the end, like I'm asking a question. Like I'm unsure of myself. I am.

"Who is this?"

There's noise in the background, as if she's at a bar. God, I hope she's not drunk. I can't deal with a slurring kid or someone who's going to be combative. Then again, loose lips sink ships.

"My name is Vicky Overton. I know this is going to sound really random, but I need to ask you some questions. About your brother. Jason." *Really*—delete.

I close my eyes and pray she doesn't hang up on me.

My sister Carolyn and I aren't particularly close. She went the way of Lawyer Mommy and Doctor Daddy and got into finance. She works in Tampa for a south branch of a big New York City firm. She makes a lot of money, which my parents like. She's engaged and owns a condo and has a boat—she checks all the boxes of perfect daughter. I don't like to talk about her.

I'd like it less if she were dead.

"My brother died a long time ago," Diana says. "Who is this again?"

"My name is Vicky. I'm an author, and I think I might know something about your brother. I know how strange that sounds, but if you have just five minutes?"

"Fine. Hang on." The sound muffles, like she's pressing the phone against her chest, and the background noise gets lower and lower until it finally disappears. "I don't know how I can help."

It's quiet now, and I know I have her attention and decide to get right to it. "I'm not sure if you remember Jason's old writing

group?" Again, a high tilt at the end. I need to speak more confidently. I've got to drag this information out of her.

"Jason was a decade older than me. We have the same dad
but different moms. I'm the midlife crisis baby. We didn't live
together. He lived with his mother full time."

"Oh. Right." I say it like I know the information. I give myself
an internal pep talk: be authoritative, don't sound like you're
doubting every word out of your own mouth. "Well, did he ever
mention an author named Kristin Bailey?"

"Sounds familiar." Quiet. "Wait, she gave an interview to the
paper when he died. So you're talking about those people. Yeah,
he used to talk about them. Why?"

I swallow. "Well I don't know if its connected, but Kristin
Bailey was murdered this morning."

"She was?"

There's less shock in her voice than I expected. Then again,
she doesn't know these people.

"Yes. At a writing conference. I don't have time to get into
the details, but some people have wrangled me and a few other
authors into finding the connection." Some people. Ha. *A Twitter
stalker is threatening our lives!* It sounds insane. "Did Jason ever talk
about Davis Walton?"

It's quiet. All I hear are the car horns from the ground below.

Then her background noise gets a little louder, then a little
more, until it's back to the pitch it was when I first called, and
she raises her voice to talk over it.

"Look, all I remember is that Jason was in a critique group
with Kristin and a few others. Tommy Johnson was one of them.
And to be quite honest, I don't want to talk about Davis Walton.
Hey, excuse me, can I order another drink?"

She's tuned me out. I was right, she's at a bar. And she also has unpleasant memories about Davis. It's connected. I know it is.

"Do you know where I can find Tommy Johnson?" I ask.

She makes a noise between a scoff and a chuckle. "No one knows where Tommy Johnson is. Hey, hi, thanks. Yes, another one of these. My tab is behind the bar. Thanks!" She's talking to the bartender again. "Look, I've got to go. I'm sorry I couldn't be more help. Sorry about the murder, but I don't want to talk about this anymore. My brother is dead, and this isn't going to bring him back."

"Wait. One more question. I promise this will be it and then I'll let you go. Please?"

"What?" Her voice drips with frustration, and I don't blame her.

I hate what I'm about to say.

"Did Jason . . . was it an accident or was it suicide?"

Bar chatter. That's all that comes through the phone for ten seconds.

"How do you know about that?"

"I don't. It was speculation, from what I read. But if you can shed any light on this, it might help me with Kristin's murder. She was stabbed."

I don't know why I think playing sympathy will work. But it does.

"I'm going to hang up. But first, I'll say this: yes, there was what police called a suicide note in his pocket. They said it was written under duress. They said that over and over when we told them the handwriting didn't match. I have to go. Don't call me again."

Not the same handwriting? Who wrote it, then? Who wanted Jason dead?

The line goes dead.

Jason's accident *wasn't* an accident. It was staged to look like a suicide. And Davis knows why—I'm sure of it.

If this were a book, we'd be really close to solving the mystery, but we'd know that one more huge thing had to happen before it falls into place. I can't help but wonder what that is.

Then there's a knock on the door.

42

DAVIS WALTON

Friday, 6:45 P.M.

Staring at this Jim Russell guy, I wonder what Vicky sees in him. I mean, she's no model, but something tells me anyone who dyes their hair that shade of purple is probably a monster in the sack. She can probably do better than this guy. He's wearing a goofy hat, and his hair is too long and sticking out the sides. In this heat, I can't imagine the hat hair he'd have if he ripped that thing off. Plus, he's in shorts and flip flops. I look like I should be on a runway standing next to this guy.

"What do you want to talk to me for?" he asks.

I narrow my eyes, then nod toward the bandage on his head. "What happened? I was with Vicky when she got your text."

His hand flies to the wound, and he pats it like he forgot it was there. "Oh. Yeah. We don't really know yet. Waiting to see if the cops can get anything off the street cameras."

"Vicky said you were mugged."

"You were with her again? After my accident?"

"Yes." I purse my lips. This guy. Like he doesn't know. He's been stalking us. "If you read Twitter, you'd know we were together a short time ago." Of course he's read Twitter. Plus, I *saw* him staring at us from across the bar.

"I've tried to stay off it today. They were tearing Vicky apart earlier, and I don't like to see that. And she's . . . well, she's taking some time alone right now."

"Right. Because you were sleeping with Kristin Bailey."

His eyes go wide, and he takes a step back. Ha. He didn't know she told us, and he's shocked.

"I don't know what you're—"

"Just stop it right now, Jim," I say with my hand up in front of his face. "Vicky told us. She said she saw the texts. She caught you with your pants down, and you thought you'd be able to get one over on her. Well, she found out. And if you think you're going to get one over on me, you're sorely mistaken, my friend."

His blank, stupid face slowly goes into a smirk. "What if I did sleep with her? What the fuck does that matter to you?"

"Because you could've killed her. You could've—" I stop, because I don't want to say he could've found out about my deal with her and Murderpalooza and Jason and Tommy. I need to suss out what he knows instead of telling him and giving him more ammo. "You could be behind this whole thing."

"What whole thing?"

"Twitter. Everything."

"Oh, so you think I started the rumors about my own girl-friend? She said an agent did it."

This guy is either a master at playing dumb or he's a bigger idiot than he looks. "Were you with Kristin last night or this morning?"

He scoffs and turns away from me, like he's going to leave.

No way.

I grab his arm, and in less than one second, he whips around and grabs my shoulders and slams me against the wall. Holy shit, I think my heart just stopped. Thank God we're near the street-level door and not visible to everyone at the bar. I'll die of embarrassment if anyone sees this. His fingers grip tightly to my upper arm, and I'll admit it: I'm scared. I didn't know he was this strong. He looks like a wimp, and I wasn't prepared for this kind of altercation. People listen to me when I talk. Jim is being defiant.

"Don't fucking touch me," he says, his blue eyes turning dark. Then the devilish smirk is back. "You have no idea what I'm capable of doing."

I lose control of myself in my fear, but it's just a trickle, so hopefully, it won't be visible down the front of my jeans. I'm trying to keep cool and let him know that he doesn't scare me, but he does. I was right all along. This guy is a killer.

He leans in close again, and the hairs on my arms and the back of my neck stand up. "Actually, you're about to find out what I'm capable of doing," he whispers.

"What are you talking about?"

"You'll see. I know more than I let on, *Davis*." He accentuates my name, and it's because he's jealous or because . . .

No.

He was sleeping with Kristin. He knows everything she knows. Fuck.

"Why did you kill her?" I ask.

He takes a step back and smiles, then takes the hat off. I was right, hat hair. He removes the bandage to show me his blemish free forehead. What the fu—

"You ever hear the saying 'believe half of what you hear and none of what you see'?" he asks. He looks like Satan himself when he pushes the tape back into place over his fake-bruised eyebrow and puts his hat back on his head. Another huge smile creeps across his face.

That's when I notice more.

"What's that on your hand, Jim?"

I know what it is. I know what it is. I know what it is. Jim peeks down at his right hand, then licks a finger on his left hand and rubs it off.

"Oops," he says. "Gotta run. Good talk."

He pats me on the shoulder in a bro way, and his smile is evil—twisted, raised too high on his left side. He's hiding something, and he's going to kill me. He exits the hotel and immediately blends into the people walking on the street and disappears. I exhale with a shudder.

That was blood on his hand.

Half of what you hear and none of what you see.

I need a drink. Something strong. I head back up to the bar, and people start shrieking. Everyone is looking at their phones, and I just know the Twitter stalker—Jim—has struck again. I open the stupid app and look up the Murderpalooza hashtag again, and yeah—there's news.

Rumor has it, there's been another murder.

Here.

Female.

My heart thumps and I begin to sweat. Jim had blood on his hand and a female is dead.

Where's Vicky?

43

MIKE BROOKS

Friday, 7:00 P.M.

I fly into the hotel, my wings and beer receipt still in my hand. If anyone wants to question where I've been—again—I have an alibi. Another dead girl? What I really need is to find Vita.

I go up to the bar, where it seems everyone has heard the news. People are standing around, reading their phones. They're in the typical groups. The ones who write police procedurals are likely trading theories. Most mid-listers chatter to each other, gathering plot points for their next books. The *New York Times* bestsellers are clinking glasses. I'm all of them and none of them at the same time.

I spot Davis leaning against the bar, doing the same with the ones famous for being famous. The ones with Instagram series and all the TikTok followers. There's a girl to his right and his left. I think one is an agent, and if my old eyes don't mistake me, the other is Joanne Lopez, the writer who won the M-TOTY last year. The three of them seem to be making small talk while looking at their phones. Heads go up, heads go down. On repeat. I take a deep breath and approach them.

"Davis," I say. "What's going on?"

I see the shift in his mood from when we were with the core four to now, when he's with fans and people who kiss his ass. I'm still a murderer to most who read Twitter.

"Mike. Where have you been? You got up and left the table about an hour ago, and I haven't seen you."

He's making people question where I've been, when another murder happened? Of course he is, he has to stay squeaky clean when he's still hiding stuff. A master at deflection. It's probably why the conflict in his book is so good. I hate thinking of him as talented.

I produce my receipt. "I was a few blocks over at Dewey's. I needed something to eat. What have you been doing? There are rumors going around." I can throw this back on him too. I've got one or two tricks up my old sleeve.

"Excuse me, ladies, I need to speak with Mike privately," he says, gives the women winks and smiles, and they do the same. My eye rolls are really getting a workout today. He takes my arm and leads me to a corner. "Did you hear there was another murder?"

I nod. "Yeah, and to be honest, I'm freaking out. The Murderpalooza hashtag on Twitter says it was a woman. I can't find Vita. She won't call me back." I look at my phone in my hand again. Nothing. I put it in my pocket. Out of sight, out of mind.

"I saw Jim. Russell. Vicky's boyfriend."

"So?"

"He had blood on his hand. I texted and called Vicky, but I haven't heard back from her yet."

"What?" Holy shit.

Davis was right; could Jim be the Twitter Stalker Murder Person? I yank my phone from my pocket and call her as well. Just like the last phone call I made, five rings and voicemail.

I disconnect without leaving a message and look at Davis. "Do you know her room number?"

"No," he says with a head shake.

"Shit." I text Suzanne. *Where are you? Vicky might be in trouble.*

Three dots. She's writing back.

Then it stops.

A minute later, three dots again.

Then nothing. No message.

I text Vicky. *Can you answer me? Are you okay?*

Davis and I hunch over my phone, both willing for something, anything, to come through. Those three dots don't mean anything. If Suzanne is injured, she could be trying to be coherent, texting us for help while the blood slips off her fingers and messes with the touch screen. If she's dead . . . oh God . . . but if she is, that could be the killer writing and erasing something. Throwing us off track.

"Where the hell are they?" I ask.

"I confronted Jim," Davis says. "He pulled back the bandage on his head. You know, the head wound from his supposed mugging? There was nothing there, Mike. Just a bandage that was painted red on the edges. The small bruise under his eye was probably makeup. He said 'believe half of what you hear and none of what you see.' He's behind this. All of it." His hand flies to his forehead. "The fake blood on his head and the real blood on his hand. And Vicky is missing."

"Should we call Pearson? I still have his card." I dig into my pocket. Damn it, I was right a half hour ago. We should've come clean.

"No. Not yet. I just wish I knew where Vicky was."

It's the first time I see Davis concerned for anyone but himself, and I wonder if it's because he really cares or because he thinks he's next. My money is on the latter.

"What if she's in on it?" Davis says.

"What are you talking about?"

"Jim and Vicky. What if they did it together, and she knows he's faking it? Remember how she acted when I mentioned Kevin Candela's book that's up for the award tonight? About the husband-and-wife team covering for each other on the mistress killing? What if she did it in a jealous rage, and he's protecting her? What if Jim did it in a fit of passion, and Vicky is covering for him?"

I roll my eyes. "A little far-fetched, Davis. We're not characters in a book."

"You didn't see what I saw. You didn't see the look on his face."

Davis's phone rings, and his eyes light up as he answers. Thank God, it's got to be Vicky.

Nope.

"Penny!" he screeches into the phone. "What's going on? Have you heard anything about what everyone is saying?"

He turns his back to me. Why doesn't this surprise me? Of course Davis forgot about Vicky already. An ass-kisser called. Hey, at least he's getting calls. I look at my phone again. Nothing from Vita. Nothing from Suzanne. Nothing from Vicky. I swallow a lump in my throat. What if he's right? What if something terrible happened to them and we could've prevented this by being honest with Pearson in the first place?

I don't want any blood on my hands, and I finger Pearson's card in my pocket.

I check the time. Just a little past seven. We agreed to meet at seven-thirty so we could sit together at the ceremony. Davis turns toward me as he hangs up the phone.

"Penelope is on her way," he says. "She wants to talk in person."

There are gushes and shushes making their way through the bar. I swivel my head left to right to see what's happened *now*.

"What is it?" Davis asks one of the women he was standing with when I got here.

Before she answers, she eyes me, the conference killer, up and down. It's definitely Joanne Lopez; I recognize the small tattoo of her dog's name on her shoulder. I remember her speech from last year's conference when she won, saying her beloved poodle died on her launch day, and she got the tattoo right after. Brutal.

"Well we shouldn't be shocked. That's what you get for trying to play with the big boys," she says with a sneer.

"What are you talking about?" I ask.

"Someone on Twitter said the dead girl is that romance writer. Julie Keane."

"Who?" I've never heard of her.

"Some self-published romance writer who's trying to be a thriller writer." She shrugs, as if this woman's life meant nothing because she self-publishes romance. Nicole loves that stuff. I don't know Julie, but Jesus, another woman from this conference is dead.

Davis looks like he's about to vomit. "Did you know her?" I ask quietly.

He doesn't get a chance to answer. Joanne talks first, while still looking at her phone. "Ha! Turns out, she was using a pen name. Her real name was Diana Fleming."

Oh, did this just get interesting.

44

SUZANNE SHIH

Friday, 6:55 P.M.

My heart is still racing after the elevator incident, and I fast walk, then run down the hallway. I stop at the door and try to collect myself, but then I can't help it, and I bang on the door.

"What are you doing here?" Vicky asks when it opens. Her hair is a darker purple than earlier today, and she's in a robe and holding a hairbrush.

I couldn't go back to my room and to Constantine. I'm too panicked, and he'd wonder why. Right now, I resent him for sending that questionnaire even though it wasn't his fault. I'm sure that's what got me locked in the box.

I can tell by Vicky's scowl that she's not happy to see me. She's been cold to me ever since she found out about my interaction with Kristin, and that's got to be double since she found out about me and Mike. I'm sure she, as well as Davis, thought we had an affair. We didn't. But that's neither here nor there.

Right now, I think she'll help me. I push my way in. I'm used to doing that.

"Whoa, whoa, I asked what you were doing here."

When I turn around to face her, I start to cry again. I don't want to, but I can't help it.

"Someone at the hotel is involved," I say through blubbering breaths.

She crosses her arms, still hanging onto the hairbrush. "What are you talking about?"

I look at her desk, where her computer is open. "Can I sit down?" I don't want to sit on her bed.

She walks to the laptop and snaps it closed. "Fine. And you better make this quick. I have a ceremony to prepare for."

I tell her everything about being locked up and the text messages I got while inside. How they knew my purse was turned over and had everything spilled out. I leave out the part about listening at Kristin's door and how I'm terrified for the ceremony tonight—she already thinks I'm a nutcase. I ask her if she's gotten any texts, and right when I do, my text goes off again.

Not Twitter Psychopath.

"It's Mike," I say. "He's asking about you. He thinks you're in trouble. I'll tell him I'm with you." I start typing.

"No. Wait. Stop writing," she says. She finally puts the hairbrush down and scratches the side of her head. "Why is he asking about me?" Her phone makes a swoosh sound, and she walks to the other side of the bed and picks it up off the nightstand. "It's Mike, asking where I am and if I'm okay. Don't answer him yet."

"Why?"

She shakes her head, eyes downturned. "I don't know. This is weird. We're meeting in a half hour. What does it matter where I am? Right after you were just targeted. Is someone looking for me to target me next? Do they need to know where I am?" She paces back and forth, her hand on her head. "Shit," she says after she looks at the clock. "I have to get ready. I might as well tell you what I found out."

"What? Tell me what?" How much worse can this be?

"I spoke to Diana Fleming a little while ago. She may have been drunk. She was ordering drinks at a bar. And she said she didn't want to talk about Davis."

A lump forms in my throat, but I'm still able to speak. "What do you think that means?"

"I don't know. I mean . . . I don't trust anyone right now. Not Jim, and honestly, none of you guys either. I need to know what's going on. There's a connection with this."

Well at least she admits it. Vicky doesn't trust me. Why would she?

She walks toward the bathroom, stops at the door, and looks at me. "I'm almost done, but you can wait here if you want. We can go down together."

I smile. Maybe she's softening to me, or maybe she doesn't want to be alone either. Whatever it is, is fine by me. I can't go to Constantine. Shit. Constantine. I pull out my phone to text him.

Hey. Caught up in meetings and I have to be at the ceremony in a half hour. I promise I'll come right up after! Or if you want to meet me at the bar for drinks, I'll text you fifteen minutes before I can leave

The least I can do is let him hang out for a little bit if I think we're not in danger. He should see what my world is going to be like. Imagine if Vicky wins the M-TOTY. I mean, hello! My inner circle will be literary royalty.

My eyes flame with the idea of celebrity. People screaming my name.

The hairdryer goes on, and I look out Vicky's window. She's on the same floor as me but on the other side of the hotel, and she gets the sunset view over the Hudson. It's blocked by buildings, but there's no mistaking that fiery orange sky.

While I wait, I decide to look at Twitter and see what the new word is. That psycho account tweeted something a bit ago, when I was talking to Pearson. Before it trapped me in the elevator.

> *@MPaloozaNxt2Die Let's tally them up! 1 dead writer, 2 dead writers, 3 dead writers . . . maybe Davis makes four? Nah. I have someone else in mind.*

What if it was supposed to be me?

What if that's why Mike wants to know where Vicky is? Is he working with someone?

I go to the Murderpalooza hashtag. Holy shit, Julie Keane is dead!

Who's Julie Keane?

Before doing any more research, I scream to Vicky and she comes out. Her hair looks great that color.

Focus.

"There was another murder! Here! Everyone on Twitter is saying its someone named Julie Keane. Do you know who she is? I've never heard of her."

She charges over and rips my phone out of my hand while saying, "Gimme that." Her thumbs are working double time scrolling and tapping. Then a tear falls down her cheek.

It's not over.

"Oh my God, did you know her?" I ask.

She shakes her head. "Not really. But oh my God, Suzanne. I know for a fact she was with Davis last night."

My hand flies to my mouth. "Is that a joke?" It's Davis. It has to be.

Her eyes fly along the screen. "Even worse. Julie Keane was her pen name. Her real name is Diana Fleming."

THE MORNING OF THE MURDER

Kristin saw Jason Fleming's younger sister Diana sitting in the third row of the conference room at the panel Kristin presided over.

They'd been emailing for the last couple months. Diana contacted Kristin and informed her that she'd written and self-published a few romance novels under a pen name but sought advice on thrillers. Kristin was more than happy to dole out advice for her late friend's sister. Kristin even suggested she come out to Murderpalooza, that this was the place to mingle and meet other thriller writers and agents to learn the tricks of the trade, but Diana said no, citing work and money.

Why didn't she let Kristin know she was coming the second she'd changed her mind?

It all felt too much like a thriller plot. The person from the past showing up.

Kristin did her best to keep her composure, introducing each writer and asking for their opinions on her panel *Trauma, Drama, and Revenge*. When she linked eyes with Diana, Diana gave her a knowing look, and Kristin knew what was about to happen.

She knew exactly why Diana had come.

45

VICKY OVERTON

Friday, 7:00 P.M.

This is impossible. I literally just spoke to Diana Fleming less than a half hour ago. *Literally*—wait, nope, that one stays, it's too important. And now to find out she was covering for herself as Julie Keane—the same one I was rude to earlier, the same one who knew Davis. Based on both of their reactions when I saw them together, I'm sure they slept together. I'm sure of it!

Davis is in this up to his neck. Jason. Kristin. Julie. That's three dead writers.

I have a few texts on my phone from him. No way am I writing him back. I can't believe I'm trapped in my hotel room with Stalkanne and I feel the safest with her.

"Don't text anyone back. There's something going on," I say. "I have to do my makeup. Just sit tight."

"Okay," she says.

"Find out everything you can." I point to the pad and pencil with the hotel's logo on the desk. "Write it down."

Back in the bathroom, I turn on my curling iron to medium while I use a nourishing oil on my face, then carefully apply my foundation and concealer, followed by a pinkish bronzer on my upper cheekbones. For my eyes, I go smoky with false lashes, but not Kardashian-like. A few coats of mascara and I wash my hands. Now I'm ready to get into the dress I bought just for the awards show. It's a white wrap dress with nude heels, and its simplicity against my violet-y hair and dramatic eye makeup is, in a word I don't use for myself often, stunning.

I wish Jim were here to see this. Half of me wants to text him, but the other half wants to change my flight back to Florida so I don't have to sit next to him on the plane. I want to get home, pack up his extra T-shirts, boxers, and his toothbrush, and set it on fire. Or in my writer's mind, find a stray hair or other DNA I can save for crime scene evidence. Nothing like a good set-up to show how pissed off you are.

I buckle my left heel and exit the bathroom. My earrings are on the credenza next to the desk, so I grab them and put them on.

"What did you find out?" I ask Stalkanne as I'm fastening. She's had twenty minutes, and she better have something good to use on Davis by now.

She lifts her head from her phone and smiles. "You look really nice."

Terrific, I'm next in Stalkanne's house of horrors. "Thanks. And?" My eyebrows rise and fall while gesturing toward her phone.

"Oh. Well, yeah, you were right. Julie Keane is Diana Fleming. God, their poor parents," she says. "Could you imagine losing both of your children?"

The thought of having one child and quitting wine for nine months gives me anxiety, and I assume I'm too young to talk about kids anyway. I'm only thirty—I've got time before I have to think about it. Even though I'm probably starting over, again. I read that women over thirty-five are considered "geriatric pregnancies," and whatever man wrote that article can fuck right off.

Still. She's right. Those poor parents.

"No one on Twitter really knew who this Julie was," Stalkanne says.

She's right; thriller writers tend not to focus on writers outside their genre. Still, why isn't the hotel doing anything? Could Stalkanne be right—is someone here involved? That's the only explanation I can come up with. "Did they mention Davis yet? Has anyone on Twitter tied him to Diana yet?" *Please, please, please . . .*

"No. The hotel said they have her phone, and they're going through her recent calls and texts and social stuff to see how she spent her last few hours. They want to see if she was targeted as well."

I'd laugh if this weren't so real. That Pearson guy is going to find out that I called her and that we had a five-minute conversation right before she died. "How did she die?"

Stalkanne screws up her face. "Huh. It doesn't say, now that I think about it."

Christ. That probably meant she was found swinging from a rafter on the roof deck.

Or . . .

Or maybe Stalkanne was right. Maybe someone from the hotel is involved, and they're trying to keep this under wraps too. Which means none of us are safe. Where are the police? I need a bodyguard, someone who will take a bullet and carry me off stage like Kevin Costner did for Whitney Houston in that awesome movie that came out the year after I was born.

Maybe I'll even get to fall in love.

I look at the clock. It's showtime.

"We should get going. Don't want to be late."

"Wait, wait," Stalkanne says, a worried look in her eye. "We're going to go down there with them? With Mike and Davis? I thought you said they were dangerous?"

I put a hand on my hip. In charge. "Yep. As a matter of fact, I want to confront Davis. I saw him with Julie Keane . . . Diana . . . today. I think he fucked her last night. And the fact that she's Jason Fleming's sister . . . how do you not want to know what the connection is? If this were a book, it's where the reader would say things are working out too perfectly. Which is why I think there's still a big finale. There's coincidence, and then there's this."

Her eyes shift. "Fine, but can we take the stairs?"

She's still afraid of the elevator. Can't say I blame her. Assuming the stalker is targeting her only, I can't take that chance being locked up with her. I have a man to throw under the bus and an award to possibly win.

I nod. "Let's go."

46

DAVIS WALTON

Friday, 7:25 P.M.

My head swivels to the people around me. Their funhouse faces are contorted, clown-like; their laughter muffled yet loud, bellowing out from deep within and echoing. I hear that plus a high-pitched shriek that I know my brain is using for defense. To keep everything else out. I pinch the top of my nose and take a few deep breaths, trying to channel what Papaya, my yoga instructor in LA, always says. *Only you can give life to negativity. Breathe it out. Tell your body there's no home for it here!*

Julie Keane—I remembered her first *and* last name this time—is dead.

Julie Keane is Jason Fleming's sister.

I'd never met her, not as Diana, anyway. She was still in high school when I knew Jason, and they had different mothers, so she didn't live with him most of his life.

Julie targeted me last night. She wasn't a super fan who wanted my body—God, that hurts. She's been following me around and trying to get back into my room on purpose. Why?

What if she was behind the stalker Twitter account? She may have been friends with Kristin Bailey. They could've met at Jason's funeral (I didn't attend, I was busy healing myself from the crash) and got to talking. What if Julie knew everything about me, and then . . . well why would she turn on Kristin and kill her?

Who turned on Julie?

"Davis!"

It's Mike next to me, loudly snapping me out of my fear fantasies. "What?"

"Did you hear what she said?"

"Who?" I'm disoriented. Wait. Joanna or something like that. She was last year's M-TOTY winner, if I'm not mistaken, and I rarely am. She's that writer next to me, still leaning on the bar, still smirking at her phone and at the fact that Julie is dead. Fuck, she said Julie's real name was Diana Fleming right in front of Mike.

When I focus on Mike, his face is twisted, his eyes aflame. He wants answers—answers I don't have. I just found this out too.

"That woman who was murdered was Jason Fleming's sister. Did you know he had a sister?" he asks.

I'm still trying to concentrate on how much trouble I'm in, but my head is in a fog and I can't shake it. The whole house of cards is going to come tumbling down like a turd in a hurricane, and I'm the one who's going to leave a shit stain on someone's house.

Mike's voice gets louder. "What else are you hiding, Davis?" Then sinister. "Where's Vicky?"

I snap out of it. *Jim.* "I have no idea! I didn't do anything. Jim was the one who—" And like an angel on her way to heaven, I see Vicky ascending the stairs to the bar. She's even wearing white; she's just missing the wings. She looks great, and she's with the kid. I throw my arm out and point. "Vicky, you're alive!" I say, half out of relief and half because now I get to be smug in front of Mike. See, I didn't kill her, or Kristin, or Julie.

She's walking toward us. No, she's stomping, in those heels, the tall, spiky ones, and wow did I mention she looks great? She's does. Until her index finger is two inches from my face.

"What did you do, Davis?"

My first instinct is to snatch that thing and twist it, but even I'm not that much of a douche—you don't lay your hands on a woman.

"What are you talking about?" I ask rather innocently. "Where have you been? Why didn't you answer me or Mike? We've been looking for you."

Her face scrunches. "No, no, no, Davis. You don't get to do that again."

"Do what?"

"You always find a way to turn the conversation around and keep the heat off you. Well guess what? Someone has been concentrating on you most of the day. You can't double talk your way out of this one. I know you were with her last night, and we all know she was Jason Fleming's sister. You better start talking or I'm calling Pearson right now to dig into you."

The kid is standing half behind Vicky and doesn't say a thing. Mike is still glaring at me. Thankfully, the people who surrounded me earlier are ensconced with others, talking about Julie Keane's death.

"Wait, what?" Mike says to Vicky, then looks back at me incredulously. "What does she mean, you were with her last night? I asked you if you knew her." Back to Vicky. "You're right. He's been lying all day."

"That's not what's going on," I say. "I barely remember last night. She wasn't there this morning. How do I know she wasn't making the whole thing up?"

My mind drifts back. Condom wrappers on the floor. Finding her lipstick. She was definitely in my room with me.

Wait, wait, wait . . . I found condom wrappers, but no used condoms. Not that I looked in the garbage, but I feel like I would've seen them somewhere. Of course, housekeeping already came and took away any evidence. I remember the lipstick upright on my desk when I came back from Clover & Crimson this afternoon, when everything was made up.

I shake my head in disbelief. "I don't think I was with her last night. Someone planted some stuff in my room. I think someone from the hotel is in on this," I say.

Vicky audibly gasps, then looks back at the kid. "That's what she said too."

I'm about done with this girl, shared opinion or not. "What does she have to do with any of this? Because she's a stalker and a Mike-fucker?"

"Watch it, Davis," Mike says, then turns toward Suzanne. "I'm curious, though, why would you say that someone in the hotel is involved?"

Her eyebrows dent with worry. "I was attacked. I got locked between floors on the elevator." She finally says something, and it's not what I want to hear.

This Twitter stalker person is going to try to take us out one by one. I'm too stunned to ask her what happened, but she regales us with her story.

"This person isn't going to stop until—"

Until what?

I'm the only one left with a huge secret.

I don't finish the sentence. I don't have to—it comes to me at once. They think the Twitter stalker is going to destroy them, but I can see the forest and not just the trees now.

The Twitter stalker is coming after me and using them to do it. Good writers can always solve the mystery.

47

MIKE BROOKS

Friday, 7:30 P.M.

"Well let's get in the ballroom and make sure we get a table together," I say. "Vicky, do they have you at a special table? For nominees?"

"No," she says, shaking her head. "I mean, well, yes, all the nominees have one of the front five tables. But we can decide who else sits there. Each is a table for six, and since Jim isn't coming, I guess there's one more available spot."

"Who's the fifth?" I ask.

"Penelope."

Davis smiles, since he's going to make it about him, because that's what he does. *His* agent will be there. Not Vicky, the nominee's agent. Davis's.

"I saw Jim," Davis says again. "Vicky, he lied to you. He didn't get attacked."

She rolls her eyes. "I was there. He was in an ambulance."

"Well I don't know what he's got going on, but I confronted him a little while ago. I saw him watching us in the bar. He knew we were sitting by the sunflowers. I think the Twitter stalker is him."

"Davis, stop making Vicky uncomfortable," I say. This guy is unbelievable. Always worried about himself. "If that's true, why didn't you tell us when it was happening? And where is he now?" My mind flashes to Nicole and the kids.

What if he *is* crazy, and he's after everyone?

I pull out my phone and text Nicole. *Everything okay?*

"He was on his way out when I confronted him. He left," Davis says desperately. Vicky was right. He's still trying to turn the conversation. "But, Vicky, I swear, he pulled his bandage off his head. He doesn't have a gash. He's faking it. Did you see the cut or just the gauze pad?"

Vicky's face falls, and she stares at him with doubt. Not doubt about his story, but her own. I won't let him do this to her.

"What does Julie—Diana—being killed have to do with the rest of us? The only connection is you, Davis," I say. "Vicky's right. Stop trying to turn the conversation onto something else. None of us knew this Jason guy. Only you."

"And Kristin," Davis says.

"And they're both dead. And so is his sister, another one who has a connection to you. I'm not sure why, but this is because of you."

Music starts to boom from the ballroom, signaling that everyone should start to get situated.

"You're saved by the bell, Davis," Vicky says, pointing her finger in his face again. She means business. "I'm going to get to the bottom of this. I'm calling Pearson as soon as this show is over, and I'm telling him everything. The Twitter account, the texts, everything! I'll tell him this ridiculous story about Jim. The medics said he gave a statement to the cops. There's a record of the whole thing. You're not getting away with whatever you're trying to do."

I place my hand on Vicky's shoulder to try to calm her down. Everything she's saying is valid, but she should be concerned with herself and her nomination and possible win right now. She shouldn't be getting worked up over this.

"Don't let Davis ruin this for you," I say. "Let's go inside." I turn back to him. "And you better follow, because none of us know what the hell is next."

I guide Vicky and Suzanne in front of me when I feel my phone vibrate in my pocket. I grab it and check, still waiting to hear from Nicole. It's her.

> *I'm fine and the kids are fine. We ordered in from Antonio's. I'll see you soon. Xoxo*

I let out a breath of air, thankful that she has other things to tend to. Not that she's a Twitter maniac, but I'm glad she's not keeping up with any of today's shenanigans, including seeing me being accused of murder. Out of sight, out of mind. It's bad enough that she thinks I'm in danger because of Kristin, and she has the new pregnancy to deal with.

So do I. I've barely had a chance to let it sink in. I can't wait until this ceremony is over so I can go straight home to my family.

People congregate toward Vicky as soon as we walk in. The same fake-ass people who tore her apart hours ago are now all *I never believed what they were saying* and *I hope you win!* and *Good for you for setting the record straight.* The same people look at me with narrowed eyes, still wondering if I'm the killer du jour, but Vicky waves off their accusatory stares and mentions how stupid it is that people believe I'm a killer too.

"You Twitter mobsters will really listen to anything without facts, won't you?" she says with a smile and a wink to the latest one who apologizes. Kill them with kindness.

Bad choice of words.

But thank you, Vicky, for defending me at all. Jim's an asshole for cheating on you. And if he's lying about being attacked just for sympathy, I won't let him forget it.

The four of us stay close as appetizers and glasses of champagne go around. I grab a chicken satay stick and a mini beef tenderloin despite my wings and fries combo from earlier. Suzanne grabs a champagne off a tray and places it on the table with Vicky's name on it, then she sits down and concentrates on her phone. Davis, of course, is working the room like he's George Clooney, and people fawn over him like he is too.

I hate to be petty, and I know authors are supposed to support other authors no matter what, but I hope someone takes this guy down a peg. I jam my mini tenderloin in my mouth and watch Davis press palms, fake-laugh, and stare intently at everyone with a concerned look on his face, like he's really listening to what they're saying. After spending most of the day with him, I know he only does what's good for Davis. Everyone else exists to further his agenda.

In the book I wrote with Kristin, the big reveal came at the awards ceremony. That the co-author—effectively, me, if this situation were fiction—was the killer. If I were writing today's events as a book, I'd make sure the reveal happened at this ceremony, because everyone will be watching.

Too bad this is real life and not fiction.

48

SUZANNE SHIH

Friday, 7:45 P.M.

Thank God for this awards ceremony right now because no one is paying attention to Twitter. Everyone is catching up and hugging each other and talking about the successes and failures they've had. New releases hitting the stores next Tuesday. Their publisher not exercising their option clause. It's like the Oscars for writers, and all anyone wants is to hold that little statue.

No one is glued to their phone in their camaraderie.

That's good, because right now, the ones who aren't here are commenting on a tweet from @MPaloozaNxt2Die. The tweet?

> *I'm sure everyone has seen* Misery. *Looks like Suzanne Shih was about to club off Kristin Bailey's feet #murderpalooza #kristin-bailey #suzanneshih*

Oh em gee.

Attached?

A few screenshots of some of my emails to Kristin and a copy of the cease-and-desist letter from the publisher's attorney.

I nervously look around the room, but all I see are glasses clinking and people huddled together in groups. Davis is off with a bunch of people I don't know—possibly agents and publishers—and Vicky and Mike are together, speaking with a few of the other nominees.

I'm alone, which is how I need it to be right now as I investigate. I scroll through tweets over and over until I'm sure I'm causing carpal tunnel syndrome in my thumb.

@MPaloozaNxt2Die OMG who did this? Who's #Suzan-neShih? #murderpalooza

Suzanne Shih never stopped! Holy shit she's off her fucking rocker. Did the cops see this yet? #murderpalooza #Justice-ForKristin #SuzanneShih #Stalker #FuckOffSuzanne #Murderer

And we have a winner! Now we know the truth, finally #murderpalooza #SuzanneShih #Murder #Guilty #Stalker #WereAllGonnaDie #whosnext

Kristin Bailey was literally stalked by this #SuzanneShih and no one did a damn thing and now she's dead. Are y'all proud? #murderpalooza

I can't believe #SuzanneShih had to resort to violence. It's never the answer. I hope someone fucking kills her next #murderpalooza

The hypocrisy is glowing like blinking neon, but no one on Twitter sees it. Looks like Mike is off the hook. They're coming for me.

Do tears come to my eyes? No.

I break into a slow smile. My name is a *hashtag*.

I'm famous.

"What's going on?"

It's Mike's voice. I turn around, and he's arrived at the table with Vicky.

"Oh. Nothing. Just catching up on my emails," I say.

"Is there any more news about Julie Keane?" He whispers it, probably unsure which name to call her.

"Um, I haven't looked."

Crap. I'm about to get caught. They're going to open their phones and search @MPaloozaNxt2Die's account. They're going to see the tweet and the documents, and I'm going to be banished by everyone else at the conference, and I'm—

The lights start to dim.

"Showtime," Mike says to Vicky with a smile, then his eyes search the room. "Where's that prick Davis?"

I follow his gaze and see Davis walking toward the table, elbows hooked with Penelope Jacques. Penelope should be here for Vicky right now, but Davis really knows how to work the room. He escorts her to the table and gives her the seat on one side of Vicky while Mike occupies the other. I sit next to Mike, and Davis next to Penelope. There's an empty seat between us. Good.

Jim's seat.

"Is this seat taken?"

I turn around because I recognize the Italian accent.

"Vita. I've been calling you for hours," Mike says with an edge to his voice, and he doesn't seem pleased to see her. How could you not be pleased to see your agent?

She nods, presses her lips together, and puts her hand over her heart. "*Mi dispiace*. I'm sorry. Lot's going on with the killings, yeah?" She looks at me, and her eyes are dragon fire. "We need to talk when this is over."

Talk about an edge to your voice. I think I shit my pants. I already know what happened; she read Twitter, and she knows what's going on. She's going to drop me. She didn't know that Kristin and I were . . . connected.

She has no idea who she signed, and what I see on her face is regret.

What's the saying? Even bad publicity is good publicity? Something like that? That remains to be seen.

The emcee steps on the stage and taps the microphone.

I smile. I'll be fine if Vita drops me. I'm famous.

49.

VICKY OVERTON

Friday, 8:05 P.M.

Thank God Vita Gallo took the empty seat. I don't think I could
bear it if I win and am reminded that Jim isn't here. Gut punch.
Still, I wonder about what Davis said about him. He couldn't
have been faking it. Why would he do that? And why tell Davis
about it? It doesn't make sense.

I try not to think about it. Damn it, this is my moment.
Maybe. Hopefully. Hopefully not. I don't know what's going
to happen to me, or to any of us, tonight. On the table, there's
a beautiful embossed card, which I know I'm taking home to
frame and hang on my wall. I'll see if the conference can get me
the PDF of it so I can get a two-foot-by-three-foot foam poster-
board made for my office.

MURDERPALOOZA
THRILLER OF THE YEAR
NOMINEES
Kevin Candela
Husband's Double Life

Marco Crimmins
When the Blood Dried

Kristin Bailey
Secrets of the Lake

Larry Kuo
A Killer Among Liars

Vicky Overton
A Friend Like You

I didn't think I was going to geek out after seeing it, but here I am. Geeking out. Look at my name, fancy and listed with amazing authors. I guess this is how Stalkanne goes through life, all starry-eyed.

Penelope is seated next to me. She's changed into a dress as well, and she reapplied her makeup, which is no longer dripping down her face. She keeps grasping my forearm and giving it a little shake while smiling. It's like she knows she's been a shit to me and she's trying to make up for it, as if I'm that starved for affection. Does she think I'm going to win, and she wants to get back into my good graces? She still hasn't apologized for ditching me with the bill this afternoon.

My head feels like it's full of oatmeal. The emcee is on the stage and people are laughing at what he's saying, but it's muffled to me. It's the nerves. I golf clap along with everyone else when I'm supposed to, and then the thunderous applause starts, and everyone stands as the president of Murderpalooza takes the stage.

Jonathan DeLuca is a tall, slender man in his early sixties. Blessed with a full head of dark hair and what appears to be a summer tan, he looks much younger. Dressed to the nines—a three-piece suit, vest and all—he exudes confidence, which he's got to be faking right now. The entire conference is a hot mess. His smile is assured when he takes center stage, then wavers as the applause dies down and we take our seats again. He taps the microphone.

"Thank you for the wonderful introduction," he starts. "As Peter said, I'm Jonathan DeLuca, President of Murderpalooza. For two decades, we've prided ourselves on being the premiere conference for thriller, suspense, and mystery books. This has always been a safe space for attendees."

The room is dead silent, waiting to hear what he's going to say about Kristin.

"As you are all aware, we lost a dear friend today—a true talent in every way. Kristin Bailey was beautiful and smart and taken from us far too soon. Everyone who knew her, loved her. She selflessly donated her time as a PitchWars mentor five years in a row and supported debut authors by featuring them on her social media platforms on their launch day."

That part is true. My book was featured when it came out last year, when I liked her and she wasn't screwing my boyfriend. She connected her fans with newer authors. She knew the power she had, and maybe I wouldn't be where I am today without her.

Maybe.

Jonathan continues. "Please be assured that I am working closely with Gerald Bivona, the head of security for the hotel, to piece together whatever we can. Kristin deserves answers and justice, and we won't stop until we know who has committed this horrible deed."

There's another round of golf claps, and Penelope dabs at her eyelids with the cocktail napkin that was stuck to the bottom of her champagne glass. She and Kristin were together for her whole career.

"I've also recently heard about another author's death, and again, we are working with the investigator and hotel security to see if the deaths of Kristin Bailey and Julie Keane are connected."

Oh, hell yes, they're connected, and as I promised Davis earlier, I'll be telling Pearson every goddamn thing about today. Let him find out what Davis's connection is to both of them and her brother Jason.

"Now we'll feature our five nominees with their thirty-second introductory videos."

The lights dim, and a blank screen descends from the ceiling. It comes to life with a countdown reel. Five, four, three, two, one, and then the first one is up. A spotlight from the side of the room shines on a table a few down from where I'm sitting while the video plays.

"Hi, I'm Kevin Candela, from Chicago, IL, and thank you for nominating *Husband's Double Life*. The story questions how far you'd go for love when trust is broken. Do the bonds of marriage really mean for better or for worse? Or does 'worse' mean you'd risk your own sanity and freedom for another?"

Everyone claps as Kevin stands up and takes a bow. Jesus, am I going to have to curtsey or something? I'm the only woman left. I can't even follow Kristin for guidance.

The spotlight trains on the table right next to mine, and the second video starts.

"What's up, everyone, I'm Marco Crimmins from Hoboken, NJ, author of *When the Blood Dried*. It follows the actions of a serial killer who falls in love with his victim's religious mother, but he still can't curb a taste for killing. Will she find out who she's let into her life, and in the end, was losing her daughter God's plan? And is God's plan sparing his life or seeking revenge? I'm excited to be nominated for this award tonight. Thank you."

He too stands and bows to applause. Shit.

He sits when the claps die down, and a lump crawls up my throat when the next video begins to play. Her voice. Alive.

In the mess of today, I forgot how beautiful she was, because I wanted to hate her. Her curly hair is pulled off her face tied with a pink bandana doubling as a headband. She's wearing a light pink sweater set, and her arms are folded at a table in front of her. Her smile is radiant.

"Hi, I'm Kristin Bailey. I grew up in Heimer, Iowa, but New York City has been my home for the last five years. Thank you for nominating *Secrets of the Lake* for the Murderpalooza award! It's a story about a summer resort centered around fictional Lake Miller in the Midwest. Every summer, the same families rent the cabins around the lake, and the main family, the Claypools, begin to learn that having insight into people's lives for two months out of the year isn't enough, and they don't really know the people they've considered friends. Especially after a first-time family is slaughtered."

With no table for her to spotlight, the video pauses at the end, Kristin's face smiling and bright. Everyone stands and the applause is thunderous. It must be, because even I'm clapping.

I begin to fidget as the tape for Larry Kuo starts to roll and he talks about *A Killer Among Liars*. Do I curtsey or no? I can't bow. Do I wave? Curl my hand like the Queen? Smile like a deranged robot? Oh my God, do I have lipstick on my teeth?

"You okay?" Mike whispers.

I lick the invisible lipstick off my top teeth. "Mmhmm."

"Don't worry. We're here for support."

"I just don't know what to expect with this whole Twitter thing. I'm a little scared. I don't want to stand up."

The clapping starts again, so I know Larry Kuo is done. Shit! Then it comes, like a damn spaceship. That spotlight hits the table as I sit there like an idiot and all eyes turn on me as my video starts. Ha, I turned this in two months ago. My hair was still mousy brown, and I'm wearing a tank top in the video—what was I thinking? Whatever, Penelope said to try to be relatable. It was May in Florida; I was probably already on my third shower.

"Hi everyone, I'm Vicky Overton from St. Petersburg, FL, and my book is called *A Friend Like You*. It follows two best friends—who couldn't be more different—into adulthood. One murdered someone in high school out of revenge, and the other helped her cover it up. But was it really revenge or was it plotted from the start? When a mysterious letter shows up, it turns out someone else knows the truth. I'm humbled and excited for the nomination. Thank you, and good luck to my fellow nominees, Kevin Candela, Marco Crimmins, Kristin Bailey, and Larry Kuo."

The applause starts and I stand and smile—at who, I have no idea. The spotlight is in my eyes, thank God, so I can't see anything anyway. I decide to go with the Queen wave, then smooth my dress in the back and sit down quickly. Thank God that's over with.

And I didn't get shot or stabbed. So that's a plus.

It's over.

It's so far from it.

Jonathan DeLuca comes back to center stage. "Our original award presenter had a last-minute emergency, but thankfully, someone familiar with the industry happened to be on hand to read the winner. Some of you may have already worked with him, even though you'll never admit it and he'll never tell." He laughs and makes a *shushing* face with his finger to his lips. "Most of you will know his name, but now you'll get to see the man behind the curtain. May I present developmental editor Jim Russell."

I knock over a glass of water, and my eyes immediately meet Davis's.

I told you so, he mouths.

What the actual fuck is Jim doing? Presenting at this ceremony? How did he know who to contact? People clap as Jim walks out onto the stage, and yes, it's him. It's developmental editor Jim Russell. My boyfriend. Ex-boyfriend.

The killer.

How do I know that? Because he's flawless, in a suit and tie, and there's no cut on his forehead. He made it up, and that makes Davis right and me terrified. He's been playing all of us from the beginning. He wanted us here together tonight. Oh no.

I turn to Mike. "What the hell is going on?"

His face is stone. "I have no idea, but I think Davis was right."

THE MORNING OF THE MURDER

Between Suzanne Shih showing up at her door that morning, and Diana Fleming's surprise visit, it was no wonder Kristin was confused.

She grabbed coffee at the lobby café with Bethany after their panel. She invited Kevin Candela and Marco Crimmins to sit with them when she saw them passing through. She didn't want to be alone. The bigger the crowd, the better. For once, she wanted to look unapproachable.

But after they'd ordered and settled in, she realized Diana was also in the café. When she caught her eyes from across the room, she averted her stare, hopefully letting her know *Later. Not now.*

Kristin needed someone by her side as she went to the elevators. She couldn't be accosted by Diana in public. She knew how it would look, so she grabbed her stomach.

"Ouch," she said, putting her other hand over her mouth.

"Are you okay?" Kevin asked.

Kristin screwed up her face and forced a burp. Her little brothers taught her how to do that when she was twelve. "Mmm,

I'm not sure. I think it was the bacon this morning. I thought it smelled funny. I've felt like crap since then."

"That's hardly exclusive to the bacon. I don't know how anyone eats the buffet food."

"I think I need to lay down." She looked at Bethany. "Can you walk me up to my room in case I pass out?"

"Oh my God, of course. Do you need me to call someone?" she asked.

Kristin waved her hand in front of her face. "No, I'm sure I just need to rest. I'm going to skip the next couple hours of panels. I'll be at *Settings: Beach, City, or Country* at eleven."

"Okay, great. Let's go."

Kristin kept her coffee cup in her hand as they left and navigated the crowd to the elevators. This time, there was a line, and she kept looking behind her. Bethany had her by the arm as Kristin played up her fake stomach illness, and after making sure she was settled in and had water, Bethany left to attend a nine-A.M. panel.

Kristin grabbed her phone and texted Jim as soon as the door closed.

I need to see you.

He wrote back immediately.

Vicky has a meeting at ten. I'll be over as soon as she leaves.

That worked out perfectly. She could be alone with Jim in her room for an hour before her next panel.

At least she felt safe with him.

50
DAVIS WALTON
Friday, 8:25 P.M.

I knew that guy was full of shit. Look at him up there, all dressed up, with no gash on his head. Just like I said, and no one wanted to believe me.

What's he planning on doing to us? To me?

What does he know?

The four of us eye each other nervously. Suzanne's mouth is open, Mike looks like he aged two decades, and Vicky is dabbing the tablecloth, matting up the spilled water, but she looks like she doesn't know whether to shit herself or run screaming.

Penelope looks at Vicky. "Hmm. Isn't that your boyfriend?"

Vicky's eyes look like a Barbie doll's, painted on and too wide. "I don't know what's going on," she answers.

Good save. She doesn't have to explain the *is he or isn't he* now. I think he's a damn murderer, but what is he planning to do to us? Why now?

Oh God. Vicky is going to win, isn't she? He's going to make her walk on the stage in front of everyone, and something terrible is going to happen.

Then why did Kristin make me sell my soul to Jonathan DeLuca to make sure she'd get the votes to win? Why? Because of Jim. Change of plans when a murderer enters the scene.

"Vicky," I whisper. "You can't go up there if you win."

"What nonsense is that?" Penelope asks, quite loudly. "Of course she's going up there if she wins."

I draw her and Vicky in closer. Let Mike and the kid huddle with their agent. Penelope is ours. "I don't think you know what's going on," I say. "It's dangerous."

Penelope isn't having it. "No, it's not. I saw what everyone was saying this morning about Vicky. It's just fucking Twitter. People also thought it was him, right now they think it's her." She points to Mike, then Suzanne. "None of it means anything."

"What do you mean, her?"

"Those stalker documents I sent you. You put them online, right? They're everywhere."

I push my chair away from the table and grab my phone and look at the @MPaloozaNxt2Die account. Sure as I'm Davis Walton, they—Jim—got access and put them online. He must've gotten them from Kristin's computer after he murdered her.

"You and I weren't the only ones to have these docs. Look, there's been something going on all day. I haven't had a chance to give you details until I knew what was going on, but someone has it out for me. For me, Mike, Vicky, and that kid Suzanne. They've been putting things online about us all day. Bad stuff, Penny."

She blinks a few times. "What did they put online about you?"

The truth? Nothing at this point. Which means . . .

Jim grabs the microphone and clears his throat.

"Thriller writers are special, as you all know. I won't say I've worked with any of you—" He scans the room. "—but

I won't say I haven't either." Small laughter. *Cha cha cha, what a good guy.* "The best thing about thrillers, suspense, and mysteries is you never know how they're going to end. In romance, they always end up together. In fantasy, the princess storms the castle. But thrillers, they're a game of cat and mouse that only a select few can figure out. You have to be looking for the twist. The red herrings." He looks at our table. "The killer."

Vicky is covering her mouth, and there are tears in her eyes. Mike has a hand on her shoulder. Suzanne is filming it.

"So I'd like to present the award for the one who did it best last year, and hopefully, they'll continue to do it for years to come." He removes an envelope from underneath the podium where the award is being housed. "The Murderpalooza Thriller of the Year Award goes to . . ."

We hold our breath. Oh shit.

"Kristin Bailey for *Secrets of the Lake.*"

Music plays, her picture returns to the video screen, and everyone stands and claps. Of course Kristin won. I knew she would because I helped make it happen. Then what's the story with Jim being here, on stage? Mike whispers something like *sorry* into Vicky's ear and gives her a good shake. Then Penelope hugs her and says it's going to be okay, maybe next year, but I'm sure my debut *Memories Gone Wrong* will be nominated next year, and no one will stand a chance against me. I don't think Vicky cares that she lost.

Jim continues. "Accepting the award for Kristin Bailey will be . . ."

He looks to the left of the stage and waves someone out.

"Kristin Bailey."

Hushed gasps turn into howls when Kristin Bailey walks onto the stage, her bright green dress vivid against her dark skin and hair.

It's not a hologram. It's her. It's Kristin.

She's alive.

She walks toward Jim, who has his arms open wide. She hugs him, and they double kiss on the cheek like they're French—Penelope does this all the time—but it's probably because they've been fucking.

I could fill a pool with the amount of sweat I'm producing right now.

Kristin is alive, which means I'm dead. Davis Walton is about to be a memory.

51

MIKE BROOKS

Friday, 8:30 P.M.

My first thought is disbelief. *You've got to be kidding me.*

My second thought is genuine. My friend is alive, and my heart gushes.

But why was she messing with me today?

52

SUZANNE SHIH

Friday, 8:30 P.M.

I rub my eyes. Oh em gee. It's really her. She's alive.

God, I love her.

53
VICKY OVERTON

Friday, 8:30 P.M.

Look at him, up there, rubbing it in. Go ahead, kiss her in front of everyone. Show the world your dirty little secret.

I just don't understand why they were screwing around with me all day. Why would Kristin fake her death?

Why the fake head gash, Jim?

Who's really behind the Twitter account? Why, why, why, why, why . . .

54

KRISTIN BAILEY

Friday, 8:35 P.M.

Well, here we are. It worked. Perfectly. Only five people knew I was alive—well, besides everyone I hired—and it actually worked. Gotta love a good non-disclosure agreement and the best publicist in the business.

I let out a breath; it's over. Everyone that the writers and agents talked to today were hired by me. Pearson, the medics, the people in NYPD uniforms—they're all actors. Thank God I had the help of the hotel manager and the head of security, and my publicist Lauren took care of handling the pubs and the real NYPD. What patrons are going to call the cops if they think the cops are already there on the scene, taking care of business? Hey, all publicity is good publicity, right? A murder at a conference, complete with a zipped body bag containing a CPR dummy being wheeled out on a stretcher, got this hotel a *ton* of attention.

I chuckle internally, because no one cared about the truth, as was evidenced all day with the retweets and the accusations. Of course, the @MPaloozaNxt2Die account—me and Jim—had a few unknowing helpers to do some of my dirty work. We watched as they banded together, then turned on each other, then came together to band against one.

Exactly how I would have executed it in a book. People can be so predictable.

Now the thriller novel I've created for today unfolds in front of me. People in the audience scream, others take pictures or film. One guy tries to make his way on stage (thanks for keeping them back, Gerald Bivona, my hotel security buddy). No one believes that I came back from being murdered because it makes them wrong. They were following the herd. Zero evidence besides a few tweets saying it was so, some fake "police tape, do not cross" over my hotel room door that I bought on Amazon, and a few actors in cop uniforms.

Fake. Fake. Fake.

I kept camp in my room behind that police tape all day, with my laptop, playing games with them. For one reason.

I whisper in Jim's ear. "We did it. Don't worry, everything will work out with Vicky," I say with a smile. "She'll understand once you explain it."

He nods and rubs my shoulder. "I know. I wanted to tell her, but she can't keep a secret to save her life. She'll see this is as much for her as it is to bust him. Ready to take that asshole down?"

I've never been more ready for anything. Showtime.

"Okay, can everyone settle down?" Jim says into the microphone. "Our award winner would like to say a few words."

I smooth out my jade dress, the one my mama always says makes my skin radiate. I wish my parents and my two brothers were able to see this, what I've accomplished in just one day, but they're still back in Iowa. I'm here, I have all the interest I want, and it's time to make everyone proud. They can read about it later online—a hoax this elaborate might even make national news.

"Hi," I say, and my voice cracks. I laugh nervously. "Sorry. I'm still getting used to being alive." There are small laughs throughout the crowd, but mostly pure, unadulterated attention. I'm the shiny new toy under the tree at Christmas, and my audience is a bunch of five-year-olds. I might as well say *ho, ho, ho*.

"I'm sure you're all wondering what happened today. I have a lot to explain," I continue. I look down at the award. It's engraved with *Murderpalooza Thriller of the Year. Kristin Bailey, Secrets of the Lake*. I'm so proud, but I also want to smash it. It's not real. "First and foremost, I want to say I can't accept this award. I didn't win it fair and square. There were bribes in play. I'll be requesting a new one to be made for whoever had the second most votes, and I'll pay for the engraving myself. If Jonathan DeLuca has a job after today, which I'm betting he won't, I'll make sure he gets it taken care of."

I scan the room of my peers until I find Jonathan DeLuca sitting at *my* table with some other Murderpalooza executives, and I stifle my laughter when he turns to give a nasty look to Davis.

Davis Walton. You have no idea what's coming, asshole.

"I want to tell you a story about how I started out, back in the Midwest. All of you must belong to a writing group in one form or another. Well I was part of a great one, one that I joined after meeting the authors at a mini writing conference. We were young and starry-eyed, and we had not only champagne wishes and caviar dreams, but also delusions of grandeur.

"One of my closest friends from that group was an uber talented young man named Jason Fleming. Unfortunately, he suffered from a massive case of imposter syndrome and never thought he was good enough. He was; he was one of the best writers I'd ever known. But not everyone in the group was as supportive as they claimed to be. Particularly, a terrible writer named Tommy Johnson." I shoot that asshole Davis a look, but he's not paying attention. He's got Penelope Jacques' ear, and he's talking a mile a minute.

You can't get ahead of this, you prick. Nice try.

"Jason Fleming died in a car accident six years ago, but not before he gave me his completed novel to read, which I still treasure to this day. I recently became close with his sister, Diana, to see if his family would let me help them find a way to publish the book posthumously for my dear friend. Diana was helpful, having been a relatively successful self-published author herself. You all may know her as Julie Keane, the romance writer."

Gasps travel throughout the audience, and I look to my left, where she's smiling from the opening in the curtain.

"Come on out, Diana. Say hello to your thriller peers."

Another resurrection, and you bet I'm helping this girl get her foot in the Thriller World door. It's usually slammed shut on romance writers. Not on my watch.

When she walks onto the stage, there's a hush. Of course, no one will say anything now that she's here, with me. Five minutes ago, everyone was spreading the gossip that she "died." Why did they think that? Because it was all over Twitter. One person from a random account (me) can say one thing on a popular hashtag (#murderpalooza), and I never had to do anything else to get people to believe it. Julie Keane was dead, murdered, and it was repeated as fact. Over and over. Even the conference made a statement about it. All because they believed tweets. Zero evidence. Just tweets.

Diana waves to everyone, and I hand her the award, and she takes it and exits the stage.

It's still my turn to talk, and she knows what's coming. She's been helping me since Jim's developmental-editor genius kicked in months ago and we decided to make today a novel. I had no idea she'd made it into New York yesterday—she didn't get to the bar until after I left. She figured it would be best to fuck with Davis in person. She spoke with Jim last night, and he had our partner in security put condom wrappers and a lipstick in Davis's room when they knew he'd be passed out in a drunken stupor. Jim came to my room in the middle of the night and told me after they'd done it, and we plotted on how to add her to the game. Diana never touched that asshole.

But it was fun to make him think they had sex.

"Anyway," I continue, "imagine my surprise when I read Jason's book. Not the first time, but the second time. How? I got an advanced reader's copy of it, about to be published with much fanfare by another publisher. I knew it was the same book because I have the original. The ARC I got was a different title. It was also by a different author: Tommy Johnson. Yes, the bad writer from the group stole Jason's book and claimed it as his own. He never thought anyone would find out because he uses a pen name too, which I found out when I saw his author photo on the back."

This. Is. What. I. Came. Here. For.

"Ladies and gentlemen, you all know Tommy Johnson as Davis Walton. Tommy, would you like to stand up?"

55

DAVIS WALTON

Friday, 8:45 P.M.

"You *stole* Jason Fleming's book?" Vicky screams my way. "Your real name isn't Davis Walton?"

"Wow, you asshole," Mike says.

"That was the connection," Suzanne says.

"Davis, what is she talking about?" Penelope asks. "Tell me this isn't true."

It's not just them. Everyone in the audience is staring at me with mock horror, over acting for the cameras that are on, the videos being taken. The murmur has gotten louder, like a game of telephone, people talking from one table to the next to the next until everyone stares at me and waits for an answer.

I look up at Kristin, who is smiling like a Cheshire cat.

That's why she made me bribe Jonathan DeLuca to make sure she won the award. She planned this, to humiliate me in front of everyone. She wanted the platform, to make sure she couldn't be questioned.

She could've just accused me on Twitter. She's right; everyone would've believed it.

No, instead she made a whole game of it. Getting Vicky, Mike, and Suzanne involved. They were used. All for me.

I have no defense, and everyone needs me, Tommy Johnson, to say something. God, I've been thinking about how I killed Tommy Johnson all day long, how I gave him up and left him behind in the Midwest and moved to sunny LA to start over. Armed with my new novel—Jason's novel—I submitted it for publication under a pseudonym, then legally changed my name. Davis Walton. It's powerful; it gave me confidence. I'm Davis Walton. I say it to myself ten times a day.

But I'm not. I'm untalented Tommy Johnson, basic as fuck.

Before I start to cry in front of everyone like a pussy, I go with a pure Davis move.

"Jim Russell has been sleeping with Kristin Bailey!" I say it because it's true. Deflect. It's true, right?

They're both staring from the stage, smiling, getting off on the fact that that's made up too. It has to be. The look on Vicky's face says so—she doesn't believe it either, not anymore. It was part of the game, a reason for the three of them to feel threatened and help expose me.

They have had suspicions about me for the last half of the day. I move to say something.

"I—"

There's nothing there. I can't write, and now I can't speak either.

I *what?* What's next? Am I supposed to say Mike killed her because that's how it happened in the book? How ridiculous. She's not dead; she's right there, on stage, ruining my entire life. And Suzanne? She's a stalker. So what? She didn't kill Kristin. I don't know who to blame to get all the eyes off me.

Penelope looks at me like I'm a monster. All eyes are on her too, and for the wrong reasons. I was making her rich, and now she sees the contracts being null and void. Goodbye, Penelope. Goodbye, Bee. Goodbye to my film agent Susan, my publisher Gary, my publicist Billy.

I'm no one. I'm Tommy Johnson.

I stand up as the shouts are being hurled in my direction. Audible boos and hisses.

Then I tuck my tail between my legs and walk out of the ballroom.

56

KRISTIN BAILEY

Friday, 8:45 P.M.

"Well, that's that," I say with a chuckle as Davis gives me the finger before he exits the ballroom. Could've been for me, could've been for everyone in this room. I hope it was for me; I'd love to be the one to claim his destruction.

Then I redirect my attention to the table at the base of the stage. "Could I have just accused Tommy Johnson with my proof? Sure. But where's the fun in that? It was much better to humiliate him where he thought he was a hero. Where everyone loved him, no questions asked. Because he looks the way he looks." I shrug. It's true.

There are light chuckles throughout the room. They know I'm right.

"Wait, folks, there's one more. When I said I didn't earn this trophy, I meant it. I blackmailed good ole Tommy Johnson to make sure I won and got up here so I could tell you my story. Jonathan DeLuca coerced people to vote for me, with promises of *the* Davis Walton to promote everything Murderpalooza so he could double prices next year. It's always about money and screwing over the real people who love mysteries and thrillers. Let's give Jonathan a hand." I gesture to him and begin the clapping as Jonathan sits red-faced. He whispers to another old male colleague and then they, too, stand and leave, to the same sentiments as Tommy.

I look over at the two people I've used for selfish reasons: to be here, where I am. Vicky and Mike. They'll get the fruits of my labor. I've made sure of it. They deserve it.

"A few personal notes, if I'm allowed." Of course I am. People are listening to me with bated breath. "I started this Twitter game this morning with the intention of banding two of my favorite writers together, only to make them suspicious of each other, and then gang up on Tommy. It worked. They got the hints I've been throwing out all day, that Tommy—Davis—was the problem. It's a great plot for a book if it's executed correctly. But for it to come together, I had to make them think they were in danger. Living in a novel."

Suzanne . . . well, I'll deal with her later. I added her as part of this game this morning to expose her stalking tendencies after she came to my room with some love poem or something. Then, when Gerald and I were plotting in my room in the afternoon, we caught her with her face pressed up against my hotel room door. What was she thinking? If I wasn't already dead all day, I'd think she *was* trying to kill me.

"First, I'd like to publicly apologize to Vicky Overton. My hints and stunts today have made her think that I was sleeping with her boyfriend, who happens to be my illustrious hoax partner and brilliant developmental editor, Jim Russell. I hope it goes without saying that I'm not sleeping with him." When

I catch her gaze, she has tears in her eyes. "Vicky, I'm sorry. Jim and I were working together a few months ago when I read Tommy's ARC and found out what he did, and I vented. Jim helped me come up with the whole plan. It was his idea to make today like a thriller novel. He really is good at what he does! For a successful novel, you need more than one player to think they're in danger. Keep ramping up the tension. From the fake texts—even the racy ones a few weeks ago—to the fake attack to him leaving and spending the rest of the day with me, well, it worked, didn't it?"

People chuckle. Everyone is looking at Vicky admirably. *What a good sport!* And finally, Penelope stares at Vicky with the hunger to make her a star, as she should've in the beginning, instead of that fucking liar Tommy. Maybe now she will.

And I'll do everything in my power to support her.

Then, with a full and warm heart, I look at my good friend Mike.

"Mike Brooks, good Lord what I must've put you through today. I'm so sorry. But hey . . . the secret is out! We wrote a book together about someone being murdered at Murderpalooza! What everyone needs to know is, it's Mike's book, really. I was just critique support."

It's not his, and that's not true. We worked on it together. But I have a feeling I'll be inundated with other publishing offers after this whole thing is over. Mike deserves to have the hit. And that manuscript *is* going to be a hit, now. He won't forget what I'm doing for him—he's too good a guy.

"To all the editors and publishers—and I recognize quite a few of you here right now—look no further than Mike Brooks. I believe his agent was going to try to sell the book this weekend. Vita Gallo is right there next to him. You know what to do."

The look on Mike's face assures me that if I had to, I would do this whole charade over again. Vita grips one of his hands, and Vicky the other. Pride.

Suzanne looks at me expectantly.

I bet she's waiting for me to say something that's going to level her up, but that bitch is crazy, and I won't do it. I had Gerald lock her ass in the elevator to scare the shit out of her the way she's been doing to me. But *crazy* doesn't get affected the same way, and since this whole day was like a thriller novel, I don't need my real murder to be the last plot twist.

I wink again at Mike and Vicky, then look back to my adoring fans. "Let's take this to the bar, shall we?"

57

MIKE BROOKS

Friday, 9:00 P.M.

My mouth hangs open as I think about everything that's happened today.

Kristin was never dead. I was never in danger. All the murder accusations are finished. This may be the best day of my life, because not only were the horror parts of the day not true, but Nicole is pregnant and I'm about to be a huge star again. It's all falling into place.

Kristin and Jim are still on stage speaking to each other as everyone stands to go to the bar. I've got to get a minute alone with her. Or an hour. Or the rest of the week. I'll never be able to thank her, despite the hellish way today started out.

I whip out my phone. Nicole will understand.

Ceremony is over. Kristin is alive, it was a PR stunt for the book. It's going to sell huge, Nic. I'll be later than I promised, but you can spend the time looking online for a bigger apartment in a full-service building. Anything you want.

Anything. My life is back on track.

"I can't believe it," Vicky says. I see it in her face, the shock and the awe that we were played and that we're about to be players.

"I know. What a day, huh?"

Vita tugs at my arm. "Let's get the superstar to the bar to start fielding offers, yeah?"

I smile. "Go ahead. I'll meet you up there in a few." I look at Kristin on stage. "I've got to talk to her about some stuff. Today was an interesting day. I'll tell you about it later."

Vita's phone rings in her hand, and her eyes widen. "It's Bee Henry. She just lost her cash cow, and I bet she needs a place to throw those Davis Walton dollars." She connects the call. "Hello, Vita Gallo speaking," she says as she follows the herd to the bar.

"I'm so proud of you, Mike," Vicky says. "I'm sorry I got judgey on you earlier, about what happened between you and Suzanne."

I decide to be honest with Vicky. "It wasn't my finest moment, but nothing like what you're thinking happened. A quick lapse in judgment."

She nods. "Most of it was Davis playing mind games with me, always keeping the attention off him. I can't believe he's a fraud. I mean, I can, but still."

"I believe it. What a douche."

Suzanne appears at our side, her mouth set in a hard line, her arms crossed, fire in her eyes. "Kristin didn't mention me. Why didn't she mention my name? I was in this too, you know. I was sitting right here."

I look her up and down and shrug. Vicky is silent, and I really don't know why Kristin didn't mention Suzanne.

"My name is a hashtag, you know. My dirty laundry was exposed too. You were both accused of murdering her, which obviously wasn't true. Davis—Tommy, whatever his name is—is finished. But me? I get to be known as a stalker now." She points her finger in my face. "Vita is going to drop me, and you better convince her not to, or else."

Oh, she's not going there. Not now. I have my balls back. "Or else what?"

She purses her lips and raises an eyebrow. "I'll tell everyone about the bar last winter."

My face drops, and Vicky steps in, saving me.

"What *about* the bar? The watch thing?" Vicky asks. "I was there when I heard it from *you* about what happened. Mike was drunk and it slipped off as you were helping him into a cab. Don't think I won't come to his defense if you decide to slander him. Anything other than what you told us earlier is a lie."

I think Vicky may be my new best writer buddy in this world of thrillers.

Suzanne's upper lip twitches in response, and she taps at her phone while not meeting our eyes. "I'm going to text my boyfriend to meet me at the bar. I'll see you guys later."

She turns and leaves, and I exhale. "Thank you, Vicky."

Vicky pats me on the arm and looks toward the stage. Jim and Kristin are disengaging. "Well I guess you'll want to talk to Kristin, huh?"

I tilt my head toward the right. "I bet you want to get up there and talk to Jim too."

She laughs. "I guess it's time."

Kristin walks to the edge of the stage and descends the three steps toward us. Seeing her this close again fills my heart with such joy. I thought the next time I'd see her would be at a wake, hands folded over her chest while clutching rosary beads. She puts a finger in the air to indicate she'll be a minute and trains her eyes on Vicky first, then grabs her hand.

"Hey, Vicky. You have to know how sorry I am about how I made you feel today," Kristin says to her. "You know I like women sticking together. The most important thing was getting rid of Tommy, but that'll be good for you. You'll have Penelope's attention again."

"I know. Thank you," Vicky says, and they hug. It's not even the awkward *I-barely-know-you-but-let's-do-this* hug, it's a real one. Genuine and heartfelt. "I was just on my way to see Jim, but you should tell Diana to have the cops do a suicide note comparison with Davis's handwriting. Something tells me there's more to the story."

Holy shit. I never thought of that. Davis could be guilty of so many other things.

Leave it to the thriller writers. We always mention the bumbling detectives in our books. Not that Pearson was real, but still. We knew it was up to us to solve.

"By the way," Vicky adds, "you look brilliant tonight. Death agrees with you."

Kristin laughs. "Thanks. I know he wants to see you. Don't be too hard on him. He did this for you too."

Vicky shifts her head toward the stage and leaves. I'm alone with Kristin and I can't help it. I pick her up in a bear hug and lift her feet from the floor. I'm afraid I may kill her myself, crush her until she falls from my arms like a bag of bones. Satisfied with my greeting, I place her down and ask what I've been dying to ask.

"Kristin. I can't believe this. Why? Why would you give up the rights to this book? We worked so hard on it."

She waves her hand in front of her face. *No big deal.* "When I was up there, I told everyone I found out about Tommy when I was working with Jim. It's true. He's helping me develop an old manuscript, the one I wrote when I exchanged with Jason. I shelved it years ago but dusted it off recently. Jim's helping me make it better. You saw what he's capable of today—everything was a story that came from his mind. And not for nothing, I'm the girl who pulled this whole thing off. I'll probably have a pre-empt offer before the end of the night off a two-line pitch. We can both be huge. I don't need to hog the spotlight alone. I'm not Tommy."

I was wrong. As fantastic as she is, Vicky isn't going to be my thriller BFF. It is and always will be Kristin Bailey. The platonic love between us is real. It's surrounding me like the music on the speakers, the chatter of the guests, the air in my lungs.

So why do I still worry something sinister is going to happen?

58

SUZANNE SHIH

Friday, 9:10 P.M.

I never texted Constantine, even though I said I would. I need time to think about how to approach Kristin. Why didn't she mention my name? Doesn't she know about hashtag Suzanne Shih?

Speaking of . . . before I head into the bar, I check Twitter.

My stomach drops. I reload the page because this can't be right. The last time my name was hashtagged was like an hour ago. An hour! Why isn't anyone talking about me anymore? I was on the verge of infamy.

Oh right, Kristin Bailey resurrected from the dead and all that. Kristin Bailey this, Kristin Bailey that. I scroll the Murderpalooza hashtag until my thumbs hurt. All anyone is going to know me as is the stalker. She set it up. She put those documents of me online.

Breathe.

I decide to find Vita and confront her head-on. Whatever, maybe she'll like a "crazy" person as a client. She already likes my writing. Imagine what I could come up with now that everyone else knows about me and Kristin.

My plan is foiled because Constantine is already waiting at the bar. He's standing alone, wearing a T-shirt with his band's name on it—*really?*—and dark jeans with combat boots. His platinum hair looks wet and is pulled tightly off his face into a small man-bun. He's holding a bottle of beer, and from across the room, I see it's half empty.

I don't know why, but I get enraged. Part of me wants to walk up to him, throw the beer in his face, and tell him to go away and that I never want to see him again. He completely ruined this for me. Why is he here? I told him to wait until he heard from me. How am I supposed to kick my career into gear if he's waiting around all the time?

Kristin sent him that form to fill out. Kristin locked me in the elevator.

Kristin.

I see her coming into the bar, and she immediately gets mobbed. God, she looks beautiful. That green dress is a stunner, and she needs to know I'm on her side. That I'm not crazy. We're women in publishing. We need to support each other no matter what.

She's surrounded by the rest of the nominees, except Vicky. Everyone is hugging her. Wow, imagine getting to hug her! I inch closer, and they're telling her how happy they are that she's alive. Well duh, isn't everyone? She brushes a few wayward curls off her shoulder and smiles, thanking them. More people come over—publishers and agents—and Penelope says something like *you gave me a heart attack, I was getting stuff ready for your estate* and then they laugh and talk about what a douche Davis—Tommy, whatever—is.

Kristin is secure in her stance. Penelope grabs her hand and leads her over to Bee Henry, who's talking with Vita. There she is! With Bee! I take a deep breath to calm my center, smooth down my dress, and begin to walk over, but *of course.*

"Where have you been?"

Constantine. Standing in front of me, clutching that beer bottle by the neck. I want to rip it from his hand, crack it on the bar, and shove the sharp point in his ear. Not now.

"I told you to wait upstairs," I say, then curl my lip like Billy Idol. He hates when I make that face. Good.

"I've been up there all day. What kind of trouble have you gotten yourself into?"

I feel like I've been slapped. "Meaning?"

"I've had nothing to do all day, Suzanne. I started reading Murderpalooza stuff so we'd have something to talk about tonight. You were all over the hashtag earlier. I saw documents and things you sent to Kristin. Did you really do that or was it photoshopped? People are saying the most awful things."

I want to laugh. Constantine doesn't get it either. "That got blown out of proportion. Me and Kristin are friends."

"People thought you killed her! And then I read she's alive. What the hell has been going on today?"

Constantine is being confrontational, and that's not like him. He's, like, in love with me or whatever. I mean, he came here just to see me. But I can't deal with him right now.

"I have to talk to my agent. She's with a huge editor. Right there." I point to Vita huddled with Bee. Laughing. Talking. About Mike, I'm sure. Why does he get everything? Penelope and Kristin have moved on to another group.

"You know what?" Constantine says and places his beer bottle on a nearby table. "I have no idea who you really are. I don't think you were friends with Kristin the way you explained it to me." He hooks his bag's crossbody strap around his head and shoulder. "I'm grabbing my stuff from upstairs and leaving. We're finished."

I've lost control of everything. Why is this happening to me? I grab Constantine's arm, and he makes a huge show of wrestling me away.

"Get *off* me!"

The look he gives me causes me to take a few steps back while nearby people look our way. My face flushes. I feel the heat and embarrassment of everyone staring, and I feel dizzy. I look to my left, and Kristin is pointing at me and whispering to everyone around her.

I know what she's saying: *that's her! That's the one who wrote those letters!*

Now everyone is staring at me. I shake it off and beeline toward Vita. I know she sees me coming—we made eye contact. But she ignores me when I get there, so I tap her on the shoulder. Her head whips around, and there's lightning in her eyes. She looks me up and down like she just scraped me off the bottom of her shoe.

"Can I help you?"

She says it like she doesn't know me. Like she didn't sign me to a contract and like I didn't have breakfast with her this morning.

"I can explain what you saw online, Vita," I say. "It's not what it looks like."

"Famous last words. You'll be getting my Letter of Termination first thing in the morning."

I'm shooed away like an unwelcome ant at a picnic. Tears sting my eyelids when I catch a glimpse of Tara skirting past me.

"Hey!" I say, all cheery like. Bubble gum happy. Remember? God, that was only nine hours ago. Why do I feel like I'm on a conveyor belt and things are moving at a million miles an hour?

Her eyes shift. "Oh, hey. I'm just running off to meet someone. We'll talk later."

She gives me a smile that doesn't land, and she disappears down the stairs at a pace faster than normal. I pull out my phone and check Twitter.

She unfollowed me.

Rage.

But . . . fame.

People may think I'm nuts, but I have over three thousand new followers. Three thousand and eighteen new follows! Crazy sells.

I'm not crazy, though. People just believe what they see online. It's Kristin's fault.

I turn around and walk with determination. Conversation stops when I reach her, and other authors band around her, shielding her.

I crane my neck around them. "I just want to talk, Kristin."

"No," she says from behind someone. It's Kevin Candela. That would've made me fangirl nine hours ago, being so close to him. To her. "Do I need to file that restraining order?"

A hand is on my elbow. My body is turned around forcibly. A man is behind me, ushering me out. In front of everyone. Through the bar, down the stairs, and to the elevator. When he shoves me in, I see his name tag says Gerald Bivona, Head of Security.

As the doors close, he says, "You'll be checked out tomorrow morning, ma'am. Have a good night."

59

VICKY OVERTON

Friday, 9:10 P.M.

I hesitate before I approach Jim on the stage. Kristin left, but he's talking to a few stragglers, maybe some other mid-list writers I'd know by name but not face.

I rarely see him dressed up, an unfortunate result of both of us working from home. If we pop in on each other for lunch, we're practically in pajamas. *Practically*—delete. He's standing tall, with his hands in his pockets. His hair is messy but combed back. Sexy. And he's wearing appropriate socks and shoes for a change.

Was the whole thing an act? The bumbling Florida boy? We've only been together a year and a half, so maybe I don't really know him. He's been working with Kristin for at least two months—that's when he said he was visiting his parents, but he was really with her. Or was that a ruse too? All the text messages lately have been fake. Planned.

Mr. Mid-list leaves, and Jim turns toward me. Twinkling eyes, huge smile—man, I thought he'd be scared shitless of me right now, but he looks genuinely happy. He extends a hand, inviting me up onto the stage. I climb the steps toward him, and he reaches out for me. I stiffen.

"How could you do this to me?" I spit with venom, still mad, for sure. I thought he was a cheater, I thought someone was trying to kill me, and then I thought he was a murderer.

His eyes look so different than when I kicked him out of the room and sent him on his way earlier today. "I did it for you."

"You saw what people said about me online. I can't believe you'd humiliate me like that."

"Meghan started it, and I came to your defense as soon as it got bad. Me and Kristin were both using the fake Twitter account. I'm the one who said to leave you alone and to look into Jason Fleming instead."

That was true . . . I do remember thinking I liked the Twitter asshole.

"You look beautiful," he says and slowly moves closer to touch me. When I don't slap him, he drags his fingers through my hair. "I like this purple color on you."

Tears come to my eyes, finally happy tears. I hug him again while whispering in his ear, "I'm still going to kill you for this." Then I laugh, because the way today is going, becoming a thriller book cliché and turning into a murderer for no reason is a distinct possibility.

"I'm sorry I didn't tell you what we were doing, but you'd never be able to zip your lips if I had you running around with that clown all day," he says while gripping both of my hands. "I didn't like how Penelope put you on the backlist for Davis all the time, and when Kristin found out about him changing his name and stealing her friend's book, I came up with a plot to get him ostracized publicly and to completely humiliate him. You had to be totally in the dark for it to work. I knew it was working when you ditched me in Times Square and said you were meeting the three of them." He chuckles. "Obviously, I had to have the hotel manager and security team in on it. The manager said all publicity is good publicity. This hotel is infamous now. It was practically a movie set today."

"Makes sense."

He puts a hand on my shoulder lovingly. "I hope you know I wasn't sleeping with Kristin, but I lied to you about visiting my parents. I did come up here when she and I signed the contract because she wanted to start off in person. And you know how I am about protecting clients' identities. No bestselling author wants to admit they need help with their plots and that they don't do everything themselves."

I shrug. "You could've just told me you had a client in New York. It's not like I would've known it was her. You're about to be the highest paid developmental editor in history. You could double your prices and I bet you'd still be booked out for years. Also," I add, "I'm glad you weren't attacked." I stroke his head where his fake bandage was this afternoon.

He lets out a howl. "I followed you up to Clover & Crimson and paid the bartender a hundred bucks to make Davis's drink half tabasco. Then I hightailed it across the park and met a couple of the actors with the ambulance. Nice guys. They thought it was funny, what we were doing. And after seeing the stalker texts earlier today, I knew you'd look in my phone to find out what I was really doing there." He pauses, then smiles. "You really thought I was a killer? A *killer*, Vicky."

I too laugh because of how ridiculous it all is, now. "I know. I feel like an idiot. But all's well that ends well? I'm so happy for Mike."

He nods. "Yeah, this worked out pretty good for everyone, huh?"

"Well not Davis and Suzanne."

He puts his hands up in front of him as if to ward off an attack. "Whoa, the things Kristin told me about that girl Suzanne! Kristin pulled a plot twist on me this morning and said she was adding her to the game just to have a reason for everyone to pay attention and expose her. The documents you saw weren't even half of it. That chick is nuts. She even emailed Kristin from her boyfriend's account after she was blocked. I was kind of afraid to have you so close to her today. I didn't want her focusing her attention on you. She needs to be committed."

I widen my eyes. "Terrific. Where is she?"

We both swivel our heads toward the ballroom exit.

"You think she went to the bar?" Jim asks.

"Kristin is there."

She wouldn't try to confront Kristin in front of everyone, would she?

60

MIKE BROOKS

9:45 P.M.

I check my watch, and it's almost ten. As terrific as this night is going—now—all I want is to go home and celebrate it with my family. Vita has been getting a ton of interest, from Bee Henry to other huge editors who have sworn more money, and the book will be going up for auction, ensuring I get paid top dollar. The fact that half of it, now, is kind of based on a true story and a real event, should make the sales go through the roof.

Vita catches my eye from about fifteen feet away, and I curl a finger to her. She excuses herself from Dara Tedward, another huge editor, and beelines for me.

Imagine me commanding this much attention again. It's like this isn't really happening to me. It's like a plot in a book. *Old has-been back in demand!*

Everyone loves a comeback story.

"What's the matter, Mike? Everything is good, yes?" Vita says.

Yes.

Part of my happiness is that I'm making Vita proud again. After being dumped by my publisher and declining sales for a decade, she never wavered. Always believed in me. Stuck by my side. Talked me up when people said I was finished.

That's not only an agent; that's a friend, and she's been mine for two decades. Hopefully, she'll be my agent for two more decades, but she'll be my friend forever.

"I've got to get home, Vita."

"No more party? You're the big star, Mike. You and Kristin Bailey, yeah? Big time!" She pumps her fist in the air, and she looks gorgeous even though her lipstick is smeared on her teeth and her cheek and her hair is a wreck. She's glowing.

I smile and pull her in for a hug. "Enjoy your night. I'll be back for the panels tomorrow. I'm actually on the panel for *Creating Tension in a Scene*, and after today, I think I'm an expert."

She laughs. "You never told me what happened today."

"Right. Kristin was a master manipulator with Jim Russell's help. They had us running around like headless chickens all day, thinking we were going to be murdered next. But it worked out. It was good. Davis—Tommy Johnson, whatever—he's finished. And Suzanne—" I pause.

Her face twists and she shakes her head. "No. Can't do it with Suzanne anymore. I didn't know about her and what she did to Kristin. I cannot represent someone like that."

I nod because I get it. It's Vita's reputation on the line too. Suzanne will have to figure it out herself after she gets some help.

I say my goodbyes to everyone who suddenly wants to be seen with me and head down the stairs just as Vicky and Jim are heading up, hand in hand. Good. I stop and hug Vicky again and shake hands with Jim.

"I'm headed home," I say. "It's been a long day, as you both know."

"Right. We're just stopping in for one drink and to make sure Suzanne doesn't confront Kristin."

I let out a bellow. "Ha. Too late. She already did and was removed by security. Hopefully, she'll seek treatment. It's a shame. She's a talented writer."

"You read her manuscript?"

"Yeah. Vita had both of us and . . ." I let the sentence trail off. Vicky knows how it works.

"Gotcha. Be safe getting home. I'm attending your panel tomorrow, but I'm sure I'll see you before then."

"Great. Do you want to have lunch?"

She nods. "Text me."

Those words have such a different meaning than they did this afternoon. I give her arm a squeeze and walk out of the hotel. The night air has lost the dreadful heat, and I stop for a moment and look up. New Yorkers never see stars, but tonight the moon is almost full and high above me, and for just one moment, I take it in. I look like a tourist—the annoying ones who stop in the middle of the sidewalk to stare up at the big buildings. But I don't care what I look like. I'm alive, and Kristin is alive, and everything worked out.

I tug my phone from my pocket to tell Nicole I'm on my way, and I realize just now that she never responded to me when I texted that I would be late. Odd. I hail a cab and dial her number. I get her voicemail right as I get in the cab.

"Nic, it's me. I'm on my way. Hope you're okay. I haven't heard from you in a while. Call me back if you get this."

I disconnect and I worry. Even though everything is over and nothing bad about today was real, from the killer to the affair

I thought she was having—nothing. I don't know why the pit sits in the bottom of my stomach like a piece of lead, but it does.

When we pull up to my building, I throw cash at the driver—probably way too much, but I want to get the hell out of the cab and upstairs as soon as possible. I say hello to my night doorman and then speed walk to the end of the lobby. The elevator is waiting, and I press the button for my floor about seventeen times in rapid succession, like it'll teleport me there instead. Sweat forms on my brow as I run down the hall and then fumble my keys, with my hands shaking. When the door opens, it's dark inside. Quiet.

Eerily quiet. Why didn't we get a dog?

I flip on the hall light by the front door. "Nic?"

Nothing.

Instead of tiptoeing around the house like I do when I come home too late, I'm like a bull in a China shop and turn on the lights while stomping through the house. I open the bedroom door and—

And there she is. My wife. On the bed.

Sleeping.

I lean against the door jamb and hold my chest—I damn near gave myself a heart attack. Now I tiptoe to the kids' room and open the door. Taylor and Tyler are both sound asleep, Taylor clutching the unicorn stuffed animal that my mother gave her for her birthday and Tyler with his favorite Lego house on the floor next to his bed. I don't leave until I observe their little chests moving up and down. Breathing softly. Alive.

I'm thankful as I close the door and go back to my bedroom. I quietly take off my clothes until I'm just in my boxers, and I crawl into bed next to Nicole and put my arms around her. She's warm and makes a happy moan. I let out a breath and close my eyes to put the day behind me.

When I wake, I'm alone, but I hear a typical Saturday morning through the door. The sizzle of bacon. The dinging of cereal and spoons hitting ceramic bowls. Muted cartoons from the television.

Was yesterday just a nightmare?

I grab my phone and google Davis Walton.

There's a video of him with a suitcase leaving the hotel. He's wearing sunglasses and sticks his hand in the air when a few people shove microphones in his face. No comment, no comment.

I scroll through some of the article headlines, the recent ones from *Murdered at Murderpalooza?* to *Davis Walton Falls From Grace* to *The City's Most Elaborate Prank?* I chuckle. It's over. I feel no urge to read about them. I want to have breakfast with my family and get ready for a full day of panels with my peers.

I toss on a robe and tie the front, then exit the room where the bacon smell wafts to my nostrils and my mouth starts to water.

"Daddy!"

Both Taylor and Tyler jump from their seats at the table and run up to hug me, each grabbing a leg. I place each hand on a head and smile at Nicole, who turns around from the pan of eggs and smiles at us. I lean down and kiss the kids.

"Sorry I was so late yesterday," I say to them.

"Can we go to the park today, Daddy?" Taylor asks.

I crouch down to her level. "Not today. Daddy has to work."

"But it's Saturday," she says with a pout, sticking out her bottom lip.

"I'll be done early. We'll go out to dinner tonight." I walk over to Nicole and kiss her, then grab a piece of bacon degreasing on a paper plate on the counter. I lumber into the living room and grab the remote and switch it to one of the news channels. The headlines are everywhere. Still. Ha.

Stabbed at Murderpalooza.

I look at the time on the cable box. It's eight in the morning. This was cleared up twelve hours ago. Why is it on the ticker?

"Honey?" I say, then turn my attention back to the television.

"This is Stephanie Cooper with NMC News with a breaking story. After an elaborate prank during midtown thriller conference Murderpalooza goes off without a hitch, we've just learned details that sometimes art does imitate life. Kristin Bailey, beloved author and originating schemer of the hoax surrounding her death yesterday, was found stabbed in a hotel bathroom this morning . . ."

I tune out.

This is on the news. Now. This morning. Saying Kristin Bailey was stabbed in a bathroom.

This happened for real.

61

SUZANNE SHIH

Saturday, 7:30 A.M.

A girl's gotta eat, right?

People may not want me here, but that doesn't mean I don't have a conference badge. It doesn't mean I don't have the schedule and the ability to freely move around. I pile my hair up in a tight bun, one to hide my pink streaks. I ditch the false lashes and the rest of my makeup. I'm wearing jeans and a T-shirt and Doc Martens, and my reading glasses are on, even though they make things that are far away blurry. I look different, but I have that badge hanging around my neck so I'm part of the crowd of cool kids.

It's not like I'm famous. It's not like people recognize me anyway.

There's a breakfast buffet set up for attendees, and I smile at the hotel employee checking badges. She has no idea who I am, but I have the golden ticket. I paid for the conference, and I'm allowed in.

The air in the room fills me with hope as soon as I cross the threshold. There are tables set up all over the floor, and my chest swells with pride, because I will be here one day, famous, wheeling and dealing, having people hang on my every word. I stop by the first service table to the right of the door and grab a cup of cold coffee and a crappy croissant. For now, I don't mingle. I don't interact. I do what Mike said I do best.

Kristin is sitting at a table with nine other people. Today she's wearing a white dress and a navy blazer. Her curly hair is pulled into a low ponytail, highlighting her cheekbones. She looks pretty; I usually only see her in her famous headbands, but she should wear her hair off her face more often. I recognize every single one of the authors at the table with her. That was supposed to be *me* at that table, with my *friend* Kristin. The popular kids' table. They're talking and laughing and comparing stories. Living life. Being famous authors.

What am I supposed to do now? Self-publish? As if. I have an agent for crap's sake. At least, I do now. She hasn't given me the Letter of Termination yet. But I'm a plotter, and I have a plan. I outlined this story in my head all night.

I sip my coffee and pretend to scroll through my phone, but my focus is really on that table. Come on, Kristin. I know everything about you. I know you have three cups of coffee every morning; you always write about it on your blog. *Coffee every day makes everything okay!* She's got to be ready to pee, right?

Two minutes later, she is. She's a strong, independent woman, and she doesn't need to go in a pair. And she's coming back, so she leaves her purse hung on the back of her chair. She exits the buffet room and walks down the long narrow hallway to the bathrooms. I check my pocket. The knife is still there.

I follow.

The door closes behind her, and I wait thirty seconds, until I know she's in a compromising position and she doesn't have her phone.

I open the door. I crouch down, and there's only one set of dark legs in all six of the stalls.

I click the front lock and wait. My glasses come off and the bun comes out. The pink is showing. It's me, Suzanne Shih. Hashtag Suzanne Shih.

The toilet flushes, and Kristin walks out. Her eyes widen at the sight of me.

"I just want to talk, Kristin," I say.

Her hands are up in front of her. "I'll scream."

"Go ahead!" I shout at her.

Now she's terrified, because she stumbles backward until she hits the wall, and her eyes tell me what I need to know. She expected me to back down, didn't she? Raise your voice and make threats, and I'll stop? Why, because I'm a newbie? No, she should've just cooperated with me from the beginning.

I pull the pocketknife and tap the button. A shiny mirrorlike surface extends, and I see myself. My smile. The sharpness of the edge. "You're going to listen to me, Kristin."

Her voice softens. "Okay. Okay, I'm listening."

I pace, getting my thoughts together. "I was just trying to be your friend. We started out as friends. I'm proud of you. I just wanted to be in your circle. Have you notice me."

"I do notice you, Suzanne. We are friends."

I scoff. "I know what reverse psychology is. Don't try to trick me. You had me thrown out of the bar last night and you had my reservation canceled. You can't go around treating people like that, you bitch."

There's a long-running joke among authors about our Google searches. If we ever get arrested, just tell the FBI we're authors so they can forgive our search history. Like if you look for untraceable poisons, how long it takes for someone to bleed out, and what charges you can be brought up on for attempted murder in different states. *Sorry, Agent Officer Sir, I'm a writer!*

A good Google search will tell you where to stab someone without nicking any vital organs. I mean, for the love of God, I don't want to *kill* Kristin. Remember, normal people don't turn into murderers for stupid reasons. I'm normal.

Still, I smile as I charge toward her with my arm above my head and draw the blade down just below her collarbone on her right side. She screams a sweet sound and falls to the ground, and I pull the knife out and give her two quick flesh wounds on the side of her belly. She's writhing on the ground now, bleeding, crying, screaming, saying the things they say in books. *Why are you doing this, you're crazy, help me, why!*

How did I get stuck as the main character in such a cliché novel?

There's pounding at the door, and I turn to open it and catch a glimpse of myself in the mirror, covered in Kristin's blood, still holding the knife. I don't drop it. I open the door.

Everyone outside screams when they see me and Kristin, slumped in a pool of blood behind me.

I gently lower myself to my knees, drop the knife beside me, and place my hands behind my head. Someone, I have no idea who, but someone behind me pushes me down on my face and holds me there. I don't struggle. I don't resist.

It'll be good for the future sponsors to see me cooperating.

People scream for help, telling Kristin she's going to be okay. They're saying to apply pressure, that they don't think I hit anything vital.

Told you so.

Cops and an ambulance are there in less than five minutes. I'm cuffed and yanked to my feet. Everyone is in front of me taking pictures and video. I smile for the cameras.

I wonder when they'll let me update my blog. Think of all the clicks! All the new followers I'm getting! People want to know about me.

Hashtag Suzanne Shih.

Now there are microphones in my face. The lights are blinding. Channel 2, Channel 4, Channel 7 . . .

I look directly at them and smile. "Call my agent."

I'm led outside, into the back of a waiting car. I hear it over, and over, and over.

Suzanne Shih. Suzanne Shih. Suzanne Shih.

I'm famous.

THE END

Acknowledgements

As always, a million thanks to my agent, Anne Tibbets, for believing in me again.

To my editor, Luisa Smith—you should wear wings. Thank you for all you've done to whip this baby into shape. I love how well we work together, and this novel might be my favorite yet. Looking forward to starting edits on number four with you! Thank you to the rest of the team at Scarlet: Otto Penzler, Julia O'Connell, and double thanks to Charles Perry for giving me a cover that I'm still completely obsessed with! Thank you to the copy editors and line editors for fixing my glaring mistakes, even after a hundred reads.

Jessica Payne and Mary Keliikoa, please know this book would be nowhere without either of you. Having amazing critique partners is so essential in this line of work and I've been blessed with two of the best. From Jessica's "no girl, nuh uh, get this out of here" to Mary's smiley faces when she likes a twist, you both motivate and entertain me at the same time. Proud that you're my friends.

Special shoutouts to the amazing authors I've worked with who were kind enough to read early and give me blurbs—Ashley

Winstead, Danielle Girard, Samantha Downing, Samantha M. Bailey, Heather Chavez, Liv Constantine, and Michele Campbell. I'm happy to know you and thrilled for all your upcoming releases. I know they will be as spectacular as everything else you've written.

Thankful for Thrillerfest, which this book is loosely based on (*allegedly!*). I'd been lucky enough to attend as an aspiring writer in the years before I got an agent or a book deal, and it does so much for the entire writing community. It was so great to finally meet authors and readers at the live event in 2022 as a twice-published author (after that 2-year Zoom hiatus). I can't wait to attend again this year and be with my people. I promise, there will be no author murders. *Allegedly.*

To the Bookstagrammers—you are all *great*. It's such a pleasure to engage with so many of you daily. I only have so many pages I'm allowed to fill, so I could never possibly name you all, but there's nothing but love for Gare Billings, Stephanie Bolen Cooper, Abby Endler, Marisha Lunde, Janelle Mainero, Dennis Michel, Kori Pontenzone, Alicia Rideout, and Carrie Shields. Also, the support from people like Sara DiVello, Kate Hergott, Leslie Zemeckis, Lauri Schoenfeld, and others who feature us on their videos, blogs, and podcasts really helps.

To the readers—I love you! Thank you for picking up this book and taking another chance on me. Feel free to reach out to me on Instagram if you would like me to Zoom into your book club! @jaimelynnhendricksauthor

To literally everyone I know—you may or may not see your name in this book. Each is pulled from someone I know. But just the name, not the personality; some characters are terrible and

I don't associate with terrible people. I'm honored to have such a great cast of characters in the novel of my life.

To my forever supportive family and friends, these books are always for you—especially since I miss you all so much after moving from New Jersey to Florida six months ago. We had a special addition to the family this year, our newest little munchkin with an infectious smile, cousin James Paul Overpeck, who we all love. And of course, this one has been specially dedicated already to Ann Marie DePaulis, my best friend of four-plus decades. I can't do life without you.

Always for my husband, John Hendricks. I love you more than yesterday.